M000318334

"Your acquaintance proposes to come in here and kill me," Gelor said. "I have no wish to fight him . . . you will help me build a fear-barrier to keep him away?"

Yahna matched his charming, crooked smile. "If I refuse?"

"A woman of your intelligence?" He laughed. "The decision is entirely in your hands."

Yahna shrugged. "I must refuse, in that case."

"Uh. So be it, then." Gelor was still smiling. "This way, if you please."

Yahna let him see her sigh, then pounced—and ran into Gelor's fist. Agony doubled her over, and Gelor had the exodermic syringe out and had injected her before she hit the floor.

SPACEWAYS

SPACEWAYS #16

THE PLANET MURDERER

JOHN CLEVE

BERKLEY BOOKS, NEW YORK

SPACEWAYS #16: THE PLANET MURDERER

A Berkley Book / published by arrangement with
the author

PRINTING HISTORY
Berkley edition / March 1984

for
DWIGHT V. SWAIN—
1 elbow, 2 knees, 6 balls
and considerable respect

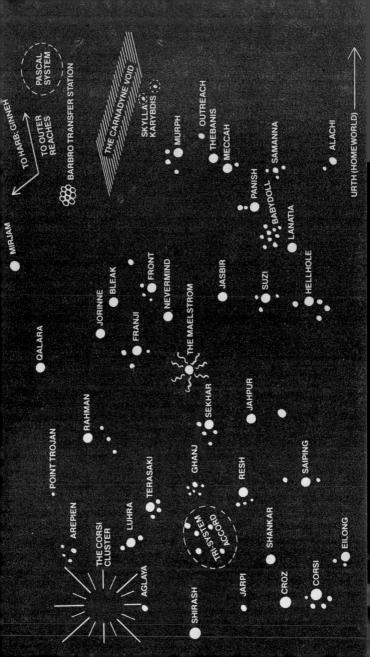

SCARLET HILLS

Alas, fair ones, my time has come.
I must depart your lovely home—
Seek the bounds of this galaxy
To find what lies beyond.

(chorus)
Scarlet hills and amber skies,
Gentlebeings with loving eyes;
All these I leave to search for a dream
That will cure the wand'rer in me.

You say it must be glamorous
For those who travel out through space.
You know not the dark, endless night
Nor the solitude we face.

(reprise chorus)

I know not of my journey's end
Nor the time nor toll it will have me spend.
But I must see what I've never seen
And know what I've never known.

Scarlet hills and amber skies,
Gentlebeings with loving eyes;
All these I leave to search for a dream
That will cure the wand'rer in me.

—Ann Morris

It's a wicked world. And when a clever man turns his brain to crime, it's the worst of all.

—*S. Holmes, detective*

SPACEWAYS

#16

THE PLANET MURDERER

1

Death, at midnight, goes a-dancing,
Tapping on a tomb with talon thin . . .

—*Henri Cazalis*

He came into the Labyrinth and onto the monitor in Pearl's
pleasure-bowl just after eight, just as the Handsome Man
had said he would. A freak. A strange broad-shouldered
near-giant over 190 sems tall. Though he was lean enough,
he showed a heavy musculature on that 1.9-plus meters
of height; a musculature uncommon except among slaves.
He looked as if he'd actually *worked*. Manual labor,
even.

The aspect that really distinguished him and made him
unique (a *freak,* many would say) was not his height or
physique. It was his skin. His skin was purple, incredibly,
with a bizarre amethyst *glow*. Swallowing, Pearl watched
him pause before the lift. He tilted back his battered,
helmet-like headgear, which was visored both fore and aft
and ridged on top. Pearl stared. His hair was lavender!

Just then he turned, and she was better able to see his
face. A clean-cut, strong-boned, friendly face with mirth-
crinkles about the mouth and at the corners of the eyes.
Those eyes also showed a certain wariness, along with
alert intelligence and wit.

So he's purple, she mused. *He's also tall, just beauti-*

fully built, and good-lookin'! What could the Handsome Man have against this fr–this unique stranger?

But that was dead-end thinking of a kind Pearl couldn't afford. Not if she was to escape this Musla-cursed planet Croz, hemorrhoidal anus of the universe, and get back to comfort and sensual excitement on Thebanis, in her beloved city of Raunch.*

In that same moment the Purple Man clapped his hardhat back on. (Pearl found it easier to think about men in terms of labels rather than names. Most of her contacts with them were brief and they often preferred anonymity anyhow.) He stepped onto the lift and off Pearl's monitor. She rose hastily and tossed aside her cloak. She'd spent her last cred for it, after that swinish slaver Vettering had dumped her here. After all, she could hardly go out on the streets clad only in skirt and red strap-titser. It still irked her, the way that smirky little Saipese clerk had fobbed her.

"Rahman green," the snip had called it. That had sounded delightfully exotic; classy. Besides, it was the only cloak Pearl had the price of. Only later had she discovered that once again her taste—or lack of it—had betrayed her. When a hust in The Oddford had referred to the cloak in none-too-sly disparagement as "vomit green," the spacefarers at the table with her had collapsed in guffaws.

Certainly it was not the thing to wear on a pickup as vital to her as this one. The abbreviated strap-titser—a Thebanian outer bra consisting mainly of straps—was a better ploy for sure. She wished only that she had more jiggle-flesh to bulge between the straps. That damned Akima Mars series had made a warhead-lover of practically every male along the spaceways!

This was hardly the time to be fretting about her figure. She had to get down below, and fast. If some other hust should decide to dig her claws into that strange stranger . . . ! That was a chilling thought that sent Pearl's hands rushing up to check her tired old Terasaki coil and gingercheck her dimple-scars. With a prayer that she hadn't

---

* Where, in the Loophole Bar, we first met Pearl, along with her friend Pacy as well as Shieda and Vettering, in *Spaceways* #2, *Corundum's Woman*.

chewed off her cerulean lipstain in her nervousness, she stepped out of her pleasure-bowl and onto the lift. It dropped. Her stomach quivered as she was whisked down to the lowest level. Wobbling queasily, she stepped out into the Labyrinth's irradialited dimness and tinkling Bergal sound.

Having solid floor under her didn't help her nausea much, here.

That was the trouble with the Labyrinth. The reason it had deteriorated from an outlander's dream of a plush luxury entertainment center to a shabby, sleazy bar in Croz's depths. The techs said the issue was something called synesthesia, an effect that somehow translated vital stims into sounds and vice versa. In the process it also made too many people's stomachs churn in what amounted to seasickness. It was not an effect to encourage drinking.

(The elaborate explanations that it was due to subliminal pressures induced at this depth by Croz's erratic rotational spin made no difference whatever.)

The Labyrinth had gone downhill in a hurry. In the process it had acquired the nickname of Hust's Haven. Most of its income now came from payoffs on the privacy/pleasure-bowls. They were suspended at varying intervals about the entrance shaft, where synesthesia was no problem. Holographic windows enabled a whore's mark to dial anything from nostalgic scenes of his own planet to Akima Mars shows or perversircs of exotic depravities.

Pearl fought the effect. Nausea was a luxury she couldn't afford. Not here; not now. Not when the Purple Man was her key to passage back to her own Thebanis!

Resting a hand against the nearest upright to steady herself, she scanned the room. She spotted him after a moment: on the far side, over by the bar. Adjusting her sagging blue-coiled Terasaki wig as she went—and fighting down queasiness—she headed for that double-billed hardhat. She hardly took note of the fact that business tonight was even slacker than usual. What few customers there were lounged in subdued—or maybe sullen, or plain ugly—silence, while the tinkling music seemed to fracture into shattered beads of sound.

The Chank barkeep saw her coming, teeth clenched, weaving her way among the tables. Conveniently he found some chore at the far end to keep him busy. She gave him a small smile and was glad she'd made her peace (or piece, she thought) with him, in a vacant bowl back when Vettering had abandoned her here.

Her path took her past an alcove that eddied tendrils of pungent smoke. Ordinarily the acrid, nostril-tingling narcostick scent of redjoy sticks would have been enough to warn her. Redhigh was a sweet-burning, mild-high "cigaret"; redjoy was a dangerous lascivicant + aphrodizzy that affected different people in different ways, some dangerous. But tonight her whole attention was focused on the Purple Man. Running her tongue along her lips, she tightened the muscles at the corners of her mouth in preparation for the swift, sensuous smile of greeting that was every hust's stock in trade. One hand moved automatically below her navel to check the hipband of her skirt.

And out of the dimness of the alcove, a hand shot up to clutch her wrist. A hoarse, redjoy-slurred voice followed.

"Hey, Purl, gurl. We din't redshift after all. Cap'm's hookin' on another pod of cargo. We got all night t'celebrate!"

She didn't need to see the man to know the voice: a spacefarer named Karim, off the merchanter *Idris* out of Luhra. Two other crudos, real animals, sat with him. Frantically Pearl sought to free her wrist. The cool she had worked so hard to build dissipated like nobac smoke.

"Let go, you—you pig, you grossporker! You bought a cycle with me, not forever."

Karim came up out of his seat and the alcove like a pouncing grat. Still gripping her wrist, he lashed out with his other hand. That slap might well have broken Pearl's neck had it landed full-face, as the flainer intended. Instead, she managed to twist just enough to escape the worst of it. At that it drove her to her knees and left her head ringing.

Dimly she thought, *Pearl, you fool! To say a thing like that to someone that redjoy makes mean . . .*

Another slap landed and her brain seemed to split into two segments. The cells in one half screamed, *My face, my face! No-o! What if he rips me, marks me?* The other focused on a booted, back-drawn foot: *Oh mother, the monster's going to boot me, kill me!*

Only then, out of nowhere, she glimpsed purple. Time stood still, or paused. Her vision cleared enough for her to see that the Purple Man had somehow joined the scene. Incredibly, he was smiling. A sardonically warm and friendly smile. And he had Karim by one shoulder in a grasp the spacefarer obviously found painful.

Baring his teeth in a snarl that would have done credit to one of those tiger-things from his home planet, Karim twisted free. He launched an enviably heavy blow at the Purple Man's face.

The Purple Man kept right on smiling. Rather than feint or dance back, he simply ducked his head forward in a sort of nod. Thus he took Karim's blow on the top of his spired headgear. The thud of impact contained elements of crispness, as of the snapping of fingerbones. Karim's high bellow of anguish quite overpowered the tinkle of music.

Now here came his fellow spacefarers, though, out of the alcove. One whipped a knife from a chest-sheath that proclaimed him a Bleaker. Pearl tried to scream a warning. In the tumult she could never be sure whether she had made a sound.

Not that it was needed. The Purple Man was definitely not blind. Now standing erect and alert again, he wore an expression of pleasure and . . . amusement? Deftly he swept off his battered hardhat. Dropping to one knee as the dagger-man moved in, he slashed upward with the helmet's rear visor.

Apparently the neckguard was razor-edged. It caught the knife-hand where wrist and palm-heel joined. Blood spurted. The knife dropped. Gaping stupidly, clutching at his sliced wrist in an effort to halt the pulsing blood, the Bleaker staggered backward. The third spacefarer, eager a moment ago to join the fray, appeared to think better of it. Shooting the Purple Man a venomous glare, he contented himself with herding his wounded crewmates toward the lift.

When he mouthed a curse over his shoulder, the Purple Man whooped delighted challenge and made a false lunge.

The fellow broke and ran. Still laughing, the Purple Man waved at the bartender—who leaned on that bar, sighting along a stopper barrel—and returned to Pearl. His face sobered with concern as he helped her up. She made it a point to sway giggily and press a hand to her still-stinging cheek.

"Oh sir—"

"Call me Jesti."

"Jesti." Pearl rolled her eyes in what she hoped would come through as sweet gratitude and adoration. "You saved my life, Captain Jesti!" And then, sham-shyly, "I am Pearl."

The man who called himself Jesti grinned wryly. Pearl had a feeling that the twist of his lips bespoke total cynicism as to her pretenses. He said, "I'm no spacefarer, uh, Pearl. I'm a kiracat miner."

"Sure does make you *strong*! And you risked your life!—I mean, those three were spacemen, mean ones, on redjoy! They might have killed you. To take that chance for me, a *stranger* . . ."

Jesti's grin broadened. "So I took a chance, stranger. An Eilan miner likes a fight. That's part of what life's all about. *Spacemen*! Huh—they never had a chance. Besides— it wasn't just for you."

Those words were like another slap in her face. She was staggered, groping despite her efforts to preserve and project her chosen image.

"Not . . . for me?"

"Firm." The smiling Purple Man slapped his headgear on at a jaunty angle. "I was spoiling for a fight when I came in. You and those tunnelworms—that just gave me an excuse."

She couldn't believe such straightforward honesty. She also couldn't tell him to go to Sheol, not this man. "I–I don't understand." She didn't, either. What a thrilling, straightforward . . . idiot!

Her purple knight shrugged good-naturedly. "Try harder. I come from Eilong. That's a planet you likely never heard of. Neither has anyone else, unless he's in the tint business."

"Eye-long? Tint?"

"Tintinnabulate alloys. They're what make high-tech spacers go. The Galaxy couldn't run without 'em."

"Oh."

That was the best Pearl could do. She wished she'd let them spin the tech tapes for her, back when she was just an unbaked little cake in the Quarter on Thebanis. But Raunch's bars had been more fun any day, and the exotic spacefarers, and to hell with edutapes.

Besides, idle curiosity was a nothing thing just now. What counted was the big shot: shuttlevator pass and ticket back to those bars! She wondered if Pacy still sort of hung around the Loophole, waggling her warheads at the more prosperous-looking spacefarers who came along. The two of them had teamed with that fat but nice and extremely strong Shieda . . . and then Vettering. That rotten sister-slicing bastard of a slaver! With luck, Pearl would get her chance to pay him back some day. A blade between the ribs would be nice. Or a shot of cyno in a drink. Or one of Shieda's exploding darts stuck up his gassy rectum.

Even as the thought flashed her, she knew she'd never carry through on any of it. She was a velvet touch, a born victim. The best she could hope for was that one way or another she'd leave this robe-happy planet and make it back home. For years she'd had her hopes set on the legendary Jonuta . . .

The important thing now was to carry out her contract on the Purple Man. This Eilan called Jesti. For that she already had her answer, and for that she had only to put her plan into operation. Gingerly, she touched her cheek. She winced at its sensitivity.

"I'm sorry. I want to stop the swelling, but I do want to hear more about Eilong. Uh . . . I've got a privacy bowl up the shaft where I can clean up a little while we talk. I'm still a little shaky—why don't you come up with me, have a drink?"

The violet-skinned man nodded. For the first time he appeared to inspect her more closely. She tried to be unobtrusive about taking a deep breath when he looked at her scarlet strap-titser and its contents.

They rode the lift up together. That made for some

cramping, of course—though not so cramped, she noted with cynical satisfaction, that Jesti's arm *had* to press so frequently against her warheads. Meanwhile, she learned more about Eilong and tint alloys and kiraoun catalysts than she had any remote desire to know. At least Jesti kept the tone light enough to be amusing.

Only when he came to his being on Croz did his manner change. Good humor and laugh-crinkles faded and were replaced by a cold-eyed, tight-lipped anger too deeply rooted to be concealed.

The issue, he admitted bluntly, was Eilong's backwardness and isolation. And its miners, the men who went below ground to gouge out the vital kiraoun catalysts. It was a worse than dangerous job. Death and accident rates ran appallingly high.

Too, exposure to the catalysts' radiation did things to the miners' metabolisms. It was responsible for their purple skin and hair, as well as some other physical anomalies. Yet the Council of Elders who ruled Eilong would hear no talk of anything so alien/progressive as cybernetic mining. They *preferred* backwardness and isolation, believing that with mechanization—remote TP cybermining by engineers and techs—would come domination by giant CongCorp. That interplanetary mineral extraction/transport/processing cartel (and presumed TMSMCo subsidiary) was forever urging change, change.

Why? Because change of any sort could not help but threaten the Council's power.

When Jesti and a handful of others had pressed the matter, reprisal by the Elders had been swift. Some "malcontents" had succumbed to "accidents." Others were remanded (sentenced!) to "rehabilitative therapy." In a few cases there had even been outright assassination, that nice word for murder.

Jesti had received a tip of impending personal disaster while he was at work. Risking his neck to ride an ore-belt to the surface, he'd slipped onto a shuttle-ship that carried him offplanet, to Eilong's space station. There he had stowed away on a freighter/merchanter slated for swift departure.

He was discovered a few hours out. The outraged captain had insisted on dropping him off here on Croz.

"I've been stranded here ever since."

The parallel with Pearl's situation was such that sympathy welled up in her. Since that was an emotion she didn't dare indulge in with this man, she stubbornly thrust it down. Of all the men to *feel* something for. . . !

They entered her privacy/pleasure-bowl. While not the most luxurious available, it included supasilient suspension, a velvasponge floor, and oversize liqualay couch-bed. Despite its sag, the upholstery's shabbiness, and the crack in the overhead mirror, Jesti was visibly impressed. (A normal enough reaction, Pearl felt, from a man who wore permanently stained work clothing and his battered miner's hardhat.)

She flicked the lift's switch to privacy position and twisted her shoulders sensuously while she half turned her back to Jesti. She had nice shoulders.

"My, ah, bandeau's too tight . . . that slap down in the bar . . . something feels sprained. Ow—I can't reach the meld. Could you loosen it a little for me?"

Jesti looked almost ready to drool as he stepped close behind her. That made Pearl feel good. He was so naive, compared with those thrice-cursed, sisterslicing spacefarers! *A man for me to control, manipulate—stead of being manipulated by him*! Pearl was only eighteen, and very aware of it.

Rather clumsily, he twisted at the backstraps, discovered the nevelcro closure, loosed it. He let go the tabs and his hands slid in under her arms to cup her bared breasts. Tentatively at first, then more firmly.

She made it a point to giggle, even as she locked her hands over his with a wriggling pretense of pulling away. Of course she let herself be drawn back, twisting so that her rearward cheeks rubbed against his fly. She noted with satisfaction that the area featured an already stiffening protrusion. Under the stim of her buttsy friction, it grew even harder.

Laughing, she slipped away from him. "That feels so

nice—but I promised you a drink, remember? Do you like orbisette?''

"What's orbisette?''

It was all she could do to keep her eyes from widening. A man who didn't know what orbisette was! It was hard to believe. *Eilong must really* be off the beaten track!

"It's a drink,'' she said, "that really puts you into orbit, you know? One plass of it and you'll flash so hard your ears ring and you hit black center.''

Jesti swallowed hard, gazing at her. "Every day and every way!'' he said with much enthusiasm. His eyes were glowing green and purple.

Pearl let out her breath. He'd committed himself. Now he had little choice but to drink the concoction. Fine for her—she had chosen orbisette because it had a fruity stingo strong enough to cover the hypnofacient the bartender had provided her. Crossing to the cabinet, she touched the button. The panel slid back and the tray came forward. Opening the pottle of orbisette, she filled the two plasses and presented the leftward one to Jesti.

It was a nice move, a neat move. Since the hypno was colorless, it had been no trick at all for her to half-fill one plass with it, earlier. That enabled her to pour the orbisette freely, while he watched. He could see that she was drinking the same thing he was. Never mind that the naïve offworlder was wrong.

He acted predictably. With his gaze and his mind on his bare-breasted host, the Purple Man gulped down the doctored orbisette. He set aside his plass and moved in on her.

Pearl made only token effort to evade him.

The key point now was to stall long enough for the stuff to take effect. His manhandling her warheads would hardly be distasteful. He was a strong man and brave. He had done battle for her. She liked that, liked it enough so that she shivered with excitement when he ran his thumbs over her stiffening, tingling nipples.

Too soon, one of his hands was groping lower. That was a bit too fast; she couldn't take the chance. She had to be sure the hypnostuff was working. Once more she slipped away, again laughing.

"Oh, *Jesti*! And *I* wanted to hear about *Eilong* . . . first. Must you be in such a *hurry*?"

Jesti followed as if he hadn't heard her. He was staggering just a little, she noted with satisfaction. The hypno was taking over. She used her own hands and mouth to ensure a long kiss—and squirmed away again. She darted past him to the couch-bed and jumped onto it. Forcing a giggle.

Blinking, swaying unsteadily, he turned to face her. Came at her in a rush, lurching and stumbling . . . and fell across the bed in a heap, unable to master the liqualay. Poor naïve innocent!

In a moment she was again on the floor, heaving him over onto his back.

"See, Jesti? You're just coming on too fast. The orbisette's got you. If you move so fast now, it'll all be over, Jesti. You won't even know what happened. And what about me—I'm a girl who likes her stims. No, no, we need to slow you down, get that first rush over, Jesti. After that . . . well, we've got all cycle, darling, and this is a place where we can take our time."

It was words for words' sake, for time's sake. Anything to keep control until the hypno was locked in solid—and yet not so tight that he hit black center and couldn't function. When his hands stopped clutching and his eyes rolled up she almost panicked, fearful that she'd let him sink too far.

"Do you miss Eilong, Jesti?" she said quietly, testing.

His eyes opened. His face seemed to fall apart. The sound that came from his throat held anguish on a level she had never seen before.

"*Eilong*!" he choked thickly. "Eilong. Why'd they do it? Why'd they make me run away? I love Eilong. I want to live there, die there. . . ." His voice rose. "Damn them! Damn their sisterslicing souls, those Elders! What d'they care if miners die, so long as they c'n run the place to suit themselves? Shiva rack me, I won't let 'em do it! I'll get back and I'll see 'em dead and Eilong free, by black Durga and Kali! I will, I will, I swear it!"

Pearl was shaken, yet knew that this was The Time. She didn't dare hesitate a moment longer. Swiftly she opened his frontmeld and tugged out his slicer . . . dropped her voice till it was low and throaty, sex-stimmed, the way an aging hust had taught her.

"Oh, what a night we'll have, you purple passion-pot! First we'll zing you, then we'll wring you, till your azle caves in and your eyeballs fall out . . ."

She took him into her mouth and her cheeks caved in, in a frenzy that was her own as much as this man who had genuinely saved her. Her tongue worked lovingly, she sucked lovingly—and in seeming seconds, hypno or no, his body was jerking. Straining, convulsing, erupting. The purple hands that so recently had sagged loose now clutched her head in a spastic spasm.

A final, explosive surge filled her mouth and emptied the Eilan. He fell back limp.

Pearl rose shakily, blinking. And obeyed her instructions: she emptied her mouth into the pod the Handsome Man had given her.

(Why was it so vital to the Handsome Man that Jesti's semen be freely ejaculated? And why taken while he was alive and at a peak of sex-stim, passion, rather than after death?) She shrugged. Questions were of no concern to her, nor the answers. What mattered was that she complete her task to her employer's satisfaction. Nothing more—and nothing less.

The sprawled Jesti was breathing deeply now, with his mouth agape. Eyes rolled up. Center-blacked for sure, she thought, straining to roll him over. She brushed away the thick lavender hair at the back of his neck and slit the skin with the tiny, ray-sharp obsidian blade. Sliding in the slender tapper, she watched the plunger's barrel fill with blood. Carefully, she emptied it into the second container.

Only then did she note the strange, slit-like orifices on either side of his throat, pulsing open and shut ever so slightly every time he breathed. After a moment she realized: gill—or their vestigial remnants. What such things were doing on a Galactic she couldn't imagine. Eilans were surely that—Galactics, humans—and it was only the stuff he mined, his being down there mining *physically,* that made him this strange color.

The Purple Man slept on. Pearl sighed. The wave of sympathy she had felt earlier was back again. A strange sense of kinship with this violet-hued man. It numbed her fingers, drew muscles tight across her stomach. *We are so much alike, he and I. Aliens both, stranded here on this offal-sphere of Croz! Each of us aching for another happier world—our own worlds! Longing for a life that logic says we've lost forever . . .*

Impulsively, she touched the cheek of the man strangely called Jesti; bent to kiss him briefly. She wished she didn't have to do what she had to do. But she did. There was no other way. Not unless she was willing to surrender herself to life on Croz forever, and that was too unbearable even to think of. She had no choice but to go on with it. The Purple Man would have to take his chances.

You poor naïve innocent . . .

At the ugly sound of the buzzer, Pearl darted to the lift-arch and checked the eyeslot. And there he was in the lift-cab. The Handsome Man. He was even better looking than she remembered. Breathtaking.

Hastily she flicked the switch to open position and stepped back so that he could enter. At the same time she discovered that her palms were sweating. So much was at stake here, so very much. *Just my whole life.* She hoped her voice didn't tremble. Just in case, she said nothing.

If the Handsome Man noticed her tension, he didn't show it. His smile was warm—radiant, almost. White teeth gleamed against the rich brown of his skin.

"Ah, my lovely one! You have good news for me, of course. Else why would you have called me?"

He was moving as he spoke in that fine baritone, almost feline in his grace, like a low-G dancer. At the same time, those black eyes gave less attention to Pearl than to the bowl, her cup-shaped room. Scanning past her to the unconscious Jesti, then on as if searching for any hint of other presence.

A sudden cynicism sparked in Pearl. Partly, it was born

of the obvious flattery (insincerity!) the Handsome Man
ladled out . . . and partly of his preoccupation with everything but her. Fearful? This, intermixed with the suspicion
and edacious nervousness that had gripped her since this
strange episode had begun, since she had become his
accomplice . . . all of it upset her more than she had
believed possible. (Besides . . . that poor naïve innocent
who had saved her face, which was her life . . .)

For the first time, Pearl viewed the Handsome Man
critically.

He's just too *handsome, too perfect.* Like a cosmetician's
vision of an ideal unattainable in nature. His features were
regular beyond imagining, the column of his neck a
sculptor's dream. His black ringlets, short and crisp, made
a mockery of the lank, greasy locks Shieda was so proud
of. He–

He interrupted her reverie by crossing to the unconscious Jesti. Drawing a slender, wicked-looking knife from
somewhere within his jerkin, he peeled back one of the
Purple Man's eyelids, clearly checking reflex response.
Pearl's heart leaped. Only with difficulty did she restrain
herself from crying out, rushing forward. It was one thing
to drug a jacko, take samples of his blood and semen. It
was quite another to play even a passive role in murder.

Jesti lay unmoving. Limp in unconsciousness. The Handsome Man released the eyelid and put away the knife. He
turned smiling to Pearl.

"Well done, Pearl. You have the containers?"

Heartbeat ragged, still quivering with apprehension, she
nodded numbly. "Pos." She wished her palms wouldn't
sweat so. "You—you brought the shuttle pass, the ticket?"

"Of course," that magnificent voice said, and re-
emphasized: "Firm."

Pearl could hardly believe his smile, his words. When
he brought out the actual credslips and handed them to
her, her relief was so great that she was going to faint. He
seemed to understand. His smile warmed and broadened.

"The . . . specimens, if you will, now," he prodded
gently.

It broke her spell. "Yes, pos. . . ."

Half stumbling in her haste, she scurried to the cabinet and retrieved his pods from where she'd hidden them behind the drink containers.

The Handsome Man tucked them away within his jerkin without even examining them. Still smiling, he executed what amounted to a pirouette of joy—or displaying his outfit to her as if he were a model. It was well nigh a designer's ensemble: dark green shirt, matching bloused green trousers, side-pleated; gloss-lustered krelhide boots, and the jerkin. It was of a black underfabric embellished with richly swirling patterns in brocade that interwove old gold and scarlet.

The Handsome Man ended his pirouette close to Pearl. "You are not only *so* beautiful, dear Pearl, but marvelously competent as well!" He leaned closer. The lustrous black eyes gleamed. His voice had become intimate, a caressing basso-baritone.

It occurred to her that her breasts were still bare. Squeezed tight in the coils of her own tension, she had forgotten to replace her halter. Now the Handsome Man's hands came up to cup those soft-skinned warheads. His eyes held hers.

"You do know you're beautiful, don't you, little one? More beautiful than any woman has a right to be. What a loss for Croz, your departure!"

She who thought she was not susceptible felt her breathing quicken.

"Not just beautiful, though. Exciting. I felt it the moment I first saw you, with your gem-like name. I knew then that I had to have you. I could hardly wait to get this whole silly business with him"—a nod in the comatose Jesti's direction—"out of the way so I could claim you."

Pearl's breath came even faster. His hands on her warheads were like fire. Even while her brain warned, *Be careful! He's a man and all men are taps, marks, under the frontmeld*, another aspect of her was saying, *Don't be a fool, Purly-gurl. He's already got the containers. He's given you your tags back to Thebanis. The business is all over. Anything he says now must be true. Even if it isn't, even if all he wants is a night here with me, what does it matter? Stash isn't that important—not yours, hust! And O Musla, he is so handsome!*

She let herself sway forward. His hands left her breasts to pull her tight against him. She could feel the hardness of him at chest and loins. Impulsively, she reached down to touch him there—and his whole body seemed to tighten. One hand moved to her shoulder. It pressed, downward.

She stiffened a little, at that. Her delight ebbed a fraction. It was not her stash he wanted, then, but her mouth.

Oh, what does it matter? If he wants that . . . well he's paid for it, and more. To get back to Thebanis . . . back in Raunch . . . that's worth anything I can give him. (And—it isn't as if I don't love it.)

Down on her knees, then. Opening his pants with a hust's skill. Easing her fingers onto his slicer, drawing it forth. Her lips parted as she gazed at it.

His hands tightened on her shoulders, pushed her back. Not far. Not letting her up from her knees, *where I belong, belong* . . . When he spoke, his voice had a raw, hoarse sound.

"Could I . . . ask a favor, lovely Pearl?"

She didn't answer. What need was there? He would ask, whether she said pos or neg, and he would do. That was the way of taps. Any hust knew that.

Already he was fumbling within his jerkin. What he brought forth made her stomach turn over.

It was a lech-noose, a Saipese lech-noose complete with arteriopads and cranial spreader. Saiping's nasty gift to its fellow planets. The last traces of her euphoria fled at sight of it. The Handsome Man wasn't just a tap! He was a depraved, perverted fobber to boot. One out to get his flashes at a girl's expense, no matter how much pain or disgust or nausea it cost her. Hooked about her throat with spasm cords leading to her wrists and ankles, the *thing* was designed to throw her into a paroxysm of near-strangulation in order to intensify his orgasmic spasms to the point of delirious frenzy.

She sighed. At least it would soon be over and she'd be free to space back to Raunch and a life in which she'd not have to endure such indignity again.

She hoped. She had just realized that she *owed* Jesti, and would help him.

In quiescent silence she let him adjust the cords. His hands were locked tight on the control-thongs. Then, with swift efficiency, she moved in on his erection.

The noose tightened about her throat to match his pulsing passion; loosened; snugged. . . . Speeding her, slowing her, intensifying her twistings and writhings and convulsive suctions as she gasped for air. She sucked, too, gliding her mouth, anxious to end this demeaning torment while she gave him such a gift. Yet way over a minute passed before she felt the spurt of his explosion, far back inside her face.

As she had known it would, the noose tightened. She made a last desperate gasp of suction, fighting frantically for air and against nausea. Tearing at the noose-thongs, breaking her nails in her frenzied efforts. She clawed at the Handsome Man's pants.

He did not loosen the thongs. He drew them tighter.

His hands drew them tighter still. When her eyes rolled up at him in mute entreaty, it dawned on Pearl in one last fading moment that he was smiling.

Smiling–!

Pearl died.

2

Stone walls may not a prison make, but they'll damn' sure keep you off the street till something better comes along.

—*Trafalgar Cuw*

The body-wrap held Jesti tightly. Too tightly for him to move. He couldn't so much as twist or pull himself together, let alone sit up. Furthermore, he felt awful. His mouth was dry. His head felt stuffed with peppercorns. Sick, giddy, and frustrated, he opened his eyes.

He saw nothing. The total blackness was beyond imagining. It was an absolute blackness that not even a kiracat miner's eyes could penetrate.

He knew what that meant—it was an augmented black. One from which all vestiges of light had been removed by inverse photophoric means. It was a phenomenon he had only heard about. He liked it better that way.

Jesti gritted his teeth. The only satisfaction he could dredge up was the fact that at least no one could see him, gloat on his misery.

Only then a voice spoke from the darkness: "So. You awake." The voice held a heavy note of satisfaction.

Jesti swore under his breath. Somehow, incredibly, he could be seen after all.

"Your name, Eilan."

Still battling giddiness, Jesti groped for words: "I can't

18

see you." And then, ridiculously, "I don't talk to people I can't see."

"Silence, scum!"

Jesti began to feel better. "You . . . want me to answer . . . and you want me to be silent. Do I have it right?"

Those words drew a choked, incoherent snarl. "Eilan scum! Offal! Do you dare to mock me?"

Jesti felt even better. He felt almost ready to smile.

"I command you! Answer!"

Jesti spoke meekly, with proper deference: "Yes, shithead?"

Stunned silence. Then a bellow: "*Shit-head*!?!"

"Is that not the proper title, sire?" Jesti kept his voice grovelingly humble. "On shipboard, they told me it was the term to use here. In keeping, they said, with the high respect in which the Galaxy holds all Crozers."

"Respect!" The unseen speaker's rage was peaking. "I'll teach you respect, you vlager! On your feet!"

Jestikhan Churt was enjoying the exchange more and more (whatever a "vlager" was; something peculiarly Crozite and peculiarly unpleasant, he supposed). No kiracat miner could resist such a situation. "I cannot rise, Lord Shithead. Someone has sausaged me in some sort of second skin. It holds me too tight to move."

"*Guards!* Lift him!"

Feet clumped through the all-engulfing darkness. Rough hands seized Jesti and jerked him upright. The sudden movement was worse than upsetting. For a moment he thought he was going either to vomit or pass out.

The voice was under control this time: "You are of Eilong. Your skin is purple. It shows no trace of subcutane dye. Only Eilong yields people with purple skin."

Jesti tried to speak. His effort produced no more than a "Hmm."

"*Your name, Eilan.*"

A new wave of nausea rose in Jesti. He tried to fight it down—then, thinking better of the situation, he allowed himself to retch. Violently. The vomit came up and out in a great gush. It smelled and tasted awful. He sagged to the left, twisting within the wrap, thrusting his head forward. A jerk and a lurch; an oath from the dark.

That told Jesti that he'd hit his target—the guard. He grinned in the darkness, twisted rightward, and heaved again.

The second guard's reaction was even more satisfying than the first's. In addition to exploding curses, he rained blows on the prisoner, half a dozen of them. Fortunately, the tightly-wrapped body envelope absorbed most of their impact. Jesti felt a lot better.

"Stop that, guard! Eilan, *again*: your name."

Something about the unseen speaker's voice told Jesti the time for games was past. He said, "They call me Jesti."

"*What*?"

"Jesss-teee," he repeated, elaborately. "Short for Jestikhan."

"That is a prime name only, a given name. What is the rest?"

"Churt. I am Jestikhan Churt."

"Not your lettered name, you anal bug!" The voice rose angrily. "I want your identitag, your number—whatever it is you stupid Eilans use to mark you from each other."

"Forgive me, sire." Only with an effort did Jesti strain the irony from his words. "Eilong is a small, poor planet where we Eilans are few in number and live mostly underground. We bear no identitags, no puterlabels. Only the names our parents gave us. No numbers. Really. Honest. I swear."

Rather to his surprise, his interrogator accepted that without umbrage. "As you will, Eilan. Name or no name, your guilt is clear."

"My . . . guilt?" It was Jesti's turn to go startled. "I don't know what you're talking about."

"Oh naturally, naturally." The smugness in the voice flowed thick as syrup now. "Leave it to an Eilan to lay waste his brain with orbisette."

It seemed a good time to stand silent. Jesti stood silent.

"To enlighten you, however . . ."

A holoproj took form in the blackness off to Jesti's

right. He blinked, again and again. Saw, tightly framed
. . . Jestikhan Churt! Sprawled on his back on a couch in
what was clearly a pleasure-bowl. The hust from the
Labyrinth—what had she called herself?—lay on her belly
between his legs with her wrists and ankles lashed together
in some sort of harness. Her head was thrown back and to
one side. An expression combining horror and agony con-
torted her face—which was black with suffusing blood.

The holoprojection cut even closer and changed angles.
A lech-noose came into view, tight-drawn about the hust's
throat. Jesti's hands gripped the control thongs.

The image faded. "A pretty picture, hmm?"

With an effort, Jesti hurled horror aside. "What sort of
game is this you're playing? I know nothing of that girl's
death. I deny guilt."

"There are questions," the voice said, as if he hadn't
spoken. "The hust had no papers. What was her name?"

Jesti tried to shrug and the body-wrap wouldn't allow it.
"She said to call her Pearl. I did." Now he was fighting to
think—this was his life!

"Why were you with her?"

"Why does any man go with a professional, a hust?"

"And you slew her."

"I deny it. I did *not* kill that nice girl."

"You do know that on Croz, possession of a lech-noose
is illegal?"

"I have never owned, used, or even touched a lech-
noose." Remembering the holo, Jesti added, "Consciously."

"Under Croz's code, ignorance of the law is no excuse
for crime."

"Like beating up innocent suspects? I have committed
no crime."

"Ah! To land on Croz without proper documents is in
itself a crime! You have no papers. That in itself is enough
to condemn you." The interrogator's heavy voice dropped
a note. "How did you come to Croz, Eilan?"

"By merchanter."

"Name and registry?"

Jesti grinned into the black. "I boarded on Eilong as a
stowaway. The captain had me locked in the airlock. He

told me nothing, and merely dumped me here. He was hardly eager to have it known I had been his guest.''

A sound that might have been a snort came out of the darkness. ''I grow tired of your inept lies. You shall not mock justice. For your kind we have special treatment.''

Light, a cone of it, drove out darkness. Jestikhan squinted, hard. The light centered on a glowering, thick-necked Crozer who hunched belligerently across a high desk that rested atop a dais. His patterned brown robe was the sort Jesti had come to associate with Crozite officialdom. In this case, at least, the cowl was thrown back. So far as appearance went, the interrogator might have been a Galactic from any of a number of planets, except for . . . *yukh*. Except for the milkily opaque pineal eye in the middle of the burnt umber skin of the forehead.

A ring of turquoise had been painted around that eye. Jesti took that to constitute a symbol of rank. He wondered whether the strange third eye (characteristic of Crozers, apparently) might also hold the secret of the man's (? Well, the *Crozer*'s) ability to see in profoundly impenetrable darkness. Maybe it functioned as some sort of sensor, like that possessed by Eilong's kirouli worms.

It was an interesting thought, one that might bear further checking, later. Meanwhile . . .

''I tire of your lies,'' the Crozite repeated. One six-fingered hand lifted in a gesture of command, the forefinger's extra joint flicking rapidly back and forth. ''Guards!''

The two attendants gripped Jesti, dragged him forward. Now that there was light, he saw the red rings about their pineal eyes. Both wore brown robes similar to that of the man on the dais. That made them policers, their befuddled captive thought, as the official gestured from his high desk.

''Bring the psychist!''

One of the guards released Jesti's arm to disappear into the surrounding darkness. He was back in seconds, accompanied by a new figure who *appeared* in the cone of light as the guard did. She paced forward.

She was the most stunningly exotic woman Jestikhan Churt had ever seen. Lithe, slender, she stood close to his own height. Maybe taller, this woman. Taller than Crozers, even. A great mass of golden hair rode her head like a spun crown, in marked contrast to the rich olive of her skin. In contrast too was her refulgent gold gown. It gleamed and shimmered in satiny beauty.

The garment was wildly out of place in such a setting. Floor-length on the left, it made a soft *whish*ing sound as she walked, almost sibilant. The trailing edge was chain-hooked to a gold bracelet on her left wrist, so that lifting her hand also brought up her hem. On the right, the fabric was slashed diagonally, from the draped left edge to a chain-link gold belt. The gown covered her left shoulder, but swooped diagonally down to the same point at which belt met slashed skirt. That left her right breast bare save for a large glowing peridot gemstone; a nipple cup that matched the great ring on her left hand's middle finger.

It was a costume to catch any eye—not that its wearer needed such help.

Her eyes, especially, held Jesti. It was as if they were sending out a challenge, a challenge just to him. Low-lidded, purple-black, they had a slant that hinted of Saipese blood. Yet her face, with its hollows and shadows and its olive hue, might have come from Resh or Meccah. The ripe-sullen lips spoke of Luhra, perhaps. Or Ghanj. Or Suzi. Or–

Long golden eardrops tinkled. The woman's right hand rose in a scornful gesture. The nail on the middle finger was at least six sems* long, and gilded.

"Is this the . . . creature?" Her voice struck a low, throaty note.

Jesti felt his face grow hot. "Permit me," he said tightly. "My name is Jestikhan Churt. I am an Eilan from Eilong, not a . . . creature."

The golden woman looked him up and down. "Indeed. Is there a difference?" There could be no mistaking the disdain in her cold eyes.

The Crozer at the desk laughed. "A good question." He leaned forward. His forefinger's extra joint flicked restlessly.

* Six centimeters: just under two and one-half *inches*, Old Style.

"Eilan, this is a time for answers. Since you do not choose to give them, you force us to other modes of probing. It is our good fortune to have visiting us the psychist Yahna Golden. A trained researcher from MarsCorp, creator of the Akima Mars dramas. She has come to Croz to check audience pulse-palps on a new production being cubed here. As a favor, she had also kindly agreed to run a brain-drain on you in regard to the murdered hustler, Pearl."

"A brain-dr–" Jesti rocked with outrage. "My mind is mine! I am no criminal! You have no right–"

"True, true." The Crozer smirked. "There are legalists who would agree with you. Later, if you are cleared, you may bring charges. For now, however"–he turned to Yahna Golden—"Psychist, proceed."

The woman nodded. "This way. My equipment is already set up." Her eyes were veiled now, her voice and expression cool and professional.

"No, damn you! *No!*"

Jesti fought the body-wrap, which was like a kitten fighting a fully grown boa constrictor. Heaving him up as if he were a valueless mummy, the Crozer policers carried him into another, smaller room.

Here, blocked up on a table, waited what appeared to be a giant crystal tube. On the stand beside it rested a metal helmet sprouting a tangle of snake-like wires that ran to a crystal disk; it was apparently the tube's cap. Additional circuitry connected to a scanner-linked control box.

"His hair must go," the psychist told the guards. "I've brought a keenr."

The nearer policer grinned. "That's for me."

"Don't cut him," she said, handing the chubby-faced fellow the instrument.

"Don't worry." He leered. "I mean, I sure woulden wanta make him vomit."

His partner guffawed. "That's right. 'e's got a touchy stomach."

The man with the keenr shoved Jesti down into a chair. "Lessee now . . ." He turned on the keenr and moved in happily.

Jestikhan tried to duck. The second guard seized him by the nose and twisted, hard enough to bring tears of rage and pain to Eilan eyes.

"No more ducking, purple-creature. 'r I'll yank yer nose off."

Both Crozers laughed. The one with the keenr bore down with it, rasping Jesti's skull bare from front to back. Lavender hair spilled to the floor.

Once they'd started, the job was over in secs. Jesti's head felt cold. He shivered within his sausage-casing—in rage, rather than with cold.

"Hey, he's havin' a chill!" the guard with the keenr whooped.

"Tha's 'cause 'is brains're freezing!"

"You mean purplies got brains?"

Yahna Golden dodged Jesti's eyes. "All right . . . *gentlemen*. The casque, now. Then load him into the insulator."

One Crozer charmer held Jesti while the other slapped on the metal helmet. Yahna Golden-psychist began adjusting pressure points and checking connections. Abruptly she stopped. Her fingers slid back and forth along the side of her subject's neck.

"What are these, these orifices?"

Her question was the sort that Galactics sometimes blurted stupidly, as if they had a monopoly on evolution. He didn't like it. In view of his situation of the moment, he didn't bother trying to hide his disgust:

"They're breathing slots. Gill slits, you likely call 'em. All Eilans have 'em. Only we don't use them for breathing anymore. Call them left-overs. Like tonsils or an appendix or such from your planet."

"Oh. I'm sorry. I should have known." Yahna Golden's fingers moved on, up and down around his (powerful) neck. And again, "What's this?"

"What's what?" Jesti's irritation was still in his voice, deliberately. God, the demeaning aspect—the ignominy. Shorn! Palpated! Stupidly queried . . .

"There's a place on the back of your neck. Sort of a

puffy little wound. The kind you might get if someone attached a sucking pod to draw blood.''

"No vampires on Croz, garden soot of the Galaxy!" a guard chortled, and the other positively girl-giggled.

Jesti scowled. "I don't know a thing about it. I'm here because I was framed, see. That must have something to do with it. And *I* see *two* vampires!"

"Oh. More likely just some sort of bite." Her fingers left his neck and she stepped back. "All right. Place him in the insulator, now."

They shoved Jesti into the tube. The disk-cap went on.

It was as if the world outside had vanished. Silence was as complete as the darkness had been. Within the casque, Jesti frowned. *What was that business about a neck wound? It must have something to do with Pearl's murder and whoever framed me for it.*

He was still wondering when something happened within his brain. He assumed that the change meant Yahna Golden had actuated the brain-drain. Like magic, all perceptions faded. He didn't know how it worked, but Jesti concentrated on the filthiest thoughts possible. Or tried to.

How long the eminently insulting process lasted he never knew. It was as if all at once he was spinning through a world of nightmare. Bits and fragments of memory, forgotten incidents, all flashed through his mind. Faces came and went: friends, enemies, work-mates, family. The long-dead were there, and the barely recollected. Men swirled up, hard-faced and rowdy. Women, vibrant and vivid as the passion they'd provided. Moments when he laughed, wept, ached with loneliness, screamed out in pain and fright. Once again he lived through mine disasters and battled with the Elders. The Crozer at the desk floated in and out. The Labyrinth and the hust. Pearl.

And above all, Yahna Golden, MarsCorp psychist. Friend of Setsuyo Puma?

How she could strike such an intense note was beyond his understanding. How long had he had contact with her? Almost, he could lay it out in seconds. Yet here she was, all olive skin and gold, gold. Cool sloe-eyes probing, appraising, mocking. Ripe lips at once taunting and scorning.

Even when he tried, he could not push back her image.

Weariness came.. A sort of fog eddied through his consciousness in strange gray tendrils. Time had no meaning for him . . . and then that too passed.

He wakened.

The crystal coffin was gone. So was the rest of the equipment. He lay on a simple table. A policer he'd never seen before slouched beside him, looking bored.

"All right? All pos?" The man jerked a thumb. "You go out that way."

Jesti swung his legs off the table. Unsteadily, he sat up. His head was cold. Carefully not touching his shorn pate, he looked along the corridor the Crozer had indicated. At its end an open doorway spilled in light from Croz's great sun, Thabit. *Crap! It's morning! All* night *here!*

The policer saw the look and laughed. "It's all yours, jacko. I go off duty now." And damned if the cool bastard didn't stroll away.

After a moment Jesti dropped from the table (unpleasantly aware of cool air on his naked head) and checked his pockets. Nothing was missing.

Except for my hair and my dignity and my miner's helmet. His mouth tightened and he shivered a little. Most heat-loss was from the head. . . .

Unsteadily, he moved down the corridor and through the doorway. Along with a row of other doors, it opened into a courtyard off the street. The building had the look of gov about it, complete to the grotesque tri-phallic emblem Croz flouted so proudly. Guards flanked the main entrance.

Behind him, footsteps clicked. Definitely female. He turned.

Yahna Golden was hurrying after him. Her exotic costume of the night before had been discarded in favor of a cloaked gold-and-scarlet travel outfit that looked functional even while it managed to make her look consummately sexy. She waved a pocket-sized packet.

"Eilan! Wait!" Urgency rode that low, throaty voice now, without affecting its sensuousness.

Jesti waited. He felt naked and vulnerable, without helmet or hair.

Her breathing just a trifle ragged, the golden woman closed the gap between them and held out the plas-pak. "You need a permapass."

Wordlessly he took it. The pass said he was CHURT, JESTI-KHAN (no IDtab) Home World: EILAN; Status: ALIEN FUGI-TIVE (provisional admission).

"Where're you from, Psychist?"

"Home planet?" She chuckled (nervously?). "Lyon. Long ago."

Across the court, a squad of policers marched in off the street. They escorted a raffish, heavily shackled group of spacefarers: two Outies, a Jarp, and a turbaned Sek. Blood and bandages were prominent on all. They also appeared to be more than a little drunk. One of the Outreachers sighted Jesti. Whooping tipsily, he waved a tattered purple shirt. Satin.

"Look! A shirt-colored man!"

"Who says it's a man?" The man from Sekhar must have stolen his voice from a frog. "Looks more like a purple egg to me."

"Eggs have yolk inside," the other Outie said. "That thing's solid rock."

"Twoo, twl'oo!" the Jarp whistled in great hilarity. The orange creature went off into a string of bird-sounds no one could understand.

Jesti burned. He started angrily for the prisoners. Roughly, one of the guards shoved him back. Yahna Golden clutched his arm.

"Are you mad? Those are pirates, prisoners! TGW brought them in for local trial this morning."

The pirates were still whooping, laughing, sneering. "That's right, Goldie!" an Outie yelled over his shoulder. "Look after that poor li'l bug. He's bruised purple already! I mean—lookit that big lump on his shoulders!"

More hilarity, while the guards shoved him and the other prisoners through a doorway into the building Jesti had just quitted.

"Pirates." Yahna Golden shuddered. "What can they do but laugh? They're dead already."

Jesti stuffed the pass into a pocket and turned away without so much as the "uh" of standard acknowledgment.

"I got the pass for you," she said, and it sounded more plea than reminder.

Jesti swung back, eyes blazing. "You got the pass for me!" The words exploded out, sneering. "Oh how wonderful of you! I kiss the ground before your bless-ed feet!"

The golden-haired woman's nostrils flared. Her eyes distended. "You shout at me? Without me, you'd still be a prisoner!"

"Without you, I'd still have my hair—my brain!"

Her face turned a lighter olive as blood drained and anger-muscles quivered at the corners of her mouth. "I had no choice and you must know it. When the Crozers asked my help, they said you'd murdered that whore. All the evidence was against you. It's in their favor that they were willing to have me run a brain-drain as a final check. I was on my way to a party—it was *my* favor to *you* that I agreed to do it."

"Favor! A pulse-palp reader for Queen Titsy's holomellers? Save your favors and push 'em right up your haughty *nose*, witch-daktari!"

That did it. Her eyes went both icy and hot. As if Sekhar's too-close sun were blazing through Iceworld's frozen tundras. Her fists clenched until that gilded middle nail stood out like a dagger poised for his heart.

"You—you *Eilan!* You dare question my competence? *Me?*—reader at the Psychesorium of Koba, with three silver medullas from the T-SA!"

"Shit! You stripped my mind, *Lyonese!* You *raped my brain*!"

"Eilan—Jesti. I had to do it. I didn't know why you'd come here, what had happened. About you, the Elders; all the trouble on Eilong. Besides, all that counts is that you're cleared now, free–"

She went on, practically babbling. Jesti couldn't hear the words. They were chaff against the tempest of his fury. The shame, the pain, the outrage—all surged into a desire to hurt, to murder. This so-cool woman with all her curves, her beckoning lips and eyes with their slow sideward glances, her costumed posturings like some wet dream from a holomeller . . . ! He *hated* her.

"You stripped me bare, raped my brain! Durga and Kali curse you!"

A mask seemed to glide into place. "Right then," she said. "Let this be an end to it. I've never humbled myself to a man before. I don't know why I tried this time."

"Wrong," he snarled, staring dark and menacing into her eyes. "It will never be an end. It's your game so far, *Lyonese*. Next turn is mine. This time, you raped my brain. But before my hair grows back, may I rot in Shiva's private hell if I don't rape your body!"

3

Not all thieves wait for the night.

—*Ifrim of Resh*

The Handsome Man, Pearl had named him. He had a name; it was Gel Gelor. He stood on the shuttle viewdeck far from Croz—high above planet Samanna, in fact. Gel Gelor was a study in physical perfection. Profile regular to a fault, black ringlets crisp and glossy, teeth glistening white against the rich brown of his skin. And the rich brown baritone of a voice.

That exterior was a mask. The euphoria and vaulting sense of power he had felt in those final, thrashing moments while Pearl died had ebbed now, dropped away into a bottomless depression. Turmoil seethed within him and verged on panic. How could he have been such a fool as to challenge CongCorp's might and fling himself thus into the face of fate?

Yet even as he raised the question, Gelor knew the answer. There was a limit to how long a man could tolerate sneers and snickers, the mockery of those who worked with him in the central compudator banks, men and women alike. Self-assurance and swagger were gifts he lacked. From the very moment of birth he had seemed destined for the world of intellect: a scholar. A deviant

31

scholar, perhaps, forever probing the far-out, the *outré*, the bizarre.

If only his colleagues could have understood! But no; one and all, they combined to put him down. That was the crime beyond forgiveness. No one questioned his skill as a compudator, but what did that matter when females mocked him as dull and found him tongue-tied?

The final blow had come from Nijah. He still remembered in churning bitterness the way she'd laughed, her red lips mocking him: "Handsome is as handsome doesn't."

It had been the ultimate insult. He was still glad he'd killed her.

At the time it had been different. For days, weeks of hours he had writhed in horror-almost-panic, certain that his crime would be discovered and the ultimate penalty exacted.

That had not happened. Nijah's death had been attributed to some druggy crewman off a departing spacer. No one had given a second thought to the idea that it might be Gel Gelor who was guilty.

He had learned a lesson from the crime: stick with husts. Avoid girls who mock and laugh—and avoid real women altogether! The trouble was that husts cost money. Especially those on a level that could arouse him. A compudator's pay didn't buy much. Yet a compudator had access to other sources of revenue. Sources such as the wealth of CongCorp itself, stellar creds beyond imagining. When a compudator was skilled enough, he could even manipulate the banks a bit and even conceal his defalcations.

Sooner or later that sort of theft must have an end. Gelor knew that. So it was that his larger dream was born. His dream of a coup that would put him beyond even mighty CongCorp's grasp and vengeance. At first conception, it had seemed madness. Then, as he pondered and delved and blocked in angles, excitement had begun to surge in him.

Ultimately he had come to know that there'd be no living with himself unless he made the gamble—for enormous stakes.

Long weeks of planning followed. An application for

leave time was freely granted because of his long record of reliability and duty, loyalty. Ah, the sensation of triumph! At last he was on his way, off to Croz. And there the preposterous wonderful luck of coming upon a stupid, stranded Eilan, rather than having to transship to Eilong itself.

Finally, the bonus of that hust called Pearl. The paroxysmal spasm of ecstasy exploding in him while she writhed and thrashed and died, died while he pulled the lech-noose tighter, tighter.

Now the last embers of that blazing murder-passion were cold and dead. It was time for the next step. The escalation his plan demanded, here on Samanna.

And so Gelor stood on the liftoff viewdeck: poised and handsome without, panic-quivering within. Of all steps in his plan, this one was surely most vital. Yet he had little idea as to how to go about it. A scholar's mind and a background in compudating had given him no background for it.

No matter! He dared not falter on his own timidity! Crossing to the viewport, he stared down at Samanna, at the spaceport area called Riverview.

It was as the edutapes had described it: a crowded yet attractive city, clustered along a lovely broad and winding river. Only it was not a river, but a geo-topographical anomaly. A ribbon-like strip of green sand that stretched down from the distant hills, remnant of some quirk of a long-ago geologic age.

The city itself also somehow captured the spirit of another period, another age, with its jumbled domes and spires and minarets. Of course it also preserved the sewers and cul-de-sacs and alleys of an earlier day, complete with riffraff and cutthroats gathered here from the usual wide spread of other planets.

Riffraff, cutthroats, and . . . the crober. He disliked the slang for an ancient and proud scientific skill, born before the settling of the galaxy: microbiology. The (mi)crober, DeyMeox, famed from one arm of the galaxy to the other.

With her and Samanna's scum to help me, Gelor thought, *I'll yet avenge all insults—and be rich into the bargain!*

Precisely what he wanted . . . and the thought terrified him. At this very moment his palms were sweating.

That realization moved him to swift action. If there was anything he could not afford, it was to allow his resolution to seep away in trepidation. Panic was his constant companion, and he must continue to fight it. He strode to the shuttleport, head held high, and stepped onto the first car down.

In Riverview at last, he asked directions to the old quarter. In a few mins he was passing through an arch that resembled an onion, uprooted and inverted. The streets beyond were narrow and twisty, uneven underfoot. The odor grew appalling. Grimly, trying to hold his breath against the stench, Gelor moved deeper and deeper into the maze.

Ahead, an open doorway belched forth strange music, mixed with a rumble of voices shot with laughter. Obvious sounds; evocative sounds. In bars, over the centuries only the sound of tinkling glasses had been replaced by quieter plass. Gelor approached.

He looked into a downer dive. Spacefarers from half a dozen planets clustered at one end. Fighting down his nervousness, Gelor put on what he hoped was a bold front, entered, and took a place at the end of the bar closest to the door. A bartender with a scarred jaw came to meet him.

"Yours?"

"I'm new, just in." Gelor forced a smile. "What's local?"

The barman reached down one of a dozen hanging tubes and filled a plass from it. He had a hand the size of an arctic mitten. "Zopa. Straight Samannish. No other planet's got Zopa."

Gelor took a tentative taste and managed not to grimace. He had no trouble understanding why this stuff was strictly local. No other planet would want it. *Should've ordered a beer, a Sam(annish) Grolz.* "Great," he got out. He moved the plass to and fro on the bar in erratic cyma recta curves. "Where do I go for a good time?"

"Husts?"

"What else?"

The barman refilled the plass, unfortunately. "With that face, you'd do better on yer own."

"Who's got the time? Besides, I like . . . special. Strangies. Freakos."

The barman snorted. "You call it, Sam husts got it." His face screwed up while he pondered. "Wait a min." He moved off down the bar.

Gelor relaxed a little. Making a show of taking another drink of the Zopa, he half-listened to the blaring music.

The barman was talking to someone in a clot of spacefarers. After a moment, a man—yellow-sashed and surely a Reshi, then—stepped free of the noisy drinkers. He came toward Gelor. A fierce-looking specimen with a heavy, turned-up moustache, he wore a sleeveless jacket that showed off bulging muscles and only half-concealed a knife. His dirty orange turban was stained in places with something that looked suspiciously like blood.

"So." An ugly guttural. "You want fresh meat."

Gelor nodded. He didn't trust his voice to remain steady if he spoke.

"Specials. Freaky stuff, huh. You want that kind of slice, it costs." He watched Gelor nod. "Right, then. Come on."

Gelor let the man from Resh lead him out of the bar. A hundred paces later, the Reshi turned into an even narrower alley. Gelor smelled vomit.

Desperately he said, "Hold on. I mean, I want something *special*. Really special." His voice shook, the way he'd feared it would, but he didn't dare follow any farther without setting up his point.

The Reshi paused, scowling. "What kind of special?"

Gelor's throat rasped, it was so dry. "TZ special. I want a woman who's on TZ."

The Reshi stared. "I won't repeat that aloud. You're on the blank, jacko. What hust's going to hold still for a mind-wipe?"

"Don't worry about that—I'll find my own hust. What I want's TZ. A good full pak of it. Get it for me and I'll make it worth your while, plus." He was fumbling out stells as he spoke. "See? I've got the cred."

The Reshi's face might have been carved from crysplas, for all the expression it showed. "That's something I don't deal in." His hand flashed up to catch Gelor by the shoulder. He spun him about till he faced down the alley. "Hust's got a bed-shed three doors along. Wild one. She'll do anything you want. Young, too. You name it."

A shove sent Gelor staggering along the alley. Frantically he threw up his hands to break his fall if he should trip or slip in vomit. Only then, as he twisted, he glimpsed the other man. With a shock, he saw the bare head. The orange turban was looped between ham-like hands.

Next instant the twisted cloth whipped down over his head, around his throat. He was jerked backward, more than ever off balance. The Reshi's beer-reeking voice rasped: "Hoy! You don't need stells, fella—not for no hust ner no TZ neither. Me, I'll hold that wad for you."

A hand clawed loose Gelor's cred-pouch. Another shove thrust him forward with such violence that slammed his head into a wall. Stunned, he slumped on his face in the alley's filth. He was only dimly aware of the thuds of running feet and the echo of the Reshi's laughter.

How long he lay there Gel Gelor never knew. Seconds only, perhaps. Long enough for his belly to knot with shame and fury. And for humiliation—devastating, all-engulfing—to flame through him. So much for genius! So much for plans. They left a man in an alley flat on his face, eating shit and old vomit.

Was this what they'd meant, those who had laughed so at him? Was this the final meaning behind that "Handsome is as handsome doesn't" line? *Am I really destined to endure humiliation and contempt forever?*

Slowly, he pulled himself up from the slime and the dreck. For a long while he sat, back against the urine-redolent wall, staring numbly into the grimy gloom. When finally he struggled to his feet, he was shaking. Not so much from pain or weakness, now, as in wrenching fury.

Clumsily, he groped inside his jacket to the secret pocket pinned there. It was still there and intact. So was the bulk of his stells intact, then, in local paper. Gelor sighed. At least he hadn't been stupid enough to trust all his funds to the pouch!

Unfortunately he still had no TZ. Without tetrazombase his plan was still only a vaporous mind-thing. Soon now, too, giant CongCorp would be on his trail and hunting hard for him—if the company ruffos weren't already.

It was a thought to bring chills to a constitution stouter than Gelor's. He had no choice now, no choice but to go on. He remembered what that slaver Jonuta was supposed to have said: *You can't keep a bad man down.* And the first step still called for a supply of tetrazombase. TZ.

Where to turn?

He brooded on that for a long moment. The answer became obvious. The treacherous Reshi had given him the clue.

Allegedly, a "wild hust who'd do anything a man paid for" worked behind the third door down this alley. Staring at nothing, Gelor nodded. Husts he knew how to handle. With a knife at her throat, she might even find some of the enslaving drug called tetrazombase.

Swiftly now, he brushed the worst of the alley's dreck from his clothes. Groping, he dug a credbill from his cache. It was a big one. Gelor straightened to his full height and strode down the alley. He knocked at the third door.

It opened a sem, after a moment. A dark eye peered at him. Gelor held the stell-note before that heavily kohl-ringed eye. "A Reshi sent me."

Promptly, the door opened wider. A lot wider. She was hardly a girl but hardly old, either. She gestured him inside. Her lips glowed red as only subcutane could make them. Her scarlet strip-dress matched.

She closed the door behind him. The red lips twisted in a sulky, taunting smile. Slender fingers reached out to caress him.

So she liked the direct approach. Gelor gave it to her. He kicked her in the stomach. The wind went out of her in an agonized gust. Clutching her belly, she doubled over. Purple-dyed hair fell forward.

Gelor shoved her backward. She sprawled onto the floor. Really superb legs, he noted, art-deco'd in multicolored arabesquerie.

He spoke coldly: "If you want to live, you'll do what I tell you."

Making vomitous sounds, she clawed her way up onto one elbow. Choking. Face averted. If she heard his words, she gave no indication of it.

"What I want," he said, pacing the words, "is tetra-zombase. Where do I get it—TZ?"

Her head came up. Still panting, still gagging and hurting, she stared at him. Pretty face, he thought—and stupid. He pushed:

"*Where*?"

Still no answer. He drew back his foot.

She brought up a shielding hand. "What—what is it—you want?"

He held her eyes with his and pronounced it exaggeratedly: "T . . . Z."

She caught her breath. Her eyes distended. "Neg!"

"Grat-shit!" Deliberately, he poised his foot for another kick.

"Neg, please!" This time it was the kick she protested, rather than his demand. "I-I swear . . . I know nothing of TZ." She paused, quaking and uneasy. "There—there is a Saipese. Sometimes he ships with slavers . . ."

"Uh. Where do I find the Saipese?"

"A girl he likes lives two doors down, across the way. If you was to wait there . . ."

"I hope he comes," Gelor said, and bent as he spoke.

With one hand, he seized her by her hair. The other he thrust down the neck of her scarlet dress, into the warmth between her warheads. He clutched, jerked, twisted, jerked again. The garment ripped the rest of the way down the front. He ignored the very naked loveliness he exposed.

When she tried convulsing into biting and scratching, he whipped her clear—by that mass of violet hair—and slapped her across her crimson mouth. At the same time he let go. She was slammed back to the floor, against the wall. Another slap-accompanied yank and he had the dress free of her writhing body. He ripped off a narrow strip. She tried to bite his leg and his foot thumped into her breast, which enveloped the toe of his boot.

While she moaned, hurt too much to scream, he wrenched one of her arms behind her. He tied the ribbon of her destroyed dress tight around her thumb. Then he lashed the other thumb to it.

A second strip bound her knees together. When he turned her over, he noticed the dye or paint on her breast. A word in blue script, outlined in yellow and artfully curving along her warhead's shape: *Amera*. Gelor stuffed a wad of Amera's late dress into her mouth and tied it in place with still another ragged strip of scarlet.

He rose and surveyed the room. A stout iron lamp fixture extended from high in one wall, bearing an A-curved neon bulb. Tying another strip of her garment to it, he heaved Amera to her feet and looped that strip's free end under the length of red joining her (red, now) thumbs. He tugged upward and she bent over. Way over, arms twisted back, thumbs high behind her.

He stepped back. She was helpless. Bound, gagged, and naked. Very sexy, really. Gelor was not in the least interested.

"Is there really a Saipese, Amera?"

Staring at the floor because she had to, she stood immobile, legs pressed together as if primly. It made her taller, relieving the strain.

"If there isn't, your thumbs go, eventually. Too bad."

Abruptly she lost all trace of hardness and maturity. Only a frightened girl, now, she twitched her head and spoke with her eyes. Black-rimmed eyes stared, huge. Rolled. Gelor loosened the gag.

"The Saipese drinks at the bar next street over. They call him Quong." Her voice was high, girlish, strained and quaky with fear.

"How your memory improves!" Gelor smiled thinly. Shoving her back against the wall, he reinserted the gag. I'll come back if I find him and he helps me. Otherwise . . ."

He left her to make his way back down the alley and on, to find that bar. His excitement was almost enough to balance his earlier, stomach-wrenching panic. *Victory has that effect on my nerves!* He tried to paste a confident smile on his face.

The Saipese called Quong was in the place just as she'd said. A small man, slight, with yellowish skin and a flamestone necklace. He looked smoother than the Reshi. Less menacing. That helped. Gelor even found the boldness to approach him directly.

Quong seemed not at all affrighted at the mention of tetrazombase. "TZ?" He eyed Gelor with a con man's bland, bright-eyed speculation. His hand came up, thumb and first two fingers rubbing each other in the immemorial sign. "Danger. That costs. Ten mil, 'tleast. You got 't?"

"I got it." Gelor felt a tingle of gratification that he'd managed to match the other's slurred slum-speak.

"Lessee the color ya cred."

Gelor showed him a bill big enough to widen Quong's eyes.

"Five now," he said. "Res' when uh ge' back. No lock on price. May come higher'n ten. Pos?"

"Negatory," Gelor came back bluntly. His voice didn't even quiver. "You go out 'ith my five and don' come back—where'm I?"

"Shaft City." The Saipese grinned. He had small, sharp eyeteeth like a cat or the creature called a Xerxes weasel. "A'righ'. You've saw the short side. I get the stuff, I bring 't here. You stake one bill'th the bar ri' now. Thass my lock so you don' change ya mind 'n' drift. Done?"

"Done."

Gelor laid out the five-stell note. Quong called the bartender and instructed him to hold it. With a final needle-toothed grin, Quong vanished out the door in a flurry of balloonpants.

Gelor ordered a beer and settled down to wait. Once again panic was rearing in him. His victory over Amera had gone flat all at once. What did it matter that he'd twisted her? The Saipese had twisted him even more, and with words, not kicks or slaps. Who knew whether the little brass-hued man would ever come back? Or if he'd bring the TZ if he did return. Or maybe come with an escort of policers. They'd have questions for a stranger trying to buy TZ! And the barman looked just the sort to go along with whatever Quong said.

It was more than Gelor could handle. Unable to sit longer, he rose and went out into the street.

No sign of Quong. Gelor was having trouble controlling his breathing. It came too fast, too shallow, and he couldn't slow it. When he tried deep-breathing his heart seemed to stutter.

What if Quong came back with some thug, a ruffo? —that Reshi! Gelor cringed at the thought. Instinctively, he knew he lacked the nerve to fight back.

A windowless building—warehouse?—stood across and down from the bar. What appeared to be buttresses thrust out on either side of heavy doors. Trying to stay inconspicuous, Gelor ambled that way. He had to walk carefully. Tension had set his bowels to churning. Any sudden move might pull a humiliating trigger.

He reached the far buttress. To his delight, its shadows provided nice cover. He could see the bar's door with minimal exposure of himself.

"Ya lookin' the wrong way," a voice said, from behind him.

Gelor spun to face Quong, bare sems away, teeth bared in an evil smirk. While Gelor groped unsuccessfully for words, Quong drew aside one flap of his coat to reveal a small, flat package.

"Product here. Your bit?"

Hastily Gelor fumbled big bills from his tunic. The Saipese counted them carefully, looked at him.

"Nine—?"

"Your bartending friend has the other."

"The deposit, pos." Quong's black eyes sparkled wickedly. "Hoped ya'd fergot." He handed over the flat packet. "Done an'done, frien'. Come 'roun' nex' time ya got some bizness."

He walked off toward the bar. Only after he had gone did it occur to Gelor that there remained a point at issue. He hurried after the man in the balloonpants. Inside the bar, he peered this way and that. No Quong. Gelor popped an agitated question.

The barman jerked a thumb over his shoulder. "He left. Back way."

Numbly, Gelor once more stumbled out onto the footway. Back in the buttress's shelter, he unwrapped the flat package with stiff fingers. It contained a plastipak holding four injectabs. A black skull was stamped into each tab. Gelor chewed his lip. Was this really tetrazombase? He had no answer. He didn't even know what the nasty illegal stuff was supposed to look like.

Quong's air and hasty exit said something, though, and Gelor didn't like it. He didn't like to think about it, either. He'd seldom felt lower, less adequate. To come this far, take all these risks, even kill . . . only to be played for a fool by a Saipese rascal!—It left him shaking with helpless fury.

And with fear. He knew it well.

Yet he dared not let himself be caught up by that fatal flaw in his character, that inner weakness he knew so well and hid so desperately. Somehow, he had to drive himself to action.

Slowly, he moved off down the footway, back past the bar. Back in the direction he'd originally come from. A mixed din of voices, movement, street sounds impinged on him from the left. Moving down an alley toward it, not quite knowing why, he entered a small, crowded open market.

A hag wrapped in a ragged sari was peddling skweez-paks of everchil pop. Gelor bought one. He drank thirstily, even though the taste of the stuff was vile. He was still sipping, walking, when a man thrust a cap of liquid flamo at him. Gelor jerked away from it: cooking heat for the poorest of the poor. Dangerous stuff. If spilled it seared the flesh in a flash, stronger than the strongest acid. The stuff had military use, too. Gelor pushed on past . . .

And stopped short. Could it be that part of his pervasive panic was born of his very defenselessness, his lack of any sort of weapon?

He turned back and bought the cap of flamo. In a niche

out of view of passersby, heart thuttering, he emptied his purchase into the empty pop pak.

A quick compression of his fingers sent flame spurting from the skweez-pak—a thin jet that fired the nearest can of trash like magic.

Like magic, too, was the feeling that welled up in Gel Gelor. Of a sudden he felt less helpless. More in command—dangerous, even. Pivoting, he left the market. Another pedlar was thrust away by a firm-faced Gelor. In minutes he was at the bed-shed of the Ganji hust who'd sent him to Quong.

The door was latched. That made him stop and step back, once more caught up in surging panic. He had left the hust—Amera—hanging and helpless. How could she have worked the latching lever?

He knew that if he paused to think that through now, he'd be lost. His lifetime companion would paralyze him—fear. He battled it. With all his might he drove his foot at the latch. The savage kick burst the hust-hole's door open. He followed, fast and ready.

The girl-woman no longer hung from the lamp bracket and the lamp was alight, in dull burnt orange and ruddy pink. Amera lay at full length on her crib-cot. The Saipese dealer half-knelt beside her.

It made sense, of course. Gelor cursed himself for a fool for not having seen the real scrute sooner. Quong—if that was really his name—was the hust's man, or pimp! That was why she had turned the action in his direction. Now he stared around at the intruder. His first thought was that maybe he'd done bad business with an undercover policer.

"You burned me," Gelor said. "The tabs you sold me aren't TZ." It was a shot in the dark, but worth the gamble.

Of course it also told Quong that this was no policer. "Thass ri', handsome." Quong was on his feet and a knife had appeared in his hand as if from nowhere. His left hand drew a slender, wand-like shaft. The black eyes glittered. The eyeteeth shone sharper than ever. "Wha' d'you think you' gointa do 'bout it?"

The old panic rose again in Gelor, but only for a moment.

"A burn for a burn," he said, and managed to keep his voice even and cold.

His fingers convulsed on the pop container. Flamo shot forth in a blazing liquid stream—straight into the bronze man's face. More specifically: his eyes. His scream was like nothing Gelor had ever heard. The sound of it was a clawing hand in his lurching stomach. He stared at the Saipese.

Quong had dropped his knife to rush his clawing hands to his eyes. Staggering, moaning with a keening sound, he beat his head against the wall.

Gelor picked up the knife and did things with it. It could have been called a mercy killing. It stopped Quong's screams, and his pain, and Quong.

With a strange sense of wonder, Gelor realized that he had never in his life felt so good. It was the first time he had used a knife on a man. Now this feeling made him know it would not be the last time. All traces of the panic that had ridden him so unrelentingly had vanished. In their stead swelled a soaring sense of exultation and exaltation. Power surged in his blood. Excitement engulfed him so that he quivered. Even the moment of his murdering Pearl was but a guttering candle beside this feeling. Nothing would stop him now.

Nothing can!

Fulfillment of his dream of triumph and domination was as if ordained. Shiva, Lord of Destruction, God of death, lived and surged in Gel Gelor. He wanted to shout it forth, to proclaim it to all this world called Samanna—to the Galaxy, the universe!

Instead, he deftly reclaimed the bills he had given Quong. Next he checked the wand-shaft the dead man had gripped in his left hand. Gelor frowned. *Too light and thin to be a bludgeon. Too blunt for slashing or stabbing,* he mused. He examined the . . . thing. Perhaps as long as his forearm from wrist to elbow, it was no bigger around than a tool-handle. Designed for a grasping hand. Close to one end protruded what appeared to be a triggering button, a rocking switch. Gingerly, Gelor snicked it backward.

A heavy spring shot out of the shaft's other end. The top hit one leg of the crib-cot. The leg splintered.

A staring Gelor understood why: the tip was weighted with a solid cylinder of some heavy or mass-compacted metal. He felt a warm glow of pleasure. This was a devastatingly deadly weapon! It was one that gave a man an unexpected reach beyond the length of his arm—and impact to shatter any skull or crush sternum or backbone! This prize made Quong worthwhile.

Rising, he forced the spring back into its handle—that took some strength!—and locked it with the trigger. At that moment Amera stopped cringing in the corner and made for the door. An orchid-colored wrap-robe rustled. Gelor whirled and acted instinctively.

The spring-thing crushed skulls, all right.

He was about to leave when he had another thought. He looked around. Checked the crib-cot. Felt, pulled, grinned. Neither Amera nor Quong would be needing all these stell-notes! Gelor hurried back out into the alley.

His impulse was to go directly in quest of the scientist he needed. DeyMeox. Yet euphoria rose high, and he instead turned vindictively in the direction of the first bar, where he'd met the Reshi strangle-thief.

As he had suspected, an alley lay behind it. Sensible; low dives *should* have rear doors opening onto alleys! He thought about that as he returned to the fronting street. He saw and heard no policer action. Good. He was in a bad area, and he had a weapon for each hand. Calling over a sharp-eyed boy from a group playing coin-toss in the filth, he held up a coin bigger than any he saw them using. The boy's eyes flicked their eager stare from the coin to Gelor to coin to Gelor.

"Wha' do uh do?"

"In that bar's a man in an orange turban," Gelor said, hoping he was right. "Moustache on him, turned up." He watched the boy nod. "Tell him I sent you to get him."

"Thassall?"

"That's all. Your job's over when you tell him."

The boy's lips parted in a crooked smile. He reached for the coin. Gelor pocketed it and produced his smallest bill.

The boy watched him tear it in half. He gave the urchin one piece.

"You get the other half when the man comes out."

"Wha'f he won' come?"

"We both lose cred."

"Unnerstan'." The boy shoved the half-bill into his grubby pants with a grubby hand and turned to trot off toward the bar.

The moment he entered, Gelor sprinted for the alley. At the bar's rear entrance he took up a stance with his back against the wall. The spring-club was close by his side, with his thumb on the nigh-invisible trigger. He didn't expect to wait long, and he didn't.

The dirty blue door opened. The turbaned head came out to peer warily this way and that. Gelor stepped into view.

"Peace," he said, raising his left hand in an open-palmed gesture. "I brought you a present." He showed the man the skull-stampéd injectab.

A guttural sound rose in the Reshi's throat. Not a word. His eyes flared in shock and fear and—knife out, he lunged. And Gelor brought up the spring-thing and thumbed the rocker-switch.

The spring released. The weighted tip rushed out. It caught his attacker in the throat—the Adam's apple. The fellow stopped as if cast in stone, instantly. Mouth horridly agape and eyes bulging. For the second time in less than an hour, an attacker of Gel Gelor dropped his knife.

Gelor stepped back and this time he lashed out with the weapon as a club, to the swine's temple. With a sound of bone shattering, the man toppled sideward. His shoulder hit the building's wall and he began sliding down.

It was easy to hold the dead man against the wall with one hand while the other slipped into the shirt beneath the sleeveless jacket. A swift riffling produced Gelor's stolen cred-pouch. He noted with pleasure that it was thicker than it had been when he had lost it. Smiling, he let the Reshi slide on down to sit against the wall, dead.

Gelor started moving. Meanwhile, he considered: the effect of the tab on that swine, for one thing. There'd been no mistaking his terror, his panic. Fake or not, the skull-stamped tab had come through to him as TZ.

If it would dupe a bottom-level thug, mightn't it also deceive a scientist?—DeyMeox, for instance. It was, Gelor felt, an avenue definitely worth pursuing. *Even more to the point is the way* I'm *reacting!*

Street-smart or not, he had taken the initiative in more than one deadly dangerous confrontation. Yet he hadn't hesitated. Hadn't faltered. The only emotion he felt was one of soaring triumph, of mastery. At last he had isolated the secret that would carry him to triumph!

Death, death, with my own hand to deal it!

For him, he had discovered just now, dealing death flashed him free of his old panic—even unsureness! The stimulant supreme, beyond food or drink or sex or intellect, drugs or booze. Death. *Killing.*

He left the alley. Shoulders back, head high, he walked taller than he ever had in his life. His blood sang. His heart thrummed. It was time to go see DeyMeox-crober!

4

Seek and ye shall find . . . trouble, more often than not!
—*Vark of Bleak*

The question was, who had killed the hust called Pearl?
Jesti knew he hadn't.

That still left a lot of other candidates. Finding the right
one might take a little doing. So, tonight he walked
Oddford's spaceport streets. Jestikhan Churt, fresh from a
brain-drain, fresh from the local lockbox, and fresh from
Yahna Golden. His hate for the golden woman still seethed
in him, a living thing.

He knew that he had meant his threat: sooner or later he
would find her, match her rape for rape: her body for his
brain. *Thereby making me . . . what?* He wondered. Soberly.
Not grinning. Jestikhan Churt, pacing through Oddford,
planetary capital of Croz.

A fragment from the brain-drain came back to him.
Something one of Eilong's Elders had argued in the course
of one of Jesti's early examinations.

"*A dangerous man,*" the longbeard had insisted.
"*Subversive at the very least. A menace to all that stands
for Eilong and to every man who stands against him.*"

Jesti wondered. Was he really that bad, that dangerous?
Or was he just another Eilan miner dyed purple from
kiracat?

It's a good time to find out.

The entrance to the Labyrinth lay ahead, in ugly darkness. Jesti turned and took the cablelift down the shaft to the bar. The Baltilana. It was empty this time of day. The (human) bartender had even run out of plasses to polish. He stood leaning against the backbar, head tilted up and to one side as if in reverie. The holocube was in the other direction.

Jesti strode toward him. The sound of his footsteps alerted the lounging man. One glimpse of Jesti imparted a greenish cast to his face. He moved off down the bar. His effort to appear casual came off as ludicrous. And Jesti kept right on beaming.

"Hey, I'll bet you didn't know me without my hair. It do make a difference, don't it!"

The barman made an incoherent sound and moved farther away.

"You know," Jesti said confidentially, following him on his side of the bar, "I liked that hair of mine. Matter of fact I'd still have it, if it hadn't been for you."

That brought a mumble. It took Jesti about three seconds to vault the bar, come down quietly, and cheerfully cuff the fellow lightly on the arm.

"Hello again."

The bartender had no choice but to face him. His eyes showed fright.

Jesti grinned. "What say we have a drink?"

"Sure, firm!" The man's fingers were all thumbs as he made a business of wiping off the polished glaze. "What, ah, what'll it be?"

"Got any orbisette?"

The very word seemed to have a bad effect on the barman. But, "Coming up," he said, and started to set out a plass.

"No plass," Jesti said. "Let's have the whole pottle."

The other man reached one from the shelf and set it down before his accoster. Fumbling a knife from beneath the bar, he snipped the seal.

"Good, good," Jesti beamed. "Let's have that drink now. What's your name, anyhow?"

The barman pointed to the tag on his shirt. *Achmet*, it read. One of a million. Millions. Meanwhile he again started to reach for a plass.

Jesti caught his hand. It was sweaty. Jesti said, "No plass, Achmet."

"Huh–"

Jesti kept on beaming. "You're drinking first. The whole pottle, Achmet."

"Th—the whole p–" Achmet choked. "Grabbles, Mirza, that'd kill me."

"Could be," Jesti said cheerfully. "A lot less than that very nearly killed me, last night." He picked up the ordinary knife with which Achmet had snipped the pottle's seal and tested its point and blade with his little finger. (He'd seen a man test a blade with his thumb, once, and cut himself. Stupid, Jestikhan Churt thought, and remembered.) "Get started, friend Achmet."

The barman began to shake. Visibly. "What—what is it you want?" He seemed to have trouble getting the words out.

Jesti grinned. "I want you to drink a pod of orbisette." He had a notion that his pause was made the more sinister by the very fact that he was still grinning. "Or, of course, you could give me some answers." He studied the knife.

"Wha—wha' kinduv answers?"

"Answers about a hust named Pearl who worked out of here, *Achmet-t*."

The barman's pallor was nothing less than frightening, now. "I—don't—didn'—know 'er."

"Don't give me that!"

Jesti spat the words. Immediately he seized Achmet by the jacket and jerked him so close their noses were nearly touching. The knife's point went tight against the fellow's throat, just enough to break the skin. A thin trickle of blood oozed.

"She was here," Jesti said, grin and cheerful tone gone, "and I was with her. *Saved* her! I want to know what happened. All about her. Now."

If the bartender at Baltilana had been afraid before, terror rode his shoulder now. His cheeks sagged. His lips quivered. His hands flapped at the knife in small, frantic gestures that mirrored his panic while not quite touching the blade.

"I—I—"

"*Who was she, Achmet?*"

"I—don' know. I m-mean—Tao's balls, she 'us just a hust. From Thebanis, I think. Some bas'ard ditched 'er here. Sometimes I'd slice 'er—free, I mean—so I'd let 'er hang around the place, you know? Or pass her some hypno to slip a loaded mark. She'd cut me in. You know how't is . . ."

Jesti twisted the man's jacket even tighter. "What about last night?"

"I don' know. Honest. She come in early, actin' funny. Smirking, sort uv, like she was onto something. Said she needed orbisette, maybe half a pod. Already spiked."

"Uh. After that?"

"I give it to her 'n' she didn' say nothing. Jus' took the pod up to her bowl. Thass all uh know. Really!"

The barman's neck was wet with sweat now. The trickle of blood from the knifepoint (which Jesti still held in place) smudged greasily in it. Breathing hard, Achmet licked his lips.

"Look, she was waitin' fa you, I guess. Thass the first time she'd came down. Then the two of you wen' back up. Thass all I know. Everything, even i-if you c-cut me." His whole voice and body trembled.

Jesti had a mind to do just that. Cut him. Yet what would that accomplish? Nothing—except maybe to bring the policers back for a man they'd love to grab again. He thought about it for a moment. Then he released the barman's jacket. Achmet sagged, slumping against the backbar as if his legs wouldn't hold him. He had the look of a man who had stared death in the face so close that he still couldn't believe he was alive.

Jesti asked, "Who else did she know? Come on—help!"

Achmet shivered again. He regained control, visibly working at it. His shoulders drew up in a shrug, probably because he couldn't lift a hand to flip his fingers. Not at Death. He swallowed, also visibly.

"It's like uh said. Uh don' know that much about 'er. She didn' have no reglar marks. She wasn' that good a slice, y'know?"

Jestikhan stared. "You asking *me*?" And while Achmet swallowed, hard, Jesti went on, "Other girls? Friends?"

Achmet shook his head. "Th'other husts didn' like 'er. Uh mean, that Terasaki coil 'n' all—she jus' wasn' Croz. They thought she was tryina play top goddess, so they froze 'er. 'Cept Zanjol, maybe. She's from offplanet, too. Tula. Sometimes the pair of 'em sort uv got together."

Jesti stood very still. "Zanjol?"

"Ahh, try The Gallus. She's got those crazy Corper twists skindyed on 'er face—green. Guess what th'other husts thinka that! They call 'er the Green Jinkle—you know, like in not worth a. Thass why her and Pearl maybe got t'gether. Lissen, I'm really sorry they shaved yuh."

"Uh huh. Want to buy me a Terasaki coil? Never mind—take off that jacket—faster! Where's The Gallus, Achmet ole friend?"

Coming out of his jacket, Achmet told him. And: "They got a thing out front with a big noose on it. You know, like they useta hang people on. Gallus."

"Oh," Jesti said, slipping on the barman's jacket.

He had to ask directions three times, en route. (The jacket he got rid of at once. He kept only the little wad of money he'd felt in it.) Each time he received a "bonus" —alleged humor about nooses, murder, Poofing. Charming.

Those were just the jokes. Reality was worse.

Inside The Gallus, zithoons squealed graveyard music. Flickering lights cast horripilating shadows of swinging "corpses." Like jungle vines, a curtain of nooses dangled from the ceiling. Waiters wore black hoods and were dressed as executioners. The bartender was . . . gray. A necrotic bluish gray. Hideous. Charming.

To get a drink, Jesti had to let an "executioner" loop one of the ropes about his neck. He didn't like that any better than the rest of it. Maybe because it came too close to home . . .

Still, I'm here, with a tenuous lead to Pearl. Assuming I can find the Green Jinkle!

He asked. Sure, they knew *her*—what'd he want *her* for? "I'm her long-lost brother, the Purple Tinkle. Our long-lost uncle just died and left us three million stells. Where is she?" He glanced about.

Some of them stared and a couple chuckled or giggled— uncertainly. They pointed. Booth in the corner. Drinking alone? Not trying to attract any taps? Frowning, he went that way, and just managed to get the frown off his face before he reached the booth. He turned, showed the bartender two fingers. Receiving a nod, Jesti slid into the booth.

She was short and chubby, with cat-green eyes and a chest on her like a soccer ball cut in half and glued onto each side. Enhanced, surely. And yes, there were the snaky green cheek-and-forehead traceries good ole Achmet had mentioned. Subcutaneous dye, definitely. Both hands around the plass of something she was nursing, the Green Jinkle was leaking a lot of tears.

"Drink it, Zanjol. I ordered us another."

"Why? Who're you?" She looked up, swollen of eye. "Great balls of Musla! What a dye-job—*purple*! You must—hey. You called me by name."

He nodded. "Because—oh, dammit!" The waiter interrupted, pretending to garrote while setting down the two drinks. Jesti glowered him away and pushed one over to Zanjol. "*I'd* call you Akima," he said, and noted that she didn't simper. He nodded. "I see you know."

"Know?"

"I called you Zanjol because Pearl did. She—" He paused. She had snapped him a wild stare. Then she snatched up her drink and drained it all. She looked at the new plass, while tears rushed and she made choky-sobby noises.

"I was with her last night. Saved her from some spacefarer named, uh, Karim, and two others. Bet you heard about that, hmm. We went up and I drank something called orbisette and passed out. When I woke, I was in jail. *Jail*, Zanjol. Someone had murdered Pearl and pinned it on me. A psychist proved I didn't have anything to do with it." He touched his dome. "That's what happened to my hair. The flainers had to shave me to—to mind-wipe me."

She was staring. "That's the damndest cock-and-balls story I ever heard, jacko."

"Name's Jesti. Jes-tee-khan Churt. Here. My clean bill of health from your robed local sadists-excuse-me-policers. Sounds like a bullshit story to me too, Zanjol. But someone killed that nice kid, and that same someone really set me up. I want him. *If* the policers ask, you know you'll tell them all about him. What about me? *I want to go after the bastard, Zanjol.*"

She stared at him. Her plump body slumped, seemed to shrink. Her mouth moved soundlessly, opening and shutting. Those green eyes filled and overflowed tears onto green-traced skin. The tears weren't green. After another second, her face collapsed. Green subcutane traceries folded in on each other like the shriveling of an old lime in the sun. Her voice was a whisper.

"Saw her . . . saw her yes-yesterday. Afternoon. She was too high to talk much. Claimed she was redshiftin' for The-Thebanis. Loved that dam' planet!" She sniffled, choked, tried hard, fought it back. "Showed me the pass. Some . . . some man was going to pay her way."

"Not a purple one, hmm?"

She shook her head, looking into her drink. "She was supposed to do a job for him," she quavered out, and Jesti's belly muscles went taut. "Don't ask. She wouldn't even talk about it. Not even to me-e-e." She wept some more.

Meanwhile Jesti's belly muscles were tight enough to hurt. He had a feeling that he was . . . almost . . . onto something. Something. What? *Who?*

"It—it had her sort of fobbied," Zanjol got out. "He—he was like out of a holomeller, she said. Only more so. That good-lookin', I mean."

"A super-handsome man," he said. "Uh. He have a name, this handsome bastard?"

"She—she didn't say. *If* she knew, she wouldn't say. She–"

"He promised her big cred to do something for him. Something that involved me, Zanjol. I want to know what, and why. And why he left me to pay the price. The psychist was just luck. Otherwise I might be here for life—in jail. No name?"

She stared. "That's it. I don't want to talk about her anymore—I don' want to talk to you anymore. Go, purple man. I yell, you're in a lotta trouble. Go. She's d . . . ead, and I got a livin' to make."

Jesti stared at her long enough to make her look down. Then he left.

Tendrils of memory left from the brain-drain assured him that possessions hadn't been Pearl's long suit. The policers had *not* found any pass or big cred. Zanjol said Pearl had talked Thebanis. Home. Zanjol said she had *seen* an offplanet pass. Jesti thought on that as he hit the street.

Passes don't just vanish and I don't have it. Pearl's was gone. So—someone took it. Who? Easy—the same man who gave it to her in the first place. Somebody so handsome he belongs in the holomellers! Uh. And maybe the same man who killed her, to frame me for her death?—not to mention taking samples of my blood and semen. For what? Why?

For some reason—because I'm an Eilan, not because I'm me. I'd bet on it.

Great. If only any of it made sense!

It didn't, and that was what made it so maddening. In turn, that left Jestikhan Churt no choice but to keep on with his probing. He had to dig deeper, and then deeper, until he learned *something. The truth! Damn it—because I have to know!*

Grimly, he turned in the direction of the shuttle station. In charge he found a thin, pallid Crozer in a blue jallabah. The fellow seemed to have no time for hairless Eilans. The ring that circled his pineal eye was white.

"Is it true," Jesti asked conversationally, "that a Crozer's middle eye gives him the power of second sight? Can he read minds with it?"

The Crozer didn't answer. All his attention remained on the routine of his work. Or so he wanted it to seem.

Jesti sighed. "Neg—that's ridiculous. Can't be so. I should know better." He put on a warm and friendly grin. "Because if you could read minds you'd know how I feel about being ignored and what's going to happen to that eye of yours in another sec or three."

He leaned across the counter as he spoke, and let his hand fall on a spiked marker weight. His hand closed. He picked it up, hefted it thoughtfully, still studying the man from Croz. And saying nothing.

A visible nervousness came on the Crozer. He seemed to be having difficulty getting the extra joints of his fingers to behave.

"All I want," Jesti said gently, "is information. Has any spacer cleared for Thebanis since last night?"

For a few secs, he thought blue-robe wasn't going to reply. Then words came, in an uncertain voice so low Jesti could barely hear: "Nothing direct. You have to go by way of Jasbir."

"So did anything clear for Jasbir?"

"Uh. Pos. Early this morning. A merchanter."

"Carrying passengers, though?"

"Pos."

Jesti tried a bluff: "And a passenger booked onto that ship, through here."

"Ah . . . uh . . . pos, pos!" The spike had wiggled a little. "True."

Jesti began to feel that he was pulling teeth out of a rock. Angrily he brought the marker weight down on the counter. It whacked loudly.

"Listen, twitch! Don't mix tricks with me! Volunteer words—quick! What did this passenger look like?"

"He—he—he was very . . . *very* handsome," the Crozer said, in an even weaker voice. And concluded by spilling almost silently to the floor in a dead faint.

It was, Jesti decided, time to move on.

Where?

To Jasbir, clearly. Either he forgot it or pretended to, or yielded to the compulsion to find the handsome man who had set him up and murdered a good-looking and mighty young girl. On Jasbirstation he might stand a chance of picking up the handsome man's trail.

The only problem was that spacing to Jasbir would cost cred—more by far than Jestikhan Churt had. Or had any hope of acquiring. To make matters worse, the mystery that engulfed him was deepening rather than clearing. His first thought had been that Eilong's Elders had gone stark, staring fobbo. That they perceived him as so important they had sent out a kill-team to set him up for murder.

That was silly. If the Elders wanted him dead, they had only to kill him. Or pay someone—and he'd seen people both last night and this afternoon who'd surely placidate a foreigner for the price of three drinks. (*Orbisette*, he thought with a grim sarcasm.) All this other business was too complicated. The chances of any such plot's failing couldn't help but run high.

If they tried once, logic told him, *they'll try again.* It was his own neck in the noose and on the block. *Besides, what would such a scheme accomplish? What effect would it—could it—have on Eilong?*

Paranoid means you think you're important enough to attract a big plot to Poof you, he reminded himself, and his grin wasn't pretty.

There was another aspect. So far, no link to Eilong had appeared. Handsome or hideous, the man who had apparently hired Pearl, slain Pearl, stolen her departure pass and ticket . . . clearly he wasn't an Eilan!

Yet he had set it all up. Why?

To get samples of Eilan semen and Eilan blood? To what end? Jesti could find no answer and it was enough to make a miner's head ache. Except that he had no time to waste on such. The only course to take (it seemed) involved tracking down the murderer, the handsome man, and wringing some sort of answer from the bastard.

Which meant that Jesti was back where he'd started: stranded on Croz, with his neck in a noose and no funds to escape or find answers.

A fine predicament. Yet somehow, incredibly, it was not in him to feel crushed by it. An element of challenge was involved, and he warmed to that. Excitement, not depression, gripped him. He paced on, thinking.

It all came down to a matter of searching out possible roads to take, and choosing the right one. The roads had to be those his adversaries (whoever they might be) would never think of. His course had to be one too mad to consider. *Uh huh—so what's the least likely way for me, an Eilan miner, to escape off Croz?*

And then, having escaped, get to Jasbir and hunt down his quarry?

It went without saying that he'd need help, and he pushed his clanking brain in that direction. Help. A psychist, for example. A person who knew how others' minds worked, and could second-guess them. And if that psychist had the ear and trust of the Powers That Be on Croz—so much the better. Ah—and even better, if the psychist had a personal debt to collect from its chosen aide. Vengeance, for instance, to exact for indignities inflicted.

(Jesti had stopped, thinking, and was staring at nothing. Thinking.)

He began nodding. The more he thought about it, the better he liked it.

Laughing without a sign of mirth, he set off in search of Yahna Golden.

5

An intelligence test sometimes shows a man how smart
he would have been not to have taken it.

—*L. J. Peter*

The (mi)crober named DeyMeox, biochemist/microbiologist
extraordinaire, famed throughout the Galaxy, lived and
worked in one of Riverview's suburbs, an enclave called
Ishkuzri. A high, alabaster-white wall surrounded her
establishment. The main entrance was set within a symbol-
embellished lancet arch. A giant cupola-canopy both provided shade and collected solar energy.

Gelor approached boldly and punched the sounder both
louder and longer than necessary. Attired in broad-
shouldered, blousy white waist-length jacket and leg-
moulding black pants, he waited.

Footsteps whispered within. An eye-slot opened. Gelor
glimpsed an over-large hooked nose and a dark-brown
scowl.

"Yes?"

"I wish to see DeyMeox-crober-daktari."

"She sees no one." The eye-slot started to close.

"Not even if he brings a message from her old associate,
Parenji?"

The slot-lid stopped. "Parenji?"

"Uh. Parenji-crober of Ghanj." Gelor smiled blandly.

59

"Perhaps you've heard of their work together on the sensing systems of Shirashi jelly-blobs."

The scowl beyond the eye-slot deepened. On the other hand, a touch of uncertainty shaded the voice. "Perhaps . . . well . . . all right, I'll take the message."

It was a ploy Gelor had anticipated. "I fear that's not quite practical." He hefted a flat portacase half as tall as he was into the eye's view. "You see, there are diagrams, printouts, worksheets."

He heard a small, hacking sound of irritation. The eye-slot closed. The gate itself opened, a half-dozen sems. A hand appeared.

With one hand, Gelor slid the portacase close to the opening and the reaching hand. With the other, he drew the late Quong's slender spring-thing from within his snowy jacket.

The gate opened wider, wide enough for a sour-faced 'Vocker servant to step into view. He was still mumbling testily when Gelor triggered the spring-thing. The tip leaped out to drive into the pit of the man's stomach. Paralyzed and fighting frantically for air, he stumbled back.

Gelor followed rapidly, closing the gate behind him.

The world inside the compound was nothing less than lovely. Fountains bubbled and glittered prismatically. A backdrop of Panishi greenery set off bright clusters of Franjese flowers. The sheer beauty of the (austere?) scientist's layout left Gelor speechless. It was, he decided, just the kind of place he would have, once he'd carried his coup through to fruition.

Meanwhile the servant was recovering his breath, after a fashion.

Gelor gestured with the "reloaded" spring-thing. "Your employer, fobber. DeyMeox. Now!"

The man from Havoc choked, retched briefly. Choking and stumbling, he led Gelor back along a walkway, then through a portico to a metal door all covered with arabesquerie. A second door lay just beyond. The servant closed the outer after them and pressed a button set into the "airlock" wall. When the inner door opened, Gelor pushed the man through and followed closely.

The room they entered was of the stuff of nightmares.

One whole wall was taken up by recordack units of the type used to store raw scientific data. Another featured cabinex isolator cages in blue and green, all occupied by creatures he couldn't even recognize. Nameless equipment stood everywhere, uncoordinated—fantastic devices whose function Gelor didn't bother trying to guess.

In the midst of it all a woman sat at a workbench, nearly shapeless in protective "clothing."

She hunched over a machine that clicked and spun lens-fields while she punched touch-buttons unnecessarily hard. In addition to the standard crober shielding, she wore a micromask.

Gelor put on his most flashing-dashing smile. "Forgive me, Microber. It is, I know, unforgivable for me to intrude on your work."

The woman looked up, clearly startled. "Who are you! What are you doing in my quarters?" She sounded more baffled than angry or even questioning.

"Sahibah, forgive me!" the cringing servant blurted before Gelor could reply. "He *forced* me, Sahibah. He hit me! He—"

"Silence, bug!" Gelor bowed politely to the woman. "My name is of no importance. I am here to propose a project. I believe you will agree that it holds advantages for both of us, Microber."

For a moment she leaned back, studying him. Her hand came up in an abrupt gesture. It signaled dismissal.

"I have more projects than I can complete in a lifetime. Go."

Gelor's smile didn't falter. "No."

"What—?!" The micromask jerked up. "What did you say?"

"I said no," Gelor told her equably. "The project I have in mind—"

"How dare you!"

She was on her feet now, tearing off the micromask to show blazing eyes. Hardly a beauty, but to Gelor's surprise her appearance was neither old nor unattractive. Solid and stocky, she was distinguished chiefly by shadow-colored hair cropped short enough to show her ears and nape and high, broad forehead, and an obvious clear-eyed intelligence of expression. He knew the apparent-age thirty-six or so did not match her birthdate.

"How dare I?" Gelor chuckled. He moved forward as he spoke. "This is how."

He slapped her across the face.

As if the blow were a signal, the servant released a choked cry and leaped at the intruder—who let him have the spring-thing's weighted end in the groin. The 'Vocker collapsed in a groaning heap.

Again, DeyMeox's (green-dyed) eyes distended, as if she couldn't quite believe that all this was happening. Her hand rose to her cheek. After a glance down at her servant, she stared wordlessly at Gelor.

"You may sit down," he said politely.

Still wordless, Crober DeyMeox sank back into her seat.

Gelor said, "My proposal is to our mutual advantage. It rests on work you've already done: your isolating a previously unidentified mycotoxin. A strain that the Annals edutapes say you prefer to Teratogenesis Six."

His captive continued speechless. Her hand remained pressed to her darker cheek, almost as if she had forgotten its presence there.

"Teratogenesis," Gelor repeated. "A fascinating word. It refers of course to the bringing into being of gross deformities and malformations of a given life-form—monsters." He studied DeyMeox. "Is the edutape correct, DeyMeox-crober? Is it true that you've isolated a strain of fungus that creates such?"

A spark of interest joined the indignation lighting DeyMeox's olivine eyes. "You have the impudence, the *audacity* to question my researches? Of *course* it's true!"

Her hand dropped from her cheek as she leaned forward. *Ruled by pride and interest*, he thought—*and impatience*. He made his face bland, interested.

"Teratogens have been known to science for generations—centuries!" she said. "Most often they were chemicals. An ancient stuff called Thaladomide, for example. Physicians thought it a harmless tranq, a sleeping potion. They gave it to women—pregnant women. Only later was it discovered that it attacked the genes. Infants by the hundreds were born deformed or crippled. Without arms, without legs, with mere flippers.''

''And,'' Gelor prodded, ''your work?''

DeyMeox spread her hands. ''Mycosis, fungal infestations, can have the same effect. The strain I call Teratogenesis Six is the most deadly of all. It induces deformity, crippling in virtually every known species.'' She broke off, her eyes narrowing. Large green eyes searched his face. ''Such an obscure subject . . . why does it interest you so strongly? You're not a crober, that's obvious. Yet you come alive as I speak. Your face lights up and your eyes are positively glowing. What is it that sparks you, aside from bullying?''

An uneasiness touched Gelor to induce a vague inner tightening. Not truly fear; certainly not panic . . . It was a feeling that reminded him too sharply of the torment that had churned in him so violently before his slaying of Pearl and Quong and the Reshi (probably Amera) had given him self-confidence . . . *control*. He swallowed.

This woman. So bright, so sharp—some said she classed as genius. Could hers be a brain too much for his to cope with? Might her insight, her discernment prove his downfall?

Almost, he shuddered at the thought. Perhaps he did inside. This was the kind of concept he dared not let himself consider.

He spoke harshly: ''What moves me need not concern you. It is enough that I am here and in command. You will do as I direct. That is all of it.''

''But how can I?'' Again she spread her hands and now, ever so slightly, she was smiling. ''If I don't know what it is you seek, I am helpless to assist you with any real competence.''

It was true. Horrifyingly, devastatingly true. In his heart Gelor knew. It infuriated him. He had a sudden, surging impulse to strike out, to slay this woman—to wipe that taunting microsmile from her face forever.

And he dared not. That would mean the end of him as well as her. Without the wealth and power that success would bring, he'd well nigh automatically fall prey to the ravening human wolves CongCorp would loose on him.

"Right, then," he said tightly between clenched teeth. "I have with me pods of a certain life-form's blood and semen. I wish you to test them to see how well that species will serve as host for the mycotoxin you've isolated."

His prisoner lifted a charcoal-gray eyebrow. "In other words, you wish me to ascertain whether my mycotoxin will attack pregnant females of that species in such a manner as to turn the young they bear into monsters?"

He nodded. "Pos. Firm."

"You rouse my curiosity." Face serene, she extended a hand. "Let me have the containers. I'll check them."

Gelor fumbled them from his jacket. Despite all efforts at self-control, he was breathing hard. This moment . . . this moment could make him. *Or break me*. It was almost more than he could do to face it.

DeyMeox-crober took the pods and looked into his eyes. "This will take time. Zhing," she said to her fallen, stirring servant. "Do nothing. No alarms."

It took time. Silent and efficient, DeyMeox moved from one nameless testing unit to another. Centrifuges whirled. Lens-fields pulsed. Data danced across several screens, in colors. Light-rays danced rainbow-like across xanthophyllic screens. Spore colonies came into being and faded in growth-acceleration flats and on 'puter simulations.

Zhing did nothing—save shoot dark glances at the handsome man who had burst in and hurt him. That individual also did nothing. He waited.

At last DeyMeox stripped off her micromask. As earlier, she studied Gelor with large, wide-open and almost unbearably intelligent eyes.

"The blood and semen, as I am sure you know," she said coolly, "are from a human being. A native of Eilong. They constitute what I should judge to be a well-nigh ideal medium for the ravages of T-Six. Perhaps eighty-five per cent of the pregnant women of Eilong infected by it would produce grossly malformed offspring."

Excitement raced through Gelor and he tried to mask it. He didn't dare trust himself to speak.

"Your next question," the crober said, "will be: Can I produce the mycotoxin Teratogenesis Six in quantity sufficient to contaminate an entire planet?"

Gelor rocked with shock. A moment before he had been afraid to speak lest his voice shake. Now he could not have spoken had he tried. *Shiva! What a woman!*

"It is, of course, a dreadful thought for anyone to harbor," DeyMeox said equably. "A being even remotely human—normal—could not help but deem it more monstrous than even the monsters my mycotoxin would create. The only issue is *why*? Why would you wreak such horror on any planet, let alone one so . . . innocuous as Eilong?"

Again, Gelor said nothing. Just not looking away from her eyes and a brain he could practically *hear* purring was an effort.

"Could it be that, somehow, devastating Eilong might bring you riches? You have the . . . look of a man covetous of wealth, at any price."

For Gelor, it was more than disconcerting; it was an awful moment. Of a sudden he was terrified of DeyMeox and her probing, brilliantly inferring mind. It was all he could do not to think of her as a witch, a sorceress. He knew he couldn't let her go on, slashing through his masks with her devastating insights. Already she had pierced and ripped away the layers of cover he had planned so carefully. Somehow he had to strike back, regain control of the situation.

Why not the truth, then. Mightn't that be the best defense—offense?

Abruptly he said, "You've heard of CongCorp?"

"The mineral extraction complex?" DeyMeox showed her surprise. "Of course. Who hasn't? It's nearly as big as TMSMCo, surely."

"CongCorp's profits come from cyber-extraction. Robomining. On Eilong, they cannot use such methods. That means that to get kiraoun catalysts, CongCorp has to buy unprocessed ore through the planet's Elders."

A horrified light was beginning to dawn on DeyMeox's face. "A—and if there were no Eilans . . ."

"The ruin need not be that complete." Gelor felt better now, less inclined to surrender to her brilliance. "It would be enough if the planet were in a state of total panic. Let anarchy take over. That's all that's needed."

"Then—*you*—would . . . ?"

He nodded. "I'll sell Eilong." Intentionally, he phrased it so that no hint of the conditional hung about the matter; as if he owned Eilong. "Planet and people, I'll sell them to CongCorp as a package."

She shook her head as if in disbelief, and heaved a sigh. "Your price?"

"Paradise. Paradise, and CongCorp's protection."

"I . . . see." Thoughtfulness described DeyMeox-crober's expression, and then a cynicism. Did those olivine eyes twinkle? "You'll forgive me if I find your faith in corporate gratitude naïve, to say the least."

Gelor wanted to hit her. In a flash, she had brought back the raw apprehensiveness that was ever a passenger in his guts.

Yet . . . not that it mattered! She hadn't guessed too much beyond the outer boundaries of his planning. If he could hold her within those limits, there'd be no problems. He bent forward at the thought, resting his weight on hands planted on her bench while he smiled his most captivating smile.

"DeyMeox: I know that science is your lord and master. Yet paradise—my kind of paradise—must still hold charm for you. I want to share it with you. Join me! Be my partner."

She stared at him as if she could not believe her ears.

He pressed on: "What do you stand to lose? Consider! All I ask is a sharing of your knowledge, your wisdom. Your reward will be not only riches, but *opportunity*. Think what you could do, what secrets of nature you could delve if money were no object! The whole Galaxy would be yours to probe–"

"You're mad," DeyMeox said.

It was her tone that stabbed so deeply. It was so flat, so

matter of fact, with no hint of emotion. An observation of spore-colony development in a growth-acceleration flat might have brought more emotion, more heat from her.

Fury exploded within Gelor.

"All right!" he raged. "Have it your way! Call me mad if you will—but die if you don't help me! That's your choice—help me, or *die*."

He had expected fear to seize her then. Yet so far as he could see, it did not. Rather, her lips twisted in wry disdain. And she continued to look serenely, directly into his eyes.

"If that is your wish, then—kill me."

Her very voice was a shrug. The moment was freighted with elements of catastrophe; an end to everything. As she must know . . .

Gelor was delighted that he had come prepared for it.

"Stain my hands with your blood? Neg," he smiled, and made it a point—for effect—to chuckle. "Oh no. I have a better solution to the problem." He brought forth the fake TZ injectab he had bought from Quong in the Riverside alley. "Do you recognize this?"

She gave it the most casual of glances. "Of course. From the skull, I assume that's a tetrazombase unit."

"Would it improve your work if I were to shoot it into one of your veins?"

This time her face opened in a full-fledged smile. "It really wouldn't matter to me." She extended a wrist in challenge. "You see, the price of a crober's life includes contact with many substances most people see as deadly. One of those is tetrazombase. Years ago I developed an immunity to its effects. So—if you wish to inject me with it, I won't even *try* to stop you."

Frustration gripped Gelor, and hurt. Once again this fiend in woman's form had him on the hip! Could it be that she was really to defeat him, after all his planning, his brilliant successes up to now?

Furiously he looked away—and looking, glimpsed again the row of recordacks along the wall. Each was neatly labeled. Zhing's job, probably.

Recordacks: storage units for raw scientific data. More—
they were most often the choice of those who did not wish
to take the slightest risk of entrusting such data to the
electronic memory of computer storage.

A new spark kindled in Gelor. He spoke carefully:
"Firm, then. You dash my dreams and I'll have only a
small vengeance as solace."

DeyMeox's face went blank. "A . . . small—vengeance?"

"Your records represent your life's work, years of effort."
He smiled gently—and gestured to the wall of recordacks.
"I shall destroy them. All of it, and be sure your computer
wipes itself clean. It is the price you will pay for bringing
my own plans to naught."

The crober's face made an interesting study, Gelor
thought. Shock flashed across it, and then panic. Her
mouth opened, closed. Her eyes flicked this way and that,
as if she were searching desperately for some way—any
way out of her dilemma.

Gelor had seldom enjoyed himself more. And, just in
case, he held his thumb near the trigger of his spring-
loaded weapon. Now her knuckles had gone white on the
workbench. She stared down. Her tongue slid back and
forth along her lips. He heard her swallow. He loved the
sound; fear, horror, panic.

"Well?" he prodded.

Her eyes remained downcast. "I have no choice. The
victory is yours."

He made sure that his own swallow was soundless.
"Good." He savored his words: "You know what I require.
How soon can you deliver?"

DeyMeox's eyes came up now. Strangely, her face once
again was calm, as calm as if he had never made his
threat. "I am a scientist. My work is my life. That's why I
can't let you wipe out my records. They're too important—
not to me so much as to humankind, the Galaxy. So, you
defeat me. I will spawn the mycotoxin. On one condition."

Despite the euphoria of his triumph, unease began again
to grow in Gelor. "What is the . . . condition?"

"A simple one. One that will exert no effect on what you plan."

"Get on with it, witch!" His body heat raced up along with his temper. "Tell me your triple-damned, Shiva-cursed *condition*!"

"A test, a simple one. No more than that." She paused: eyes wide, serene gaze on his face. "Before I begin production of T-Six for you, I wish to make a celloscopic transcription of your brain-wave patterns, for microelectro-pulsive study at some future date."

Gelor stood very still. Words, at that moment, were beyond him.

At last: "You mean . . . you'd treat me as if I were an unclassified alien life-form?" His voice trembled in his efforts to control it. "A—a hallucinotic lunatic? A speci-men in a bionarium?"

"If you wish to phrase it so."

"But *why*?"

"Call it a scientist's curiosity, my dear." At long last the crober was again smiling. She smoothed her short-cropped charcoal hair back from her high, broad forehead. Touched her cheek where he had slapped her. "The issue is contradiction."

"Contradiction—?"

"That contradiction/contra-indication between the face you show the Galaxy and what's behind it. You are more than handsome—you know that. Women who give heed to such must rape you in their eagerness to share your beauty. Inside though—oh, that's another story! Inside you lies rottenness to put a sewer to shame. I trust that is not insulting—I believe you revel in it. Where other men lust for woman-flesh, you lust for horror, multiplied by millions: a whole planet–"

Control fled and Gelor struck out at her, a savage blow. She sidestepped. The swing missed, even offbalancing him briefly. She did not try to take advantage of that and he knew in the same instant that she had planned even this. *It was her* intention *to bait me into violence*! But—where was the logic? He wasn't sure. He knew only that he dared not play into her hands. If she sought violence, then he must eschew it.

He stepped back, carefully deep-breathing. For a long moment they only gazed at each other. Only one of them wore that tiny, maddening smile. . . .

"You asked me to permit a test." His voice sounded strange and strained, even to him. "I refuse."

"Then I refuse to help you." She was still smiling.

"There are persuasive sufferings."

She flipped her fingers. "Of course. But will they give you Teratogenesis Six? Or will you learn too late that the spores you've laid down on Eilong are harmless?"

Gelor's impulse was to do murder. He enjoyed it, he needed it—and he dared not act on the impulse. Not if he hoped to attain his goal. Hope existed.

"Right, then." He was quivering in cold fury. "If that's your price, I'll pay it, just as you will pay mine. But if you play me false, you'll be a long time dying."

DeyMeox smiled her cryptic smile. "So. At last we understand each other. Zhing: do get up and let me give you an injection."

Zhing obeyed, Gelor said "Wait—" and started forward, and DeyMeox used the exodermic syringe. She also surged forward to catch Zhing, who began at once to collapse. She lowered him to the floor, and looked up at Gelor.

"You hurt him, and he needed that sedative. Of course now you need not worry about his interfering, or making a call for help. He will be unconscious for hours. I really do want to make that test, you see." Squatting there beside her servant, she gestured at the door at the lab's far end. "Will you carry-not-drag him in there, please? We test in there."

Tight-lipped, he stared at her. While fear was a score and more of worms in his vitals, he sought to sort out his feelings.

The test, whatever it was—that didn't matter. In the last analysis his resistance was a matter of pure ego. The fear factor, on the other hand—that sprang from DeyMeox herself. Her brain was too good, her mind too shrewd. He knew it: he could not match either. Furthermore, no matter what this woman said and no matter how straightforward her manner, he knew that he dared not trust her. He drew a deep breath, expelled it.

Yet I have no choice but to use her. Without her, my dreams and schemes are ashes. Time's running out, too—already the company's wolves may be howling on my trail.

So. Let this bitch run her precious tests, perhaps to make him forever famous, then spawn her hellish fungi. He had other steps to take. With a nod, he took up Zhing's dead weight, noted that the fellow was breathing, and gestured for the crober to lead the way. He'd not be locked in a closet!

She said "Curie," and the yellow-tan door opened. He was right behind her, and they entered almost together. She said "Curie" again, and the lights came on while the door closed. Wanting to drop Zhing, he instead squatted, eyes directed at DeyMeox, and eased the man to the floor. And rose.

"I've heard reports of a cryogenic unit you've developed, Crober."

DeyMeox shrugged. "Not developed. Tested. As a favor to old colleagues."

"But it does work?"

"Of course." Her manner said that the question—the process itself—was too trivial for attention at a time like this. "It was merely a matter of synchronizing differential cell metabolism with computerized permafreeze techniques." She couldn't even be bothered to flip her fingers.

"The specimens arrived unharmed?"

She nodded. "At all levels, from ameboid to full-grown Jarps and Terasak slaves."

"Wonderful," Gelor said. "Now, since I am to be tested . . . it is you who must strip."

"What?"

"I assure you I am not interested in what you will display, Crober. Surely testing me will put me at some disadvantage, and I want to take some small steps to equal that out. You will be so much more vulnerable, unclothed and barefoot."

DeyMeox heaved a sigh. "Shall we strip together, then?"

Gelor laughed because he couldn't help it.

Besides, his thoughts were a delight: *Once you've completed preparations for our experiment on Eilong, we'll use your own cryo-unit to put you and your so-loyal associate . . . into cold storage! A temporary measure; knowing you're safe here will free my mind for other vital work.*

Specifically, there was the voyage he had to make to Nevermind, and another female, the andrist Shemsi . . .

6

Take care! Strangers are coming!

—*Capt. Theophilus Conneau*

At night this way on moonless Croz, the building that
housed Oddford's policers loomed big and grim and dark.
When a flyer passed over to land on the roof, its shadow
loomed huge as some dreadsome monster of myth.

Cheerily, Jestikhan Churt urged along the psychist named
Yahna Golden. For the severalth time, she balked.

"I *demand* to know!" she whispered fiercely. "What is
it that you're going to do? I have a *right*!"

"As I had a right when you slapped the brain-drain on
me?" Jesti's laugh was not endearing. "I'm the one sets
the rules this time, Golden. You'll know what I think you
need to know when I think you need to know it. That's it.
Your first job's to play Yahna Golden. Surely you can
handle that. Just tell the shift men what I told you. Stall or
speak out of turn and I crack your kneecaps. Hurts!"

As emphasis to those words so pleasantly spoken, he
twitched the electronic bond that linked her to the control-
pak in his pocket. She jump-skipped a pace and shuddered
big. He pushed her roughly forward. Catching herself
barely in time to keep from falling, the leggy woman
stumbled into the building ahead of him.

"*You don't look your best*," he muttered, and saw her

73

pride force her to straighten and, as he'd said, play Yahna Golden.

A guard sat at the desk commanding the entrance. Drab in his slate-blues, his attention perked at sight of the marvelous-looking woman who approached—accompanied by the freak.

Above a willowy but arrestingly feminine body her face was lean with pronounced bone-structure and high cheekbones. All around that face and her rather broad shoulders bloomed that halo of deep yellow hair that was so impossible—and who cared? Certainly no male. While her waist was not deeply indented as so many women's were—not, admittedly, as a gift of nature—she had been well supplied in the chest. The conical swells there were dramatic and widely separated. At a height of about 185 sems*, she was pushing the height of her shockingly purple companion with seemingly endless legs as long as his. Couple all those physical blessings (and enhancements) with the fact that she wore a skinnTite in a variety of colors including intriguingly placed bands of black net, and the man behind the desk was suddenly happy to have pulled night duty.

He stood at once, sucking up, pushing out his chest, striving to stand tall. He did not have to work to look completely attentive.

"I'm the psychist who was here last night," the vision said. "This man—" a nod indicated the Eilan freak with her—"has something more to say. Your captain may want to hear it."

"Pos and double pos!" The guard dropped back into his chair, pushed scanner buttons, and hopped back up to gesture. "That door there. Three down and on your left."

Jesti's hard look kept the guard from staring at Yahna's rear—and from perhaps noting that she was being led.

The mismatched pair made its way down and to the left. There, a seemingly busy Crozer with a turquoise eye-ring looked up from a desk, startled. Then he raised both hands in welcome and was swiftly on his feet. His slate uniform

---

* 185 centimeters. About six *feet*, one *inch*, Old Style.

was embellished with red stripes and braidwork as well as a shining black belt.

"Psychist—Yahna!—you honor me! What may I do to help you?" His smile was nearly as radiant as her hair.

She gave him a ripe-lipped smile to melt policers, not to mention the stone walls that this prison made.

"How charming of you, Captain Aswan! I came back because of something this Eilan creature said. I thought you should hear it, too." She turned. "*Eilan?*"

Jestikhan made it a point to hang his head contritely. In the process, he noted that his battered miner's helmet rested on a table in one corner of Aswan's office. A sour nostalgia touched him. Silently, Jesti resolved to reclaim that beloved old hardhat before he left Croz. If he left.

Yahna Golden repeated, "Eilan?"

He scowled, looked at the captain. "The pirates you brought in this morning? I recognized one. One of the Outies?"

"You did—? Which?"

Jesti shrugged. "I'd have to see 'em to tell you." He hesitated. "I think he may know something about that Thebanian girl? The hust?"

Golden said, "It happens this way sometimes, Captain. Delayed response. It's a corollary of brain-drain, sometimes a problem—but you surely know that."

The Crozer was already excited. Swiftly despite his bulk, he came around from behind his desk with eyes alight.

"This way."

Jesti noted with a certain cynical amusement that the Crozer so positioned himself as to maintain a steadying grip on Yahna Golden's arm. That way the hand occasionally "had to" touch her breast. (Already Jesti had made a mental note about Yahna's acting ability—superb! A woman to be wary of.)

He followed close behind them along passageways and past doors, through doorways and past a supply room. They reached a great plasteel lockbox at least a hekto long. Prisoners glowering out of metalmesh cages.

Captain Aswan gestured guards aside. "Down this way, at the end."

They passed more cages. Another barrier with guards in floppy pants. Two prisoners were polishing worn pre-plasteel fittings with a portable tank of liquid glo-gloss. They came to a bigger cage, the kind known as a tanq. It housed four captives: a Jarp from Jarpi, a Sek from ever-hot planet Sekhar, and two men from planet Outreach. Outies, a determinedly flamboyant breed.

The pirates rated a special guard. He sat in a metal box high above the floor and beyond the prisoners' reach, maintaining surveillance of them through an unbreakable plas-mass window. He also controlled the tanq's locking levers. Entry to his coop was down a ladder from above.

The Outie in the torn purple shirt had been lying down. Now he scrambled up. "Visitors!" he called. "Our old comrade the purple egg! Shall we fry 'im or poach 'im?"

The policer captain snorted. With some irritation, Jesti thought he detected laughter in the sound. The captain turned.

"Well, Eilan? Is this the man you spoke of?"

Jesti moved closer to the cage and peered through the metal mesh. Uncertainly, he shook his head and worried his lower lip with his teeth.

"Can't be sure, Cap'm. The fellow had a mark . . . I just can't be sure through this webbing."

Again Captain Aswan snorted—in irritation, this time. He wheeled and signaled to the guard up in the control box. Jestikhan Churt held his breath . . .

The guard's electronic controls opened the tanq's door. At Aswan's gesture, Jesti stepped inside the big cage to peer at the man in the purple shirt. Suddenly he pointed.

"Here! Look! It's this one!"

Aswan had been speaking to Yahna Golden in a hushed voice. (Jesti rather doubted that the topic was official business.) At his call, the heavy-bodied Crozer captain moved to step across the cage's threshold.

Jesti bent and pivoted in the same instant. Driving hard, he slammed his shoulder into the man's middle. Aswan crashed backward against the doorjamb with a grunt and ·

an ugly sound of impact. Jesti seized his arms and held him right there. The policer was a powerful man, but hardly a match for an Eilan miner.

The four pirates gaped, quadruple studies in shock. Yahna Golden looked shocked, too. Impressed, perhaps.

Jesti spoke through clenched teeth.

"If someone was to anchor this fobber here, that guard upstairs can't close the door. Not unless he wants to throw the lockbolt right through his captain's gut." He raised his voice. "He won't sound an alarm, either. At least the captain hopes not."

That shattered the spell that had frozen the pirates. The Sek lunged in to pin Aswan's shoulders. The polka-dotted Outie kneed him in the gut. The Jarp did things to his throat that had him choking under a double-thumbed hand.

That left the Outie in the purple shirt. The one with the mouth.

Jesti straightened. "Let me tell you something about purple eggs," he said, in a pleasant voice that matched his expression. "Before you cook 'em, you have to crack 'em. Like this!"

He punched the Outreacher in the nose. Not full force, but hard enough. The chesty man hit the cage-mesh behind him, bounced, tottered, hit the mesh again, and slid to the floor amid a jingling of mesh. Blood spilled from his nose.

"Colors," Jesti said. "I'm purple. Now you're red. That doesn't mean we can't get along, so long as you understand who runs the show. Right?"

The fallen man only blinked. The words seemed to cut something loose in the man from Sekhar, however. He let go the Crozer's shoulders and started for Jesti. His mouth twisted nastily, very dark above his drab white tunic.

Jesti kicked him in the shin.

The Sek bent double. Jesti kneed him in the chin.

One Sek, down and out.

Jesti stepped over to the Jarp and the other Outie. "Next customer?"

"Not me," the other Outie grunted, wrestling the Crozer captain more tightly back against the doorjamb. "I've got this policer type to dance with."

The Jarp held up its hands, palm out in Stop posture. "So you're purple and mean," its translahelm said, "and I'm orange and not. You don't have anything to prove to me, sweetheart."

Jesti grinned. "Shall we be moving out, then? You bugs resist rescue as if you really love this place!"

"You won't move far," Captain Aswan mumbled.

Jesti showed him the grin. "On account of our friend up in the chicken coop?" He rolled his eyes up toward the guard-box slung above them. "I hope you're wrong, Cap'm-sah! For your sake."

Captain Aswan blinked. "What—"

"This," Jesti said.

Deftly he flipped a loop of line about the Crozer's thick neck and drew it nice and tight. The other end he threaded through the metal mesh of the tanq-cage, high up, and drew it tight. So tight that Aswan had to stand on tiptoe in order to continue breathing.

Now the guard up in the armored box had his nose pressed against its plas-mass window, peering down at them. He wore a frozen look.

"You see?" Jesti spread his hands. "This is what we call an impásse. Your guard up there can squeal for help. If he does, you'll be hanging dead by the time anyone can get here. Gas us and you sag and die faster. Right now he just can't make up his mind what to do, Captain."

"What he needs is company." (That from the purple-shirted man.) "We've got to get that fobber out of his roost." He snatched the end of the cord from Jesti. "Here. Let me have that."

In seconds he had it tied about his ankle and was swarming noisily up the rattly cage-mesh. Then out onto one of the framing beams that held the guard-box. That action broke the guard's paralysis—hastily, he swung a needle-beamer round in its port. He brought the laser to bear on the pirate.

The Outie's response was an impudent thumb-to-nose. A swing of legs balanced him to fall on the far side of the beam if the guard should shoot him down. (A nice touch, Jesti mused. Even dead, the falling pirate would pull the cord taut across the beam and hang the Crozer captain.)

Apparently the guard got the message, too. He backed off from his lase-beamer.

Now it was Jesti's turn. Trotting back to the glo-tank with no heed to the two cowering prisoners, he slung it on his back. Then he too swarmed up the mesh. Balancing on the beam, he crossed to the guard-box.

Neat rows of ventilator holes perforated its roof.

Ignoring the entry hatch (clearly, it was locked), Jesti emptied the glo-tank onto the cage's top. In secs, the liquid was dripping down through the ventilator holes: spattering the guard, puddling on the box's floor.

Jesti spoke through the holes: "Hey—Guard! You have another choice! Would you rather surrender now, or have me flash fire down into that nice snug little room with you? Glo-gloss flames up mighty hot indeed, they say. If I fire it, you won't have any more trouble with decisions—or anything else."

The guard's voice came faintly: "You don't understand! I can't unlock the hatch. The sector vector has to let me out at tour-term."

Stepping away from the guard-box, Jesti emptied the rest of the glo-tank's contents onto the floor below. That brought a trill of bird-like whistles. The Jarp executed a series of small dancing steps and flipped a (something that flamed) into the puddle.

Smoke puffed up in a nice billowing cloud.

Within two secs it triggered a sensor. An alarm started clanging loudly, somewhere close by. Jesti dropped through the haze to the floor.

"Back in the tanq," he commanded the pirates. And to Yahna and Captain Aswan: "You two, too."

Sullenly, the Crozer obeyed. Yahna's expression indicated that she was more intrigued than upset. Also excited, Jesti thought. *So now you're right in a* real *Akima Mars meller, Yahna-yahna!*

Now the sound of running footsteps echoed through the lockbox. Hastily Jesti twisted loose the glo-tank's jet and handed it to Captain Aswan. The tank itself he left out of sight behind the Crozer.

"We're your prisoners," he clipped, staring hard. "You backed us down with that glo-gloss squirter. *So* sorry about the smoke and alarms!"

He had no time to say more. Already two guards, slavetubes in hand, were coming on the double. Jesti hoisted his hands and took his stand against the cage's wall of metalmesh webbing.

The guards must have seen the scene as self-explanatory. Intent on rescuing their officer (or at least making a good show for him), they came charging recklessly in.

Five secs later both were sprawled on the floor. One unconscious, the other moaning. Jesti took charge of the slavetubes and looked at Aswan.

"Shall we be going, Captain?"

"This way," Aswan snarled. The turquoise ring around his pineal eye seemed to glow in his rage. "You still won't make it out, Eilan. By now the whole area's cordoned."

Jesti said, "Uh," and waved a salvetube. They went.

Only one man stood watch at the lockbox entrance. A quick twist of a slavetube relaxed his vigil. Beyond him, the supply room lay deserted. With a swift moving bend to take the guard's cap, Jesti waved his party in. He flipped a wrist-wrap from the rack and turned to purple-shirt.

"Hold out your hands."

The man started to say something, reconsidered, closed his mouth, and extended his hands. Jesti slapped on the wrap—then snipped the web that linked the two wrist-tapes.

"So long as you hold your palms together," Jesti said, turning to repeat the process with the Sek, "the illusion of security is perfect. Pull 'em apart and you're a free man." He turned to the Jarp's outstretched hands—orange, six-digited. "Pull 'em apart before I want you to and you're a *hurting* man." He glanced up. "Or Jarp," he said, and "secured" the other Outie.

He also secured himself in the same way, and strung the five of them out on a chain. Yahna Golden watched nervously all the while. Captain Aswan stared with barely repressed rage.

"We're still your prisoners," Jesti told him cheerily. "I'm sure you'll want any of your friends we meet to know that." Hands together, he waggled the slavetube—most of which was invisible between his close-pressed palms and wrists. "Or would you rather see what I can do with this?"

The Crozer's answer didn't bear repeating.

He, Yahna, and the coffle of "prisoners" left the lockbox area. They reentered the administration building proper and Jesti bade Aswan take them to his office. He enjoyed the look of bafflement that crossed the policer's face.

Aswan led them there, and a great weight seemed to lift from Jesti's shoulders at sight of his helmet, still lying on the table. Without a word he hefted and donned the battered hardhat. It felt wonderful—and a little big. Well, it was the *next* best thing to having his shorn hair back.

Helmeted and somehow more impressive, he looked at them and winked.

"Let's go."

His little group resumed the trek. When their course took them past a room with a window, Jesti paused long enough to peer out into the moonless night of moonless Croz. "Uh." Policers lined the street. A cordon all right, tribute to the trouble in the lockbox. Jesti glanced at Aswan.

The captain said nothing. His smirk told it all. He even managed to rub briefly against the golden-maned woman, Jesti noted; a sure sign of reviving spirits. *Huh. He ain't seen nothin' yet!* And they kept moving.

When they came to a lift-shaft, Jesti turned to the policer.

"Captain: to the roof, please."

"The roo—"

"The roof."

Wheels were spinning almost audibly in Aswan's head as he keyed the lift. Jesti's party boarded in silence. They went up.

On the roof, the flyer with Croz's blue tri-phallic emblem stood off to one side. A guard with a ceremonial symitar slouched beside it. Jesti strode toward him—and the aircraft. His fellow escapists followed.

Apparently the weight grew too heavy for Captain Aswan. Heedless of his own safety, he bellowed a warning. Instantly Jesti yelled "Free yourselves" and the guard came out of his slouch, swinging his weapon up. Ignoring Aswan, Jesti was already lunging toward the guard—pulling off his helmet.

Dodging the blade, he smashed his helmet into the Crozer's face. The guard reeled back. Jesti clutched the symitar and wrenched it from the man's grasp.

"Silly ass. If he'd had a stopper or plasmer it'd all be over for us. Damn! Night-air's chilly!" And he eased the helmet back on.

Then the pirate crew was with him. Beating down the guard. Scrambling onto the flyer. The Sek brought up the rear, dragging Yahna Golden with him. He was wearing a Crozer officer's cap and slate-blue coat. . . . Aswan stayed behind, apparently resting. He was lying down. In moments the polka-dots-clad Outie was at the controls.

"Hang on, gang! I know this ole Model R like the inside of my mouth!"

Spinning on its own axis, the craft pinwheeled into the air. The other Outie, he of the torn Jesti-colored shirt, now wore a guard's cap and held a guard's collarless blue-gray jacket. He proffered it to Yahna.

"I hate to see you cover all that up, but you look about's cold as my everchil Sek buddy there." He threw Jesti a mock-salute that was not mocking. "Where to, Captain?"

"*Captain!*" Jesti echoed, and laughed in the same spirit of camaraderie. "Since when do kiracat miners have captains?" He peered down at the sprawl of Oddford and its spaceport—Croz's spaceport—falling away below them in twinkling lights. "You do have a ship, though? The one TGW pulled you off?"

A light came into the pirate's eyes. "You know it! It's up there—" he waved skyward—"where they docked it. On the wheel. Crossport."

"Uh. So if we put in at the shuttle's flyer station . . ."

"Firm! We could take the shuttle up to the wheel and snatch our ship back." A dyre-wolf would have envied the good-looking Outie's grin. "Eilan, you may not have shipmaster's ID or captain's rank, but you've sure got a captain's head. A *pirate* captain's!"

"Name's Jesti," the Eilan said. "Jestikhan Churt. Let's do it."

The pirate raised his brow and pursed his lips. "Hmp! Not a bad name at all, for a non-Outreacher." Grinning, he turned to his fellow Outreacher: "Petri! Set course for the outbound-shuttle's flyer station."

"Double-theta," Yahna Golden swore in a murmur. "I'm being kidnapped by pirates!"

The Jarp tried, but its translation helmet botched the "Heh-heh."

7

High heels were invented by a woman who had been kissed on the forehead.

—*Christopher Morley*

High heels must've been invented by *men*—probably some man in love with women's calves!

—*Alanni Keor*

By the time it was over, Yahna knew that the pirate ship was an old and cruddy-looking converted ramscoop merchanter. Now its shabby exterior belied its excellent SIPACUM, tachyon conversion systemry, and defense systemry (DS). The name on the battered craft's prow was *Slicer*. (*How gross can these creeps get?*)

She also learned that *Slicer*'s master was the doll in the purple shirt, whose name was Hieronymus Jee. Second in command was the one with the polka dots, Hieronymus's brother Petronius. She was familiar with the ornate Outreacher name-pattern, but these had to go down as her least favorite.

As for the rest of the crew, the Sek answered to the name of Musla, for Musaphur. He was in charge of DS and life-control systems. Twil'im of Jarpi helped him and took turns at con duty, with limited ability. The departed crewman had been the rather flamboyant Kai Mayyasi, computrician. His flair for self-dramatization had led him to shoot it out with the TGW boarding party at the time of *Slicer*'s capture. That was why he was the late Kai Mayyasi.

That was also why Petronius Jee was subbing as computrician, and not happy about it.

Yahna could not be certain whether her presence was a matter of accident or intention. When she asked Jesti to leave her onstation rather than taking her onto *Slicer*, he refused, saying that she might prove useful both as hostage and psychist. On the other hand, he flatly refused Captain Jee's suggestion that they lash her to the main hatch to discourage small-arms fire. . . .

She had to wonder a bit about the Eilan. Could it be that he was keeping her beside him for . . . personal reasons? And if so—should she be pleased or outraged?

All such revelations had of course come in bits and pieces. To begin with, there'd been the shocking affair of the seizure of the shuttle.

"Shocking" because Yahna could not have dreamed it could be so easy. Obviously it had not occurred to Croz's security force that anyone might attack the shuttle's off-base flyer station. When the escapists had swarmed down from the flyer, therefore, the staff had contented itself with a lot of quivering and quaking, rather than resisting. The pirates kept it that way by taking the staff with them. In addition to preventing news of the raid from getting out, that also provided them with a fine supply of hostages when they reached the orbiting docking wheel.

Reaching *Slicer*'s berth had involved a nerve-racking trek out though the D-spoke tunnel to the wheel's perimeter and docking berths. Jestikhan had played little part in any of this. Though the others made a show of deferring to him as rescuer, he was clearly far more at home in a mine than on a space station. Or starship.

For awhile it had appeared that they might get away unchallenged. About the time the drive had been synced for redshift, though, someone down on Croz had commed up for a check on station Crossport. That left the Brothers Jee minimal options. The one Master Hieronymus chose was to blast without clearance. That was an experience to whiten hair. It also demonstrated conclusively that *Slicer* wasn't the bucket of bolts it appeared.

Back down the enclosed ramp to the station went the hostages. Airlock and hatches were zipped up behind them like traps snapping. Hieronymus Jee flung himself into the master's chair to flip switches, mutter, push buttons, engage links, and depress keys with flying fingers. Console lights flashed in a dexipattern like the stars of an exploding galactic arm.

Slicer dropped, spun, side-slipped, all in a lunatic pattern that even autogunnery would have been hard-pressed to follow. In secs it was threading a laser-edged trail through the planet's maze of powersats. In mins, slashing a light-track out through space to a destination that could only be described as Elsewhere, Fast.

For the moment, Yahna was left alone. She took advantage of the time to inspect the ship's quarters. She found the forward cabin equipped with pulsar lights and holoscreens, plus cubes representing a dozen worlds. All circuitry to the reepr panels, she noted with raised eyebrow, was heavy duty. A Lhote coil controlled the pulsars.

It was a setup to make any psychist happy. Especially a MarsCorp psychist who had manipulated audience pulsepaps with a fear-trap, on behalf of Setsuyo Puma and the Akima Mars production company. Yahna Golden smiled. Double-theta, but it was lovely to have some little extra edge under such awful circumstances! This edge would be even better than the other . . .

The . . . other. Automatically with that thought she ran her thumb along the gilded eight-sem nail of her right hand's middle finger. It was her last resort, her final refuge. She had adapted it from something she learned about the felinoprimates called HRal, and she hoped she'd never have to use it.

But . . . *Captive of pirates! Booda's belly*—Me!

She discarded morbid thinking and set the screen for an airy pastoral scene. She positioned herself within the prismirror's orbit, adjusted a heavy magnetic lamp, and began smoothing her extravagant halo of golden hair. Since she had chosen to wear a multicolored concealing/revealing

Indraba skinnTite today, her coiffure could do with a bit of rearranging.

It wasn't that she enjoyed such "feminine" preoccupations. To the contrary! However it was part of His heritage, one of the ridiculous habits He had left her with: the business of being sexy. Somehow she had never been able to break it. (Maybe she didn't want to—really.) *Damn Him!*

The hatch opened behind her. She turned—slowly, with the air of poise and casual grace He had taught her. No haste. No air of fear or even startlement. Naturally it was the purple man who entered. Naturally he was grinning. It seemed to be a habit of his. Strong, jocular . . . freak.

At least he had taken off his hardhat.

"Women and hair," he said. "They do go together."

Doubtless he intended no insult, but Yahna's lips went thin. Bad enough that he should catch her *preening*. To comment on it was grossporker manners, to say the least.

He stopped grinning. "We've got a problem. We need you as computrician."

She gave him a cool eyebrows-up look. "Indeed."

"Uh. Dead man's job. Right now Petri's filling in, but Hieri needs him in mate's chair, as second. Musla has to hang back there with DS. Twilly doesn't qualify, and I sure don't. You do."

"Well, I hear your logic," she said, frowning, trying to analyze her feelings.

She found them mixed, to say the least. All of it was so close to a plot for an Akima Mars holovid melodrama—a holomellerdrammer! *Except that Akima would know just what to do, damn it.* The whole mad adventure couldn't help but prove intoxicating. Part of her pulsed with the excitement of it. To lance off through the void this way—a captive on a pirate spacer! What adventurous woman could resist co-starring in a holomeller become real?!

Yet it held an edge of another kind of tension: the rape threat. It was considerably harder for corporate psychist Yahna Golden to analyze that aspect. For Yahna Golden, woman, it was even harder. Emotion made analysis impossible. And . . . she chose to smile. A good smile, properly calculated—with just the right touch of scorn.

"You still have a problem, O Leader."

"What?"

"I won't help you pirates!"

That, she had hoped, would throw him into a rage. Instead, this strange, never predictable man merely stood very still, gazing at her.

"You really don't have any choice," he told her in a nice voice.

"Because you'll rape me if I don't?"

Jesti didn't answer. Jesti only stared, flat-eyed.

"Rape," Yahna said, "is a crime of violence and aggression. Its sexual content is marginal at best. It appeals to men who doubt their own masculinity. They hate women."

"Oh."

Yahna smiled gently. She put warmth and sympathy into her voice. "Let me paint you a portrait of a rapist, Eilan. He is a being—a *being*, you understand, not a true man. When he looks at himself in his mind's eye, what he sees frightens him. He doubts that any woman could truly want him, love him, *him*. Yet this piteous creature wants love desperately. When he can't find it, it does things to him. That's why he comes to hate all women. So—" She gestured. "Hate breeds frustration. Frustration spawns a frightful drive to violence."

Again she smiled. She spread her hands, gazing coolly at him.

"There you have it, Eilan. Portrait of a rapist. A being, not a man. Because a true man doesn't doubt himself on the rapist's level. He seeks out the woman who wants him as much as he wants her. But if it's rape that flashes you, if forcing your way into a body is all that counts . . . then I am only a woman. I cannot match your strength or stop you."

She gazed at him, waiting. It was a game she had played before. Each line, each movement of face and body and hands was experience-perfected. Always she had won. What man could maintain lust in the face of the denigrating picture she painted? And now, with this purple man . . .

Oddly, her heart was beating faster. While, maddeningly, his violet face remained expressionless.

"Really interesting lecture. Odd time to deliver it, though. You're the only one here who mentioned rape. What I mentioned was the need for a computrician on this ship, if we're to survive. You've got two mins. If you're not out by then, I'm coming in again." And he stalked from the cabin.

A shiver ran through the staring woman. This strange man—he *bothered* her in a way she had never known before (*purple, onionheaded, arrogant, lower class*) even while he excited her, too, in a manner and to a degree that was alien to her. (*No, no—that's* fear *I feel!*)

Of a sudden she knew that he would indeed be back.

Unless I'm ready merely to surrender, I must be prepared! The purple, onionheaded, arrogant lower-classed . . . miner!)

Swiftly, she crossed to the door. Switching the Lhote coil from the pulsars to the heavy-duty reepr panel, she attached it to the inner doorframe. She knew what she was doing, and it took barely a min. Lips only faintly corner-tilted in a smug smile, she resumed the smoothing of her irrepressible hair.

Seconds, ticking by . . .

Across the cabin, the door opened. *He* stood there, in the entry. Staring.

"You heard what I said?" Jesti said, and it was not really a question. "About working."

"I heard," Yahna said, and was careful to coat her tone with scorn. "I'm waiting."

Jesti's eyes went cold. He stepped into the cabin . . . and stopped as if he had run partway onto the point of a rapier. He twitched, eyes suddenly wide and lips parted in a grimace of exploding consternation. His face showed . . . fear.

It was a moment eminently worth waiting for, Yahna thought. A just vengeance for all women down through all the ages; women terrorized by men. Ah, look at the bastard suffer, feel the pangs of raw, inexplicable fear!

Only then, incredibly, over there in the hatchway, something *happened*. Though bent almost double and assaulted by her scientific arts, the man named Jestikhan Churt wasn't quaking or shaking or sobbing with fear.

No. Unbelievably, he was moving. Stepping forward, forcing himself a slow and agonizing step . . . out of the field . . . then the barrier, the fear-trap, was behind him. He straightened, took in a great breath, and came striding to her.

It was Yahna's turn to feel panic. She stumbled backward, hard against the cabin wall. Involuntarily, her hands rose to shield her breasts. Because she worked with Setsuyo Puma, possessor of the well-advertised Biggest Pair In The Universe, she had sought contrast. The arts of cellular engineering and arrangement made Yahna's actually resemble *warheads*; taut, widely separated cones.

"That hurt," the purple man said tightly. "That circuit hurt almost more than I could stand, psychist. Good thing I'm an Eilan. Anyone else would have burned out. Of course our piratic crew would have killed you in retaliation— after using you sore and bloody—but that would have been small consolation to the man you destroyed. Fortunately *for you*, then, you picked an Eilan. We've got special neurons, haven't you heard? Special brain cells, they claim, along with purple skin and gill-slits."

A new thrill of terror raced through Yahna—and not just of terror. She held her breath without knowing it, waiting for his violent violet hands to seize on her.

"Thanks for the lecture. One is always happy to learn. And your courage overwhelms me." She came erect: head up, chest out, hands nervously at her sides. "Go ahead, then. I'm ready."

For what seemed an interminable moment, the purple man stared at her. Then, abruptly, he tilted back his shorn head and laughed.

To call that a first for Yahna Golden would be to use words far too pale.

His laugh was worse than hot hands by far; worse than

any white-hot iron. It rang beyond believing, beyond accepting, beyond enduring. The sound it brought forth from her was like nothing she had ever voiced or heard before. Spasmodically, her nails dug into her skinnTite, into the cleft between her ever-outthrust breasts. Wrenching, ripping.

In stunned disbelief, she realized as if watching some-one else that she was tearing away the fabric. Baring her body to this violet monster.

"Damn you, you grat—no, plithit!—you monster, you—you creature!" she screamed. "Rape for rape, you said! My body for your mind! Or aren't you man enough to take a woman?"

The shock of her words showed on Jesti's face. She was well-known. He knew she was free and proud-unto-arrogant and competent. And he had never heard of either Ayn Rand or Havelock Ellis. Incredibly to Yahna, he stepped back. His stare raked her nakedness up and down. And it was total nakedness; her body bore no trace of hair below the eyelashes. She looked all bosom and lean torso and what looked like about 85 sems of leg.

"Rape?" he lashed. "You think I'd rape *you*? No, thanks! You're not a woman, you're a stone-splitter, Golden—a ballbreaker! You'd be a lousy lay. Your head's the only part of you that counts, so far as I'm concerned. You've got a job to do as computrician, Golden."

Turning his back on her, the incredible man started for the door.

She stared, mouth forgottenly agape, and she was quiver-ing all over. The wave of heat that washed over her was like fire. Her brain ceased to function, if it had been. Snatching up the magnalamp, she hurled it at him with all her might.

It struck him dead between the shoulders, so hard that he staggered under the impact.

He tried to turn—and Yahna kicked for his groin. Barely in time, he twisted enough to take the blow on his thigh. It still hurt, and it threw him off balance. Already staggered by the magnalamp, he banged to the floor. His hands, clawing for support, caught a bare knee. She too fell, with a crash and a kicked-cat sound.

He hung on to the knee and his other hand groped, found a hold, dragged her to him.

His voice rasped in her ear: "You psycho psychist bitch!"

She got out one word before her eyes flared wide: "You—*uh*!"

They came slapping together. Writhing. His breath gushed hot on her face and his clothing was rough against bared skin. The hardness of him impaled her despite her thrashing. All breath, all possibility of forming words was driven from her by that violent invasion. Now it was she who was disequilibrated—and feeling bisected. He drove, pounding, seeking her very core. Depths of excitement she hadn't known she had possessed her while her flesh flowered, stretched around his.

She clutched him, not clawing but dragging him deeper, deeper, gasping and groaning from her dry throat, and did all she could to drive her prostrate body upward. Until she could stand no more. A paroxysm caught her and she shuddered in it, keening. The paroxysm convulsed her in spasm after spasm. Her keening scream was not of pain. And he shoved, and began twitching atop her, inside her even while she twitched and gasped in climax.

He dared not linger, in that temporary weakness of completion. Shakily, he dragged his sweaty body free. Wary of her legs, he rocked back, and rose to stare down at her.

She looked absolutely magnificent and she knew it.

He said, "You have work to do, psychist. Work as a—computrician."

She lay back, breathing deeply. Aware of the juddering surge of bared, flushed breasts. Of her wide-forked legs and his marks on her.

"And you, *Eilan*? What of you?" she taunted. "Do you still think my head's the only part of me that's useful?"

The words *I don't know—I haven't tried it yet* came to his mind, and he swallowed them. The expression on his face was something to behold.

"For a psychist, you lack insight," he told her. "All this talk about rape—I don't rape! You're the one it turns on, not me. Because you can't let go like other women. The man's got to take you. By force. The only way you can ignite and flash is to put the blame on someone else. So—*you won*."

He broke off, staring bleakly at wide-glaring eyes and open mouth.

"I meant what I said about you working, Golden. So far as I'm concerned, it's your head I want, not your body. Something you're skilled at. It's time you took your shift as computrician."

8

All women are good: good for nothing, or good for something.
—*Miguel de Cervantes*

Yellow fields of azaafrunn under yellow skies streaked with gold and fluffed with white made Nevermind seem a pleasant enough planet. Gelor supposed that one might soon grow bored with so much yellow. Too, he was aware that the few powerful Factors—capitalized, here, as an almost regal title—ran things. Life was not exactly great for the azaafrunn farmers plodding along without decent machinery and owing their souls to the Factors' stores. (The Factors, of course, were responsible for the anti-mechanization legislation.)

So? Gelor didn't give a running damn about farmers or Factors. And things were nicely different here in Nevermind's capital, Newhope.

He did give damns about the andrist Shemsi, insofar as she could serve his plan. He was delighted that she was a joy to behold. Petite, delicate, with not-quite-black hair looped in a graceful chignon and a very pale azure "mask" of dye around her eyes and upper cheeks, she wore a wide-eyes air of continual surprised delight. As if just being in a man's presence constituted an ecstasy almost beyond enduring. (She also wore a mauve dress that clung lovingly to what it covered and marvelously framed what it didn't.)

It was she who suggested that they hold their meeting in a char-par, and who chose a curtained booth where they could be free of prying or even glancing eyes. Gelor only partially masked his delight and neglected to give thanks to that unladylike lady called Luck.

Tentatively, as they sat down, he let his fingers touch hers. Rather than pull away, she clasped his hand. A stone-faced 'Minder waiter saved the disconcerted Gelor from having to decide how to respond to her response. Shemsi asked for the local tea, *char*. She also said she liked it strong and black. Gelor shrugged and asked for the same, and the waiter left.

Pushing aside the great garnadine pendant that hung in the hollow of her throat, Shemsi lifted Gelor's hand and pressed it to her breast. He was re-astonished—and sure he felt the nipple swelling. Clearly, she wore nothing under the wetcloth sari of deep red-violet. Gelor blinked, then almost automatically cupped and squeezed that pointy breast. It was superbly shaped and felt wonderfully soft. No, firm. Firm-soft, then.

Shemsi dropped her eyes demurely, she who was about as demure as he. New color came to her *cafe-au-lait* (and azure-"masked") cheeks.

Simultaneously, her free hand felt Gelor's leg beneath the table. Her fingers tightened on it briefly, to match his pressure on her perky pointy warhead. A moment later, her hand moved higher. Gelor's mouth went dry. It was all he could do to keep from panting.

Shemsi raised her eyes to meet his. "You . . . wished to discuss some project with me?"

"Yes," Gelor answered hoarsely. "Yes, yes." His mind wouldn't seem to work. He couldn't get past the one syllable.

Shemsi smiled. It was a gentle smile. One that spoke of infinite experience, boundless understanding. She gave him a final squeeze. Her hand relaxed.

"So. I am an andrist. Your interest must be in my specialty, robopathic androids."

"Yes." Gelor heaved a breath deep as a sigh. "I need three totally realistic units." He dropped his voice, leaned forward. "You understand, all this must be entirely confidential. No one must know about it."

Shemsi smiled again. "Such projects are not unfamiliar to me. I handle them on a very private basis. No assistants work with me on the secret aspects. Nor has any client every regretted placing trust in me. We maintain the most intimate of relationships." Her fingertips flicked at Gelor in a way that both reinforced her words and pointed up the concept. (Her nails bore the same color as her dye-mask.)

Gelor swallowed hard. "What I require," he said with a desperate effort to concentrate, "is—first—a dupladroid of me. A döppelganger. It must simulate me to perfection, to where it can pass as me once it's programmed."

Shemsi arched a skilfully lined (jet) eyebrow. Her face took on a thoughtfulness, an intelligence that Gelor hadn't seen before.

"It will be difficult, of course. Most would not attempt it. Yet it can be done. I admit that I will enjoy it—you are a most attractive man." She broke off to toy with her very red pendant. Her eyes met his then, in a gaze as forthright as any DeyMeox had directed at him. "It goes without saying that it will be expensive. A hundred thousand stells, I should think."

Gelor had his nice pat answer ready for that. He shrugged. "I accept that as my problem."

"Shall we discuss terms, then?" Again, she was absolutely straightforward.

He made his best effort to hold his voice wooden, without tension. "As you will, Andrist. I stand prepared to sign over twenty thousand as down payment."

"And the remainder?" Ah, sweet, wide-eyed ingenuousness . . . simulated, he knew.

"Another thirty thousand on delivery. The rest thirty days thereafter."

She sighed. "Oh my. That won't do. Thirty days afterward! That's like a Tok spacefarer telling a hust he'll pay her next time he hits port. No competent andrist works on such a wet-dream basis."

"I'd think thirty days is a fair time for me to assure myself the 'droid is perfect."

"You shall have a written, publicly recorded guarantee."

That precluded the "on approval" dodge, then. "What kind of wet dreams *do* you work on, then?" he asked.

Her face sagged for an instant. The next, she released a trill of soft laughter. "No wet dreams, voyager. We prefer hard—reality, shall we call it? Half when we start. Half on pickup on the completed dupladroid—guaranteed perfect."

The hand on Gelor's leg squeezed and kneaded. The other moved his palm from her breast in a slow glide to a point excitingly lower. Her hips writhed.

"If," she said, "you catch my meaning, you understand."

It was the end of a magic moment. *She talks of husts so freely because a hust is what she is*, he mused grimly. *A smart hust, a clever hust—but a hust, still.*

Hustlers were a type he knew how to deal with.

The more than lovely Shemsi was still chuckling softly. Her hips moved and her hand continued its kneading.

"I flash to you, voyager. Building your simulacrum could be a sizz for both of us. The cred would be the least of it. Still, I can hardly just forget the payoff! You're no charity case. You have cred. Share a little for a professional job, that's all I ask. Just share a little." A final, pulsating squeeze then, and: "Because when you do, I'll share too, believe me!"

Gelor chuckled. All traces of his earlier skittishness had faded. "I believe you." With his free hand, he stroke-patted her knee. "Before we seriously talk price, though, there's the matter of the second and third 'droids."

"Sec–" She showed surprise. Then: "Yes?"

"The second offers no problems, Shemsi. I see it as nondescript. Of indeterminate origin. No particular racial/ planetary type. Appearance just commonplace. Nothing distinctive as to physique."

"And the third?"

"A big brute." Gelor made it a point to hold his voice level while excitement rose. "It's to be made in the image of a Bleaker. Complete with chest dagger and armored glove."

"A big brute of a Bleaker—?" For the first time, Shemsi looked and sounded baffled. How bright and sharp and swift and businesslike—and how easily she could look . . . otherwise!

Gelor leaned back, relaxing. It was like the day, back when he was a boy, when an old bot-fisherman had showed him how to let the line go slack just before he twitched to set the hook. He smiled and forced himself to look straight into those melting eyes, all outlined in their blue mask under the so-shapely black brows.

"You must give him a few distinctive touches, of course. I had it in mind to let him have a Rahman-green birthmark across the left side of his face, from the outer corner of his eye to mouth to earlobe. That eye, the left, is blind—burned out by—never mind. I have a holopic for you to go by." With a small smile, he handed it to Shemsi.

Her face froze in a mask of shock. "*Dravan!*" she gasped low. "Dravan the Marked!"

"Correct." Gelor basked in the warm glow of the moment. "It should constitute an interesting project, no?"

"But—the authorities . . . TGW–" Shemsi's hands were actually fluttering. Below the dye-mask, her cheeks had lost color.

"Right. In view of the price on Dravan's head, they'll take a dim view of the simulacrum." Gelor smiled lazily. "On the other hand, what does it matter, so long as it remains our secret?" The smile vanished as he leaned forward. "You *do* guarantee professional secrecy, do you not, Andrist?"

"Oh pos. Of course," she said, seeming to shrug off her tension.

(Gelor noted how her fingers continued their nervous fumble-fondling of her garnadine pendant. Her hand dropped at the same instant and her tone became brisk, businesslike.)

"The price for the three will be a half-million stells."

He kept his face bland. "A rather drastic upsurge in price. You suspect me of some devious purpose?"

Shemsi shrugged. "I stated a price . . ." Her face was just as open, eyes bland, arched brows at rest.

"Done, then," Gelor said stiffly. She did assume an

illegal purpose, he knew, and now he knew that she'd do it anyway. For enough cred. What rate she stated mattered no more to Gelor than what he promised.

"When do you wish me to start work?"

The shift in her manner amused him. All business, now. She rated better as an actress than many a holomeller "star" he'd seen. Only her abrupt acceptance of the clearly hazardous commission and her lack of quibbling or questions, even response to his suggestion of "devious purpose," showed how fearful she was—or how devious, he thought. *Ready to call the policers the first chance you get, my carefully sexy lady?*

He pushed the point a bit further: "The method of payment . . ."

"Shelve that for now. It doesn't really matter—not on a job that is this genuinely exciting."

She was fumbling with the pendant again. Again her voice held a small, raw edge of tension. She studied him with eyes that were somehow veiled despite the candor of her manner. "Why do you want such a simula, though? Musla's beard, a Bleaker outlaw! You must be planning piracy, at the very least!"

Ah. And that interests you, carefully sexy lady? A hust, then, thinking as all husts did. Always searching for a path to greater profit. He kept his smile inward. As of this moment Shemsi knew too much for him to let her back out . . . or get out of his sight. Left alone for five mins, she'd have policers on him. *If I were so stupid as to give her the chance.*

Oh, he wasn't about to kill her. His need for her was too great, and besides, an alternative existed. Hardly an ideal solution, true. But it would serve as an acceptable field expedient.

Coolly, smoothly, he leaned forward in a way that coaxed her to do the same. Their mouths met, open. Tongues probed and flickered—while he moved his free hand down to the spring-thing beneath his jacket and brought it to bear on the spot where this too-clever woman's legs merged with her torso. Meanwhile she was crushing his other hand into her there, searching for his throat with her tongue. A swift jerk brought that hand free of her grasp. Palm and heel, he rammed it hard against her breastbone and broke the kiss by pinning her to the back of her seat.

His other hand swooped in to let her feel the spring-thing then, twisting it cruelly against her.

"Shall I ream you a new stash? This thing will do it, stash."

Her eyes stared at his, wide. Shemsi didn't move. She didn't speak. He could *feel* the terror in her.

"If you want to live," he said tightly, "*and* keep this narrow channel unblooded and smaller than a doorway, you'll do precisely as I tell you." He prodded with the spring-thing, saw her wince. He spoke as he rose: "Come on."

Shemsi's eyes distended. "No!"

Gelor allowed himself the luxury of a small bleak grin. He brushed her nipples with the spring-thing.

Shaking, quaking, fumbling with her crimson pendant, Shemsi tried to rise. It didn't work; apparently her legs wouldn't hold her. He prodded. She grunted, but was sensible enough not to cry out even as she writhed. That did not, however, aid her legs in straightening to get her onto her feet.

Tight-lipped, Gelor caught her by her hair. He dragged her erect thus and shoved her ahead of him toward the curtained entry. Holding her so that she must stare at the chamber's ceiling, he eased back the drape and thrust his head out to check the hallway. And something struck him hard on the back of the neck.

The violent blow sent shock and pain joining to blur his vision. Desperately he twisted sidewise—and glimpsed the (Never)minder waiter. The fellow was lunging at him, teeth bared and eyes wide and glaring. With a frantic effort, Gelor brought the spring-thing around. His thumb shoved the trigger button forward. The spring-head slammed into the waiter just below the breastbone. His mouth leaped open and made ugly noises. For an instant, he hung poised on tiptoe, like some strange folkloric dancer.

Erect now, Gelow swung the spring-thing. Its weighted

tip lashed out, whip-like, to the vulnerable point behind the 'Minder's ear. Gelor felt death in its impact . . .

And at the same instant became aware that Shemsi was trying to wedge past him. Savagely, he jerked at her chignon. Set him up by taking a "private" booth with a waiter-imitating-guard in attendance, had she? His mind raced. The man had not been there when he had and known to strike Gelor when he had. Somehow, Shemsi had alerted him.

How?

With the thought came the answer. The pendant! He snatched at it. A violent wrench broke the delicate chain. The garnadine flicked in half on minute hinges. Inside snuggled the button of a silent siren.

Gelor cursed aloud. Desperately he looked this way and that. (Shemsi tugged. He yanked at her hair. Her mouth emitted a gagging noise. She ceased tugging.)

He narrowed his eyes at the large lacquered panels set into each of the walls of the booth. Spotting a slot running along the lower edge of one, Gelor tucked in his fingers and tugged. The panel slid upward to reveal an auto-dumbwaiter. Fitting, he thought, and tossed in the pendant. Without letting go of Shemsi, he seized the dead 'Minder by the collar. He dragged him to the chute, and in a sudden movement sent Shemsi staggering face-forward into the backmost corner of the booth. By the time she was coming close to getting herself together, her confederate had followed the pendant to . . . somewhere.

Gelor slammed the cover just as sounds of a sudden small tumult rose from char-par's entrance area. Naturally Shemsi chose that moment to turn around. A glance at her opening mouth told Gelor she was going to scream. He hit her, good and hard.

She sagged and he gave her a better one, a nape-chop to make sure she was unconscious. Fumbling an injectab from his pocket, Gelor stabbed it into the hollow at the base of her throat.

The sounds from the right, the entrance area, grew louder. A policer came pelting down the corridor. He carried a thumper-pistol. If she'd glanced in the right direction she couldn't help but glimpse the action in the booth, Gelor knew. With the drape only half in place, the nipper saw nothing. Her attention was focused too tightly on the hall's far end.

Good! Gelor swung Shemsi's limp form up and slung her over his shoulder like a sack of topatoes. He raced for the entrance. Outside, a policer van stood at the curb, pulsers throbbing. Its driver looked young and nervous.

"Quick!" Gelor snapped. "This one's badly hurt. Your partner said get her to hospital, fast!"

He was dumping Shemsi into the rear seat as he spoke, and scrambled in beside her. It was a good spot for him. It put him right behind the youthful nipper. Already the fellow was snapping coordinates. The van swung out into the street.

Gelor waited till they had covered a half-dozen blocks. Here, the cargo shuttle from the surface spaceport to the planet's docking wheel towered high above them. An open gate yawned eighty meters ahead. Shifting to the edge of his seat, Gelor spoke urgently to the driver.

"My patient's worse. Pull into the port. I'll have to use the aid unit at the intake station."

The young policer nodded without glancing around. He wheeled the van right through the gate. The policer insignia did its work. The gate guard waved them through and the van never slowed.

Great masses of cargo rose in building-high blocks on either side of the avenue leading to the intake station. Alleys jutted off at right angles. Loader-lifts rumbled to and fro, picking up and depositing goods from a dozen satellites and planets. Gelor braced himself.

"Watch it!" he shouted in the driver's ear.

The nipper went rigid. Gelor thumbed his spring-thing's triggering button. The spring-head shot forth. The driver's skull shattered with the brittle sound of breaking ceramic-ware.

Gelor lunged. He shoved the policer aside and seized the steer-bar. He spun the van rightward with a jerk and swung into a loading alley. The vehicle swayed so wildly that for a moment he thought it must overturn, then careened into a massive case, righted itself, and ground to a halt against a row of bright blue synthetic chemical drums labeled BULK BORQ (*unprocessed*). The impact flipped the lid from one big canister. Gray-blue borq crystals and preservative oxytabs spilled out across the pavement.

Gelor grinned. This was a better break than he had any reason to hope for. Hastily, he glanced this way and that. Not a soul, not a vehicle was in view.

Gelor dragged the unconscious Shemsi from the battered van and hauled her over to the borq drum. He heaved her up to drape her over the big barrel, head and arms hanging within. He scooped out borq until he could crowd the slim woman below the rim, knees to chest. Ripping off her wetcloth sari, he draped the dark fabric loosely over her head and tied it—loosely—about her neck so that the borq crystals couldn't get into her eyes or nose or mouth.

(It was a long, long time later before Gelor realized that he hadn't even noticed her bared breasts or any other aspect of her nudity. He was a man who knew how to concentrate his energies and his thoughts . . . and in whom the sexual imperative ran fourth to greed and self-love and his *need* for violent mastery.)

The drum's lid had been popped upward by impact. It was not damaged, and he snapped it into place as neatly as if it had never suffered the impact of the van. He bent down the sealing clamps and made them click. Not even the most powerful of men could get out of the canister now, with no leverage and no tool.

Gelor used a broken trim-strip from the van to score the drum's bright blue surface with an erratic series of scratches that would seem accidental—while making it eminently recognizable.

He was barely panting when he stepped back to inspect and admire his hasty work. He had a right, Gel Gelor thought, to be in a self-congratulatory mood. Not only had he eliminated any possible danger where Shemsi was concerned . . . in the process he had come up with the perfect way to transport her to Jasbir!

Unconscious, sealed in a drum of borq, she'd be completely free of official attention. And thanks to the oxygen-generating tablets essential for any interplanetary shipment of the chemical, odds were strongly in favor of her survival. Even though cramped and uncomfortable in the lightweight plasteel barrel, Shemsi-andrist would live to carry out the work he assigned her, at no cost above the lives of a couple of mindless 'Minders.

All I have to do now is get her onto an outbound merchant spacer.

Gelor hurried around the van to check the policer. Dead. Good. He donned the fellow's cap and jacket and stowed the corpse out of sight in the rear of the van—the detention space. With that zipped up, he swung back around to lift the stopper from its seat-holster—to hell with one of those ungainly thumper-pistols designed for crowd control!—and thrust it into the inside pocket of his new jacket.

Stepping out into the main avenue leading to the intake station, he hailed the first loader-lift that passed. Nothing happened; the dam' thing was cybernetic and Gelor had to get out of the way fast.

The next one had a human driver. Relatively speaking, anyhow. She pulled her huge vehicle to a stop.

"Trouble?"

"Double." Gelor spat on the pavement in what he hoped was an appropriately 'Mindish manifestation of disgust. "I was s'posed to pick up a can of this borq"—he gestured— "for shipment to Jasbir. Super-speed order, y'know? Instead, I dodged one of those damned cyber-loaders and trashed my van." He shifted from foot to foot in a calculated show of embarrassment and hesitation. "I'm awready in trouble. Help a dumb bug out and get the can on the shuttle for me, willya? That way I'll have time to take care of the paperwork at the intake office. The ship's already stowing cargo. Gotta admit I'm at yer mercy— it's my ass if I miss roll-off."

The loader-driver's snort said worlds about the intelligence of policers, and of anyone who'd assign one to get anything onboard a shuttle. Still . . .

"Y'know—you mighta done us a favor! Union's been tryina find a way to fight all these sisterslicin' cyber-loaders, anyhows!" Her voice was an anomaly, along with the pink button on her drab green coverall and her language: she had a voice like an eleven-year-old. "Now one's essed up a nipper goin' about 'is duty! Outta the way, jacko. I'll handle it!"

She had the loader's magnetic clamps around the drum in seconds. In moments she was speeding down the roadway into the tangle of carriers crowded about the shuttle's cargo area. The blue synchem drum vanished from Gelor's view briefly, then reappeared: jouncing up the ramp to the left onto a crawler.

Exit one andrist: bulk borq, unprocessed, outbound for Jasbir.

So much for the carefully sexy Shemsi. At least, Gelor decided, for the time being. Right now he had more important matters to consider.

Specifically, it was high time he set about contacting CongCorp to begin negotiations for the sale of the planet Eilong.

9

Women, all the world over, are what men make them.
—*Sir Richard F. Burton*

Things were less than good onboard spaceship *Slicer*, in Yahna's view. Tension rode heavily on them all. Nerves rasped raw with strain were poised ready to trigger violence at the slightest provocation. There were provocations.

Hearing a series of frantic bird-whistles from Twil'im, Jesti found it backed into a corner of the DS station. Musla of Sekhar was threatening it with a knife, a *kris*. Jesti managed it so that no one got stuck.

The issue was the manner of Twil's rubbing against Musaphor, in passing. Musla was convinced that the Jarp had designs on his devoutly Muslim body. Twil insisted that nothing could be further from the truth; it had merely lost its footing momentarily. Its flailing hand had only happed upon Musla's backside. All an accident, all innocent. As a matter of fact, Twil avowed, it preferred women. *Oh wonderful*, Yahna thought. She had never seen Jarps as sexy at all.

Hieri calmed the pair down, eventually. After that, though, Sek and Jarp walked wide of each other.

The next incident involved Yahna. Seeing how her dress was torn (after her episode with Jesti), Hieri had concluded that she was ship's woman. That meant available for trysting:

slicing. Jesti disagreed. Harsh words were exchanged. Hieri backed off—making it obvious that he did not consider the matter closed. And again, Yahna Golden's emotions were mixed.

It was nice, somehow warming, to know that she'd aroused at least a degree of protective feeling in Jesti. On the other hand, she wasn't sure she wanted it. Hieri was a handsome man. Her phantasies would accommodate him nicely. Still . . . she was *not* ship's hust. Once that sort of thing began, where might it end? A career as crew's hust on a pirate spacer offered little future even if a woman embraced the concept, which Yahna definitely did not.

She even retained mixed feelings about Jestikhan Churt, after his (Assault? Violation? *You won*, he'd said. . . .)

Of his courage there was no doubt. He'd proven that beyond question, and a vast resourcefulness. His intelligence was something else again. Where did inborn ability in this *miner* leave off and acquired knowledge begin? She had a notion that he was very possibly her equal in innate capacity. What he lacked was background, sophistication. Class. Obviously a life spent in the mines of Eilong limited experience! Oh, he had his own brand of class, and time spent ranging the Galaxy in *Slicer* would fill the gaps soon enough, with her filling any crucial information gaps. Working with MarsCorp had given her a range of insights and plenty of lore—and she was an educated woman. She would *not* succumb to the simplistic kneejerk of *Whatta Man (sigh!)*.

It was in a different dimension that Golden ran into trouble. Emotion and feeling—as brought into focus by her extra-long, gilded nail. Unhappily, she lifted her right hand and looked down at that middle finger.

Her associates took it for granted. One more affectation, a flamboyant *shtick* like her periodot nipple cup or her crown of aureate hair, all designed to catch the eye and project that ShowBiz image. Only she knew the truth about it: that nail was a lot more than a normal horny sheath protecting her fingertip. It was her secret armament. A razor-edged plasteel sliver molded to the actual nail and sheathed in its gilt coating. Not much less dangerous than a HRal's retractable claw!

So. She had her weapon. So—why hadn't she used it last cycle, in those moments of writhing violence on the floor here, while Jesti forced her?

It was a question she had no answer for and didn't like at all. Certainly she hated the Eilan for what he'd done. Yet, incredibly, a degree of ambivalence clouded her reaction. And her feelings, now.

For one thing, there was the matter of the change in him. *Then*, his words and stance had projected cold anger. *Now*, his manner had reversed totally to wry humor. As he had put it: *"We're even now, Golden One. You raped my mind, back there on Croz. That hurt my ego. I had to have payment from you for that. That's why I flashed so fast when you gave me an excuse to rape your body. Ego-bruise for ego-bruise. Now, that's over. Out of my system. I've had my revenge. You got the rape you wanted. It clears the board. We can forget it, without debts. Settle down to being people."* And he had laughed, eyes bright with affability and humor between friends.

Friends? Well. . . . Was apology, a left-handed one at that, enough to make up for violation of a woman's body?

The answer, of course, was a vehement *Negatory*.

Add to it the things he'd said, the accusations as to her motives. What right had he to probe her secrets, to show such psychiatric ability to drive through her mind-locks, her need for rape, her powerlessness to explode her tensions into orgasm without a foreplay of violence?

She hated him for those coldly verbalized perceptions. Above all, she hated him for being perceptive—being right.

Yes, she knew that. For her, passion would not release itself in simple copulation. She found no pleasure in the routine joining of two bodies. To gain release, to soar to ecstat, her secret self demanded the catalyst of brute force. Specifically: rape.

Of course it was only lately that she'd been able to admit that to herself. To face up to the facts of her conditioning and what had happened between her and Fahrood.

It was the kinship that had made it so bad, left the guilt and need for expiation. She was a child and he a grown man: uncle, cousin, in-law—something. Kin. Even now a family conspiracy of silence surrounded him. She'd never be able to get the bloodline clear. What counted was the way he had come into her bed when she was only eight years old.

He with his great man's body and his huge-seeming hand across her mouth. Coaxing, cajoling. Soothing. Threatening. Until at last there was nothing for her but to give in.

Then the pain. The shame and tears. The anguish. If she could have killed herself then, she'd have done it. Him, too! Yet a child of eight—what could she do? He knew that, of course.

Other such nights followed, so many of them. At first, he swore that each would be the last.

The worst had been the business with her mother. Her mother, who had claimed to love her so, yet wouldn't listen. She accused her daughter of lying; she punished Yahna for lying. Then her mother wept and wailed and clung to the girl, as if mother were child and child were woman providing solace. Begging her to keep the nasty truth a secret. Not to reveal what had happened . . . what was happening.

Why had her mother done such a thing? Again, Yahna wondered. Fear, she now supposed. Her mother had been intimidated. Imploring silence lest her husband slay the man—whoever Fahrood was—and in the process, destroy the family. Better merely to destroy one member, Yahna. . . . Besides, the child need feel no blame, no shame. She remained a victim only, feeling no passion and no pleasure.

The nights went on. Months, years of nights for Yahna, whenever lust stirred within Fahrood.

And then the night came when her body became a woman's body, and she was a child no longer. The night when nerves pulsed to life, and senses woke, and muscles twitched and spasmed. After a time Fahrood began to fear that she would fill with child, and who dared mention an anticoncep shot for a girl barely at puberty? And so he disappeared. He left a ripe, aroused, passionate child-woman. A woman who ached for man as an addict lusted after its eroflore.

Only later, when boys her age approached her, did she learn the nastier truth. Her body was a woman's body, ripe to overflowing with a woman's passions. Yet let a man so much as touch her and tension was at her throat like a Ghanji tiger: the tiger was a mind-block called guilt. The pain and shame of all those nights with Fahrood had left a legacy she had not even realized.

It was more than surprise and shock; it was too much to bear. Better that her body should ache with longing than that she should feel the pain come through as secret sin. So it was that Yahna erected a wall of cold disdain around her. Friendships faded. Intimacy lost its glow for her. Even when acquaintances admired her mind—her brilliance, sometimes—they walked wide around her.

Later came another truth. A fellow student, the nice-looking Thebanian called Djalor at the Psychesorium of Koba. Djalor watched her; Djalor dared; Djalor pressed against her. Instinctively, she thrust him away. That was too great a blow to the male arrogance of youth. Djalor slapped her. She reeled, lost her balance, fell. Her temple struck a table. She spilled down into blackness.

When the blackness cleared, she realized with horror that the boy was doing things to her body . . . and that even worse, her body was responding. She could not prevent its delighted response. His fingers toyed and eased in and out of her while he nursed or pretended to nurse at her breasts, and every nerve in her went ecstat. She heard her moans and gasps and little whimpers, and there was nothing of guilt or pain in them.

· He knew, of course. When he reached the point at which he could no longer wait to be in her, the tiger forced her to resist. That got her a hard-clamped breast and a forearm across the throat, and a vagina full of hard youth. Since she was helpless and forced and couldn't do a damned thing to deter this *use* of her body . . . she enjoyed the hell out of it.

He knew that, too. It was clever of him to tie her up,

once he had flashed. With the resilience and potency of his age, he was ready to begin again at once. It was also flaining well nice of him to tie her up, though he didn't know it. . . .

She felt no guilt. She was helpless. This hyper-horny boy was to blame, not nice (not-so) little Yahna. She was relieved of all participation; of guilt.

It was a night to top all nights. It ended only when Djalor lay shaking with exhaustion and utter depletion. Yahna thought she'd die of pure ecstasy. She too was exhausted, drained. She did nothing while he untied her, even chafed her cord-marked wrists and the breasts he had bared and bound. Then he left.

Next day he had slipped an arm warmly about her waist, and moved it up toward the breast that he had owned but a few hours previous.

She broke his arm with a testing bar.

By then, she knew the truth. Her childhood years as Fahrood's victim had forged shackles on her brain. Violence alone could break them. The immediate violence of the thing called rape. With most females, it was a phantasy not really desired. With Yahna, it was necessity. That was the sullen lurking tiger in her mind.

It changed her life. Turned her into a tacit temptress. From pure research she moved more and more into applied techniques. The job she sought and won was as a psychtech serving the cynical sensualities of MarsCorp . . . doubly rich multiplanetary corporation born of the sensuality of another woman: Setsuyo Puma. "Akima Mars." The Biggest Pair In The Universe.

Off went the sedate mode of dress her family had imposed upon Yahna . . . along with the family name she hated anyhow, for its dishonor. On came flamboyant styles that cried out to lust, that appealed to passion. With them came the halo of gold, and the surname to match. This was Yahna Golden. She yearned for—begged for—rape. It never happened. She was too successfully *daunting*.

Until now. Now she fared through the purple abyss of space on a pirate ship, with men whose hands dripped garnadine red with blood. All of which brought her reverie full circle. Back to Jestikhan Churt and her ambivalent feelings about him. The man she had not daunted, but dared too much, pushed too far. At last!

She could not see him as a pirate. He was not in the same class as the crew of the sneerily-named *Slicer*. And he had protected her from Hieri. A man of honor and old-fashioned principles!

And raped me.

Ah, but had it been rape, really? Could she be wrong about her tiger, her mind-lock? Might her need for violence not exist first and foremost in her imagination?

There's one sure way to find out!

She contrived to "fix" her clothing. Since it was ruined, torn and rag-taggy, she turned the fine lovely dress into a double-strap halter and a hip-band skirt, short. A bit of skindye, carefully applied, created an interesting atomic symbol around her navel, in yellow and linden green. And in the most casual of ways she contrived to place herself close to Jesti. Found excuses to stretch and twist, to display her body at its most seductive. (The halter displayed little cleavage. It didn't need to.) She let him catch her with her low-lidded gaze on him—challenging, tempting, taunting, tantalizing. Ran her tongue along her ripe-sullen lips in clear and open provocation/invitation. Found transparent excuses to lean back against him, body touching body, in a manner that left no question of intention.

She could feel him stiffen, the second time she did that, when she twisted. His arms came around her, one palm flat against her bared belly.

Her muscles tightened by pure reflex in the same instant. Cat-lithe, she twisted free of his embrace and clawed at his face. (Death of a dream. The tiger remained triumphant with its claws firmly in her mind.) Sidestepping swiftly, Jesti dodged the slashing nails. The rising desire she had glimpsed moments ago had already vanished. His old, mocking grin was back as he caught her wrists and pinned her tight against a bulkhead/wall.

"Have mercy, woman! You're raping my mind again. I can't trust you for a moment."

"Who's raping whom?" she kneejerked. "Whose hands were pawing my body?"

"Who cares who did what? This spacer's not big enough for us to fight each other. I mean, for right now us mad rapists got to stick together."

He was chuckling and winking as he said it. And all at once, quite in spite of herself, Yahna was laughing too.

Again, Jesti was right. Even more importantly, she'd learned her lesson. She was what she was. A tiger was a mind-lock was a tiger. From here on, she would face it. Live with it.

That cleared the air between them. Yahna made it a point to be present any time Jesti was sleeping and to stay in the con-cabin with him when he was oncon, with his back necessarily to the door. In turn, he persuaded her to don a (man's, large, but not loose everywhere) shirt, and pants that bagged on her everywhere save rearwardly. Regardless of what the real situation was, he told her in manner salesmanly, to the others she had *looked* as if she was flaunting herself, and that would likely lead only to trouble. And he, Jesti told her, would be involved. She swallowed, almost wanting to hug him, and agreed to the loose clothing. (No, he did not apologize for having ruined her dress.)

The situation with regard to the rest of the crew came to a head the third day out.

Jesti was oncon. Running shorthanded as they were, he had little choice, qualified or no. Besides, if SIPACUM signaled danger, all he had to do was hit the alarm for help. On ship's day three, Yahna was playing computrician. Abruptly SIPACUM began flashing a ruddy telit and beep-beeping. Alarm.

Captain Hieri was asleep, and he needed that sleep. Petri, as ship's second, had the duty. He was in and keying before she had reacted. He adjusted the scanner and his voice rasped with excitement:

"Theba's cold warheads! It's a spacer—a 'Vocker. Foundering, it looks like."

Jesti pushed back in the con-chair. "So?"

Petri's grin would have done credit to a hungry dyre-wolf. "So there's no such thing as a 'Vocker that doesn't carry ice emeralds. Ships from Havoc pay their dock fees

with 'em. Saves them stells.'' The wolf-grin broadened.
"With their ship in trouble this way, it must mean their
drive-train's out. That locks their DS, too."

Jesti spread his hands and repeated it: "So?"

"So all we have to do is change course long enough to
come alongside, lock on, and pick up those gemstones.
Like taking candy from a baby."

Yahna could see the shadow of a frown touch Jesti's
forehead. "I thought we made a deal. I saved your necks.
You carry me to Jasbir—or wherever."

"Firm. But–"

"No piracy, Petri. That wasn't on the tapes."

"But *ice*-emeralds . . ."

"No," Jesti repeated.

Petri stared. He wore a stopper. His hand touched its
grip, thrusting up out of the violently crimson and yellow
sash he wore. Jesti smiled. It was a dangerous sort of
smile, Yahna decided (feeling a little rush). The Eilan
swiveled around in the captain's chair. His hand lay in his
lap. So did his own blue-gray cylinder. Petri looked at it:
Jesti's stopper.

Yahna had heard of echoing eternities of silence. This
was one of them.

Then Petri snorted, angrily. Wheeling, he strode from
the cabin.

Still smiling, Jesti let his eyes swerve toward Yahna,
and swiveled the first chair back to face the console. Back
by the wall—she'd gotten out of Petri's way at the
SIPACUM interface, fast—Yahna relaxed. And ever so
silently, the con-cabin's door reopened. Stopper in hand,
Petri stepped inside. He leveled the weapon at the back of
Jesti's bare head. Very bare head.

It seemed to Yahna that she stood frozen. Yet that
couldn't have been. There wasn't time. Blood pounded in
her ears. She couldn't breathe. She didn't even dare scream,
lest Jesti turn and Petri tighten his grasp on the stopper—
all it took to beam Jesti. With a Three, she'd bet. Already
she could see the Outie pirate's knuckles paling as he
started to squeeze his weapon's grip.

Yahna Golden pounced.

It was not a conscious act. She hardly knew what she was doing. She had to do *something*, and her legs did: they drove her at Petri. Her right hand was out and thrusting its middle finger. The one with the six sems of plasteel.

Petri glimpsed her movement out of the edge of his eye. He stiffened, started to turn . . . and with all her strength she drove home the deadly nail in a slashing thrust to the side of the throat. The razor-edged plasteel "fingernail" sliced through the skin and deep into flesh. It found the carotid artery.

Petri's head went back. For a fraction of a second he hung rigid. Then another instant passed and a spasm hit him. He jerked frenetically. Jetting blood drenched Yahna. Then the man who had been Petronius Jee was tottering, crumpling, falling. He was dead before he hit the deck.

Yahna would have fallen too, only somehow Jesti was out of the con-chair and catching her, grasping, supporting her. Seconds passed before she realized that the captain was standing in the cabin doorway. If he felt emotion as he looked down at his fallen brother, Hieronymus Jee didn't show it. He didn't even bend to make sure Petri was dead.

Yahna tried to speak. She couldn't.

Jesti spoke for her: "Your brother had it in his mind to kill me, Hieronymus. From behind."

Hieri's face remained wooden. "Petri lacked judgment. That's why I am in command."

Jesti's gesture was helpless in frustration. "What can I say, Captain? Stopper's in his hand. I'm sorry, sure, but that won't bring Petri back. And I'm not hypocrite enough to claim I'd rather I was lying there instead of him."

"Oh? Indeed." Hieri's face remained stony.

"In deed." Jesti rubbed the back of his neck. His eyes seemed to draw deeper into their sockets. "Don't make it a blood feud, Hieri. That buys no points for either of us."

(*His tone*, Yahna thought—*it's close onto pleading*.)

Hieri's expression didn't change. "Don't worry. Outies feud only with equals. Purple subs don't rate more than a Poofing."

Jesti stood very still. "That sure does sound like a threat. Do I dare turn my back on you now?"

"You're right both times, Eilan. With me, you'll see it coming."

Jesti nodded once, and shrugged. The faintest of tight-lipped smiles had replaced his conciliatory manner. His thumbs were hooked in the royal blue sash Petri had given him yesterday—not bright enough, Petri said. Now that sash bore Jestikhan's stopper.

He said, "Your decision, Captain."

SIPACUM's *pingg* sounded in the same instant and as swiftly changed the focus of attention in the tense cabin. As one, Hieri and Jesti swung to the scanner. Hieri made hasty adjustments, stared.

"Theba's butts! The 'Vocker ship's gone on its way, and directly behind us is a CongCorp relay station—and there's a ship coming in fast, heading directly for us!" He banged open inship comm. "Musla! Stand by DS! Unidentified spacer closing fast." His fingers were also racing over the keys. Come on, SIPACUM, damn it—give me an ID on that spacer before we find out it's TGW the hard way!"

10

I find that the best virtue I have has in it some tincture of vice.

—Michel de Montaigne

Jesti was in no mood to give Hieronymus Jee credit for much of anything. On the other hand, there was no questioning the Outreacher's competence as ship's master. Computrician Yahna had gone to work, too. Jesti could only stand and feel out of place. *About as helpful as warheads on a buck grat*, he grumped mentally.

Then, somehow, SIPACUM identified the oncoming craft. A repair ship, heading for the comm-relay station floating so huge and yet tiny against the vastness of space. The station had trouble, then.

"What the vug's a comm-relay station?" Jesti heard his voice say, and wished he hadn't.

Surprisingly, Hieri answered. Without turning from the con: "A fixed pseudo-satellite that handles all message traffic to and from CongCorp headquarters, that's all. In–dis–pensable! They even have equipment to tap in on CC's mainbanks. That's why the thing's set up like an unmanned fort in space. So—it has problems, and here comes the repair ship. All we have to do is get out of the way."

Before he was aware that he'd had the thought, Jesti said, "Wait."

Hieri swung around this time, staring. "*Wha–at?*"

Aware of new tension, Yahna wished she had taken Petri's stopper . . .

"I said wait." Behind his grin, Jesti's mind was racing. "You told me you were a pi-rut, Captain! What's on a repair ship? Probably some just shockingly valuable equipment . . . either mighty usable on *Slicer* or mighty salable, surely!"

Hieri kept on staring, blinking. "Eilan, I've plain misjudged you. Your brains aren't really purple. Or if they are—well, I think I'll see if I can work out a celldye job to make mine the same color." He swung back to the con. "You know what else? This is going to be so easy it'll be almost embarrassing. Musla! Open DS! Stand by to bracket that ship. We're *taking* it, mind, *not* trying to blow it away!"

"*Hoo-hahhh!*" Musla's voice came back, and mere moments later one, then two bolts lanced out at the repair ship.

Hieri hunched forward. "Welcome, repair ship! We who are about to blast you, salute you!"

After a moment the voice came back, worse than startled: "*Blast us! What kind of—what are you t—what d'you want?*"

"Now that is a most sensible attitude, repair ship. What we want is onboard your ship. We're between you and the station and we're monitoring. You try sending them a message and we'll send you to atoms!"

After a moment's silence, the voice came back from the other ship, tiredly, resignedly. It gave the invitation: "*All right, pirates . . . Red Rover.*"

"Coming over," Hieri said, "Stand by to receive a link."

Jesti hadn't heard anything familiar in minutes. He learned as the operation moved forward (with Musla disgruntled that he wasn't going to get to blow anyone away). "Red Rover" meant "We're coming over," as in boarding the other ship. "A link" as Hieri used it this time was the

S-tunnel that linked one ship's airlock to the other. It enabled the pirates to walk across. Or swim; the spinner or torque-inducer that simulated gravity on both spacers had to be cut off while they linked.

Jesti threw up and got to stay behind.

Yahna did not, and furthermore knew more about electronics equipment than anyone on *Slicer*. Ready or not, like it or not, she got to *Red Rover*. She did give Jesti a look that was different from the others' stares—she glanced at him as if he was a genius. He assumed that he'd misinterpreted Yahna's look.

And that was how he began his active career as a space pirate: sitting oncon, his throat hurting from the acid of his vomit, hanging on against floating (and told that if he threw up in freefall he'd clean it up—once G-for-gravity was restored and it stopped floating around), while all the action took place without him. Having already cleaned up Petri's body and blood, he was not anxious for further cleaning details.

Hieri was right, too. It was all so easy that it was almost embarrassing. Almost. No one looked embarrassed, however, except Jestikhan Churt.

It *was* weird to see all that equipment coming over from the smallish repair craft—floating. The electronic *thing* Yahna pushed easily along and into *Slicer* must have weighed a half-ton. She guided it to her own quarters, rather than the hold. And here came Musla, with more, and a grinning Hieri, with more—and a prime element off the other ship's comm. It could race on to the relay pseudo-satellite and babble its news of being pirated, but it certainly wouldn't be saying anything until it arrived!

"Settle the cargo!" Hieri ordered. "We've got to get the flyin' vug *out* of here!"

They were far, far away by the time their victim reached the CongCorp comm-relay station, and a grateful Jesti was again enjoying the feeling of weight. It not only enabled a man to walk, it stopped his innards from floating.

Two hours later Petronius Jee had been "buried" in space and Jesti was in Yahna's cabin, where she was telling him what a genius he was.

• • •

"You were right, Jesti. A relay station is built around a message center, and it's linked to CongCorp Central. Where, for instance, there just must be information concerning kiracat ores and the planet Eilong."

She moved to a mirror and smoothed her crown of very yellow hair, suddenly pretending to be oblivious to his presence. With her butt poked back that way. Sure.

Jesti said, "Could be." And gazed at her outpoked bottom atop legs long as his and a lot better looking.

"Could indeed. Why, that data might even prove pertinent to a fugitive Eilan who keeps wondering why anyone would conspire to steal some of his blood and semen—and then plant false evidence so he looked guilty of a particularly nasty murder."

Jesti's palms were wet with sweat, just like that. His pretense of understanding, of calm inquiry, redshifted at speed. "You mean you think CongCorp's behind it?" His voice came out raw despite his efforts to the contrary. He had also lost all interest in backside and legs.

"You know I don't. It lacks C-Corp's characteristic bludgeoning style, for one thing. The approach of whoever worked out this plot is a great deal more subtle."

Jesti said, "Uh," and was pretty proud to get that out.

"But there's still a tie to CongCorp, somewhere. There has to be." Yahna turned to face him, spread her hands. "After all, *why* did you have to flee your own planet? From what you've said, it's because you pushed for cybernetic mining. You *know* CongCorp would've heard about that. They've got ears everywhere. So . . . they'd naturally poke around, trying to find out what's going on. Keeping tabs on Eilong—and their 'friends' and 'enemies' there. And everything they learned would go into the central data banks we're going to tap."

Jesti felt his heart jump as he watched her move to the electronic thing she'd brought over from the robbed ship—and ensconced here in her own quarters onboard *Slicer*. She was smiling, too.

"You chose well when you brought me along, Jesti. Psychists are trained in working with computerized statistics.

That's why Hieri was able to throw me into his computrician's slot. I can use those same techniques to tap
CongCorp's banks—*and their own equipment*.'' She patted her acquisition. Her smile became a grin. ''Good
God—I stole it! I *am* a pirate!''

''Best-looking one along the spaceways too,'' he said,
and wished he hadn't. He saw the flash of her eyes, the
stiffening. *Oh lord. Now she's all ready to challenge and
dare and fight again!* ''Maybe I better stay off that subject
and say you're the most competent pirate along the
spaceways, Golden One. Tell me about that machine.''

She shrugged elaborately, wearing a silly ''so what''
look. ''This? Only a certified genuine CongCorp all-circuits
deepscan computercomm link. If we're lucky, Jesti, it may
help us find out who your so-handsome friend is—the one
who took it upon himself to lay Pearl's murder on your
doorstep . . . a CongCorp employee, maybe?'' Abruptly
her mood seemed to change and she flipped her fingers.
''We may not be so lucky. If that's the case—I don't know
what we'll do. Jasbir's too big for us to get anywhere just
asking questions!''

Jesti wanted to shout ''Go to it!'' rather than stand there
swapping gazes with her. He forced himself to say, ''Well,
Yahna-psychist-computrician-pirate . . . let's try and find
out.''

With an elaborate gesture, she swung to the all-those-
words-she-called-it *thing*, and depressed two keys, then a
third, shook her head, hit a fourth and another. Lights
flashed on and the portable console said *chung* and began
purring.

''Hmm . . . let's try innove.''

''Sure. Just what I was about to say. What's innove?''

She didn't laugh. ''CongCorp for 'innovational.' That
means any twist the company thinks they can steal a stell
with. I'd say your case falls into that category.'' More
key-depressing, headshakes, re-starts.

Jesti stood in sweating silence, hearing only the electronic hum—of whirring disks? The reader screen didn't
even light up. Yahna tried another tack. Jesti stared. His
palms dripped and his legs had gone clammy inside his

pants. Yahna tried again, *tick-tick-cli-tick*. And the screen came alive, dutifully going indigo and flashing a string of words in eye-eez green:

PROJECT EILONG . . . PROJECT EILONG . . . PROJECT EILONG . . . CONTACT MADE NONIDENT. FREELANCE OPERATOR CRYPTONYM HAJJI KALAJJI. MEET SET FOR JASBIR AREA TIME/PLACE/DESIGNATION TO COME

"The pilgrim of Kalajji," she whispered. "Jesti, it's a start. All you have to do is take the discs and drive and screen, here, and feed it into SIPACUM." She glanced up. "It isn't as if we can keep this thing, you know."

He was staring at the onscreen message. "You stole it," he muttered, but it was an automatic response, made without thought. His thoughts were very much elsewhere. This was a win; a skirmish won. The real war lay ahead. Tracking him. Finding this "Hajji Kalajji." Was he also a hyper-handsome, double-dyed, card-carrying, certified villain who went about strangling mere innocent slips of husts and laying the blame on fugitive Eilans . . . after stealing samples of sperm and blood?

It seemed a distinct possibility. A strong one. One to be pursued, just as soon as *Slicer* reached Jasbirstation and one Jestikhan Churt could get himself down onplanet. Jesti grinned. He could hardly wait for them to lock in on Jasbir's orbiting spacedock wheel.

That was when the next nasty scene started, with Hieri storming in to storm that their use of this dam' device might well enable CongCorp to put a trace on them. Knocking Yahna roughly aside, he shut down the computercomm terminal.

And turned, and froze, staring.

"Ah, Jesti . . . you cleaning that thing?"

Jesti looked down at the stopper in his hand. "No, Captain. See, you want to get to Jasbir to sell a few little things. That's wonderful—I need to get there to ask a few questions about my frame-up back on Croz. That fancy putercom-thing just gave me a lead."

"And maybe it's traceable, Eilan! Maybe CongCorp can get a fix on us, backtracking that machine."

"If that's the case, Captain, I'm truly sorry. But–"

"They can't," Yahna said quietly. "That's not the way it works. There's no 'beam' to trace."

"Shut the vug up, Goldie!"

"Captain-sah, that's why this stopper just sort of jumped into my hand. Somehow I seem to've made myself responsible for all of you, by breaking you out of prison. Now I've made myself responsible for her—I'm the one who kidnapped her, after all. You wouldn't *knock* Musla out of the way as you did her, and you wouldn't Twil, and you sure wouldn't knock me out of the way."

Hieri stared. "I might," he said, from a mouth that barely moved.

Jesti restored the stopper to the belt he had slipped on in place of Petri's gift; wearing the sash hardly seemed bright, since it had been Hieri's dead brother's, and he was dead. The Eilan shook his head.

"No, Captain, you wouldn't."

After a long, long while of staring, Hieronymus Jee half-turned. "When we go down onto Jasbir to sell some merchandise, that goes with us."

Jesti flipped his fingers, a gesture he was learning. "Sure, Cap'm."

With a curt nod, Hieri left the cabin. Jesti and Yahna looked at each other. Another skirmish won. Another war to come.

11

The weak in courage is strong in cunning.

—*William Blake*

A spaceport cargo hauler brought the two drums of bulk borq (unprocessed) to the place Gelor had chosen as his base on Jasbir. It lay far out on Marmot's outskirts in the parklike area adjoining the new Bionarium, the interplanetary zoo. Originally it had been palace-in-exile of Ghanj's old Prince Palkivala, last Ghanji ruler of the Q'riim dynasty. After his death, his horde of wrangling offspring had lost it to a rental syndic. Gelor had leased it from the syndic.

He liked the place despite the fact that it had seen better days. Its high walls rendered it secure from prying eyes. An unparalleled security system guarded it from intrusions. Nor did it hurt that within those walls the grounds surpassed those of DeyMeox's luxurious Samanna estate.

Interior palace walls and partitions were thick and soundproof. A feature that particularly pleased Gelor was a result of the old prince's long and vengeful memory: a dunge-on!—three small cells deep beneath the palace proper. Each was equipped with its own locking system. Though hardly up to present standards, they looked sturdy enough to keep his captives safe.

Gelor liked that. It meant he could sleep without

apprehension. Eagerly, he flipped the lids off the borq drums.

Both captives were alive and well. Gelor considered it intelligent to re-clothe each limp, thoroughly confused woman. Only then did he give each a shot of stim. Soon he was leading them to their cells. He opened a door and turned to DeyMeox.

"Your quarters, Crober."

Though she surveyed the chamber with marked distaste, she entered without voicing protest. Gelor unlocked the second cell and gestured Shemsi inside. Unlike DeyMeox, the andrist showed no particular irritation.

"It's hardly luxury, Shemsi," he said coolly. "Still, I think you'll find it comfortable enough."

She shot him a sidewise glance from lowered, lavendered lids. "Agreed. Hardly set up for passion, though, is it?"

That took Gelor aback. "I didn't plan it with passion in mind," he advised stiffly. (That bothered him, too. He recognized a tendency in him: taken aback, his face stiffened while his voice tightened.)

"What's planned and how things shape up later can be two different things," Shemsi said, and leaned against the doorframe. Almost thoughtfully, she took her captor's hand and pressed it to her breast. "You do agree?"

Angrily, he jerked the hand free. "No. You're here to work not . . ." He groped, searching for a euphemism while he felt heat and knew he was reddening at the ridiculousness of having to grope for dodge-words at such a time.

She completed the sentence for him: "Indulge ourselves?"

He glared. "I hardly see why you should introduce the subject."

"You are a man . . . aren't you?" Shemsi smirked. "Hardly a bad-looking one at that. Good-looking or not, though, you'll never get her."

"*What*?"

"You heard me." Shemsi's lavender-dyed lips twisted in a small smile of mockery. "You're not her type, handsome. And really—vice versa."

He went even tighter. "I don't know what you're talking about."

"Oh, of course not. A man like you, what do you care about stash? You probably wouldn't know what to do with it if you got it."

Gelor's face went hot. "You seem to want to be hit. Or are you so concerned about my welfare?"

"*Your* welfare!" Shemsi's laugh was caustic. "Don't flatter yourself, handsome villain. It's not your welfare I care about—it's mine."

He looked questioning until her slim shoulders lifted in a shrug—and with a mocking, triumphant look she watched his gaze drop to her breasts.

"What else? Her Majesty and I are stuck here for the duration of your project, right? It's going to be hard on us, at the very best. If on top of that you're panting for Her Majesty all the time and she flats you, the word for it becomes 'impossible.' You'll take out your hots on both of us, in meanness. And you are a mean man, a genuine double-dyed villain. If you were halfway normal, I could enjoy cooling you off in bed myself. You're not. You proved that when you rammed that awful spring-thing up me, back in Newhope. So, we've got to take a different route." She leaned close and traced patterns on his chest with a fingernail dyed to match her lips and eyelids. Her voice dropped to a confidential level:

"I'm an andrist. What I had in mind is an android—a dupladroid. Of Her Majesty DeyMeox, you see. I can build in a sexulator that'll give you a ride three times better than she could. It'll even say the right things to you. Nice purple lines that would make even a Bleaker hust blush."

Gelor's mouth had gone dry. Furiously he seized her shoulder. Shoving her bodily into the cell, he slammed the door behind her. He was shaking as he blindly moved up the corridor and stumbled up the stair to his own quarters.

What bothered him most was the gnawing fear that the mocking bitch might be right. Maybe he was caught up in a lust for DeyMeox, a yen he dared not admit. He could *not* afford such involvement, he thought, reaching his own luxurious quarters and at once pouring a drink. What he was attempting was perilous enough and required much concentration. Complicate matters further with a woman and he might as well write out an invitation to disaster.

Yet what could he do about it? What man could stand against his hunger for a special woman—who was also available to him?

Unless . . . *Unless I can exhaust my passion, really sate any lust I may have for her—in her!* At least, it would do no harm for him to go to her bed. To find out for certain . . . Gelor pushed the concept around in his mind for the next thirty minutes, with another drink.

Then, shivering at the thought in spite of having decided, he arose and went back down the stair to Prince Palkivala's dungeon.

He was partway down when he heard the sound of voices. DeyMeox's and Shemsi's. He frowned. Catfooting a step at a time, he went on down. Peered around the corner, down the dungeon passageway. He swallowed: the door to DeyMeox's cell stood open! So did Shemsi's. Tension leaped in him and he ran to check the cells. Both were empty.

Gelor cursed. What a fool he had been to assume that mere locks would hold these two—one a genius and the other at least super-bright!

Not too far off, female voices tinkled in laughter. The sound came from the far end of the passage, where a second stair rose. With a care for quiet, he hurried to it. The stair led into the palace grounds and the door at the top was open. Gelor peered out to see his prisoners—ex-prisoners, he corrected bitterly. They were strolling casually through the gardens!

His natural impulse was to charge out and accost them. He stifled it. Better by far they not discover he knew they could get out of the cells. *A change of locks?* No. That would only set the precious pair to working on new plans. *All right then, how do I control them?—rather,* best *control them!*

Obviously leg-chains or drugs would do the job. The trouble was that either would also reduce efficiency, at a time when he needed top performance.

It was a problem that made for a sleepless night.

By morning, however, he thought he had the answer. As a matter of fact he held it in his hand: the property of a deceased policer. A stopper. When he brought them out of their cells, he greeted them with a bow and a warm smile.

"You slept well, I trust, despite the . . . primitive accommodations?"

DeyMeox shrugged and looked away. Shemsi gave him a glance that came through as pure venom. Gelor kept right on smiling.

"As all three of us know, you are both highly intelligent and resourceful. That's why you're here. I needed top talent, not mere bodies."

The women made no comment.

"I recognize that there will be a temptation for you to try to escape," he went on in the same cheery tone. "What you need to understand is that any such effort will prove, I assure you, futile. Futile. Not, I hope, fatal." He smiled. "Shemsi, you lovely sexy creature, how much experience have you had with stoppers?"

Shemsi remained silent.

"None, perhaps? Then it's time we broadened your education." He took out his weapon and displayed it. "I'm setting this at its middle level. It is called simply Two—or Dance. Let's use it to explore your terpsichorean talent."

He squeezed the grip of the simple-looking cylinder.

Shemsi's eyes went wide, her face stiff and agonized. Her eyes distended and her whole body began to shiver, to twitch and jerk. Gelor let her hang so for perhaps fifteen secs before he eased up. The andrist's limbs were instantly limp. She crumpled, tears streaming.

"You see? You didn't realize you had such dancing ability, did you?" He moved his gaze to DeyMeox, thumbing the stopper down to One. "Mere dancing is beneath a crober's dignity, I think. You deserve a demonstration more in keeping with your status. A degree of statuesque poise, as it were." And he squeezed the stopper's rubbron grip.

Hit with Freeze, DeyMeox stood as if carved in ice. A unique ice formation, however: it seemed to ripple in its tension. Again, fifteen secs. And again he deactuated the simple and fantastically effective little weapon. DeyMeox spilled to the floor as limply as had Shemsi. Fear gleamed in her eyes.

"That was setting One: Freeze," Gelor advised, in a conversational tone. "Stoppers have a third setting. It's called Fry, but regrettably I cannot demonstrate . . . because you would be vaporized and I'd be without the help I need! You will just have to take my word that it is not as unpleasant as what you have experienced, but absolutely permanent—final."

They stared at him. They believed. They knew.

Gelor sighed. "Naturally I regret that I have had to subject you to this ordeal. I knew of no other way to show you the problem that will arise should you decide to abandon our mutual project. Consider: all around our compound's walls I have had a series of stopper units mounted. Each is set in Three—Fry, that is. The pattern in which I arranged them is erratic. *Please* don't seek to approach the security barrier they provide. They will stop you, permanently. You will have delayed me, but not defeated me. I hope you'll agree that such a step isn't worth the sacrifice." Again he let them see his warm and friendly smile. "Now, ladies, shall we get to work?"

The look the two women exchanged gladdened Gelor's heart. Wordless, they settled to their tasks.

For DeyMeox, that meant preparing a sealed spore chamber in which to culture her deadly T6 fungus. She also set up a rank of temperature/humidity/pressure-stabilized two-step canisters. These were for the transportation of the lethal product to Eilong, for the murder of a planet.

Gelor found Shemsi's fabrication of the three dupladroids of more immediate interest. She began with the modeling of the ghastly Bleaker, Dravan.

A menacing figure, Dravan, with his blinded eye replaced by an ugly optic covered with a "blind" film, opaque to the viewer; the heat-scar he had *chosen* not to have removed, and his weighted glove and familiar grooved chest-dagger. Pirate, murderer, and sadist—not to mention raving mad, according to TGW's psychists. That in no way prevented the devil from being every bit as diabolically clever and as ruthless as any disciple of the legendary (?) cult of Kali, those devotees of death-dealing called *thugs*.

Gel Gelor held Dravan in high esteem for four good reasons.

First, he had vanished from the spaceways a good seven years ago. The odds favored his being dead, naturally, though no one had proven it. Second, the very mention of his name was enough to strike terror into whole planetary populations. Deadly and unpredictable as he had proved himself in many a bloody fray, even the boldest rovers tended to feel a chill at thought of his possible reappearance. Third, because of Dravan's reputation and record, CongCorp would be disinclined to question any depredation—no matter how madly improbable or dangerous—so long as his imprimatur was on it.

Finally, Gelor had the full specifications from which to duplicate mad Dravan. TGW had shared them with CongCorp several years ago, when he had been held prisoner—briefly. ("Briefly" because Dravan the Marked had sliced three throats with a broken eyecorder case one dark night, and made his escape in a handsome and state-of-the-art-equipped TGW pinnace.)

Today, watching the simulacrum taking shape under Shemsi's skilled touch, Gelor knew he had chosen well. Even fully conscious that he was looking at a simulacrum, a droid, he found the figure terrifying. CongCorp's reps would likely benasty their collective underwear when they faced it.

Gel Gelor went away smiling. Shemsi stared after him. She wasn't smiling.

Next day when he returned to find her at work she was entirely naked. Absolutely refused to wear that "filthy rag" any more, she snapped, without looking at him. Gelor didn't remind her that he popped their garments into the autocleaner every night, and provided them with smocks *and* nightgowns so that they could sleep clothed.

Instead, he used the stopper. After he'd executed the Setting-Two step for twenty secs, she was willing to put on the smock and return to work. Sullenly. Gelor went away looking triumphant.

Yet as the days passed, he grew to feel a prisoner in his own palace. More and more his nerves were rasping raw. Tension kept rising in him and he was afraid to use any drug. Not with those two on the premises! Of course they were the source of the tension. The damned women. Now that their first fright had faded, they saw through his mask of menace. Sensed his weakness and *tested* him constantly. They knew he dared not kill them, at least not until their work was finished. So—they played with him.

Shemsi was worse. Teasing was her ploy. Her attire developed fascinatingly-located tears. Her smock dangled open; oh my, she had "forgotten" to sash it. First she would lead him on, then balk. When frustration sent him into a rage and he sought to force her, she gave in instantly, all warm flesh and simulated passion . . . until the moment when he lurched into his panting climactic rush. Then somehow there was a twist or sag or sideward lurch that brought ecstasy crashing down to the ache of a spoiled, foiled spasm.

Twice he had thought a beating might cure that predilection in her. No; she transmuted blows and stopper-Dance into vomiting, twitch-tics, and blind stagger-gropings. And she would *shriek*.

In consequence, the progress with the dupladroids was slow. Worse than slow. Endless new synthetics must be obtained; special tools became necessary. Plastiflesh became "unsatisfactory." Servoslaves were "clumsy" and Jasbiri supplies inadequate. Three body-torsion drives broke down. Or were they sabotaged by the lovely, brilliant . . . viper?

With DeyMeox the problem lay on a different level.

So far as Gelor could distinguish, she worked efficiently. On the other hand, her superior intellect kept creeping in.

It was she who pointed out what should have been obvious to him from the beginning: it was not enough that he ravage Eilong with her mycotoxin. To sell the planet he must make it habitable again, afterward. He must clear it of Teratogenesis Six. Otherwise, no pregnant female could be safe on the planet, ever.

Developing such an antitoxin would naturally involve research—time. Yet it had to be done. C-Corp's experts would demand a demonstrably effective countermeasure to the awful T6 fungus before they'd approve any deal.

Her forthrightness drew Gelor to her—while her acumen made him edgy and worse. Though she lacked Shemsi's flowerlike beauty and sensuality, DeyMeox was not unattractive. He liked her clear-eyed frankness (which helped her look better). Stocky or no, the firmness of her spoke of robust good health. (And Gelor saw that they were all fed well. Better than well.) Even her short-cropped hair, in disarray any time she left her lab and stepped out into Jasbir's (created) breeze, tempted him to run his fingers through it.

He commenced to attend her more closely. To no avail— even a hand rested on her shoulder while she worked was enough to draw her eyes to him. Not in outrage, which would have been bearable, but in bemusement. That was worse than screams or curses. Once he tried to embrace her, to cup her breast. DeyMeox didn't say a word. She merely whipped a knee up into his groin.

He lurched away, groaning. DeyMeox returned to work.

"Each of us has private property, right?" she said over her shoulder, without even raising her voice. "These *appurtenances* are mine. I hope *your* appurtenances have learned that. Fondle your own."

He went away, and did. Fuming even while feeling sorry for himself. Shemsi and DeyMeox. Andrist and crober. Gelor came to hate them both.

Yet he could not dispense with either of them. Between them and his great dream of pelf and power, they had him hung on the horns of a dilemma so gut-piercing that he sometimes despaired, wondering if he could survive.

I will, he grimly assured himself, and mockingly bought

a pair of thoroughly baggy, singularly unattractive khaki coveralls for each of his laboring geniuses. After that they wore nothing else. Mockingly?

Well, he would survive. Meanwhile he had business to conduct; business with giant, multiplanetary CongCorp. Dangerous business.

12

Don't oppose forces; use them.

—Buckminster Fuller

Jasbir. A pleasant green planet orbited by two moons, one settled, while the planet orbited its single sun, Huygens. The home world of Badakeacorp and perhaps the best calculators in the Galaxy; a world where government was no friend to the people. A world where slavery was entirely legal and integral to the planetary economy.

Question: How could a pirate spacecraft dock at Jasbir-station when the Word was out on it?

It was a problem to ponder and Jesti pondered it. It was made harder because the CongCorp reader/coder had provided no further word on the mysterious Hajji Kalajji and his incredible offer to *sell* Eilong. What did come through were bloodcurdling indications that C-Corp had no intention of taking lightly the looting of its repair ship.

Despite the extreme unease their situation brought, Jestikhan Churt remained hardcore certain that all issues could be resolved once they reached Jasbir. It was simply a matter of staying loose and not getting fobbied. That state of mind plus the right combination of daring and skill—and luck—would accomplish all. He felt certain of it. A word had been applied to such a situation once long ago: Serendipity. That was the kind of break he needed now.

The first step toward achieving it was to work out some means of transportation onto the station, onto the planet.

It was almost enough to make a man wish he were a spacefarer stead of a miner—*Durga forgive me for harboring such a thought!*

He said words to that effect to the assembled complement of *Slicer*. Musla glowered and grunted. Twilly tootle-wheeled, finger-flipped, and looked pointedly at Jesti's crotch. Yahna—in the interesting short tunic/dress she had made of a seafoam-green bedsheet—shot the purple man a glance that might have been a warning. The exception was Captain Hieronymus Jee.

The mantle of barely controlled rage he had wrapped around him when he had first learned of his brother's death seemed to have been doffed. Back were his black humor, the raised eyebrow, the sardonic twist of lip that characterized the Outie. He wore a Jesti-hued tunic over baggy yellow pants.

"Don't fret about Jasbir, Eilan. You'll like it. It's one of my truly favorite planets."

"Even with CongCorp and prob'ly TGW scanning for us all along the spaceways?"

"That's their problem, not ours." Never had Hieri's smile been more urbane. Leaning forward, he noted telits and studied the screens above the control console. "Well, well . . . look at this!"

Leaning over his shoulder, Jesti studied the image that Hieri brought into better focus. It was without doubt the clumsiest-looking, scrungiest craft he had ever seen. An ancient ramscoop wallowing along through space and time (a lot of time, that duck-billed platypus of the spaceways!) for all the universe as if there were no hurry and no tomorrow anyhow.

Hieri was checking the craft's ID. "*Effluvium III*," he announced.

"Effluvium?" Jesti frowned. "Doesn't that mean something like garbage?"

"It means stinking mess," Hieri said cheerfully. "It's a conwaste carrier. Make it 'garbage scow' if you'd rather— 'conwaste' means contaminatory waste products. See, most trash can be converted, but with some you run into stuff that's too dangerous—poisons, toxins, super-pollutants. Those have to be shunted. Some suns don't care what gets dumped into their hearts."

"Uh," Jesti said, staring at the ramscoop spacer. "So this rig carries that kind of, ah, cargo."

"Right. Headed for some nice stable star with no planets—a perfect dump. The ship's ideal for our purpose."

Jesti grinned. *Serendipity*? "*Tell* me about it, Captain!"

Hieri laughed aloud. "As you said, docking at Jasbirstation is hardly practical, in view of our popularity. So—we need alternative transport. There it is. Ole *Fluve the third* is our transportation!"

Jesti's smile was wry. "Sounds good so far. And–?"

Hieri spread his hands. "We're pirates, remember? So this time we pull a really low-profit snatch—we pirate a garbage scow!"

While Musla snorted a laugh, Jesti said, "And dock it at Jasbirstation?"

"Negatory. Conwaste carriers can't dock there. Jasbir's moon Ruby is settled, and they have special loading ports for . . . garbage scows. If Effluvium's empty, we go in to Ruby asking for a load of sludge. If it's full—we pretend it isn't!" Hieri adjusted his screen. "Shuttles run down to Jasbir from Ruby, see. Once we've taken over *Fluve*, we've got easy passage."

"Uh . . . Cap'm," Musla said, obviously thinking. "We could get in trouble if we take a loaded ship onto Ruby or if we're off schedule or somethin'. Why not report a problem on, uh, *Effluvy*, an' limp into Ruby for repairs?"

"Give that man a diamond from the heart of a dead star!" Hieri called, still working oncon. "Great idea. *Fluve*'s crew will play it our way too, because we'll pay 'em off. If TGW ever asks any questions, they can claim we held 'em hostage. Who'd try to resist a mean-looking bunch like us?"

Jesti asked, "What about *Slicer*?"

"No prob. We'll make the pickup in open space, then move *Slicer* to The Sponge till we need it again."

"The Sponge?"

Hieri and SIPACUM moved the coordinate markers to pinpoint the second moon circling Jasbir, the nearer one. "That skungeball. No one lives on it! The ray-ray level's too high for anything short of spacer-level shielding." Seeing Jesti's frown, he translated "ray-ray": "Radio-activity. You've heard of that on Eilong, haventcha?"

Jesti opted for lighthearted sarcasm: "Just the *real* big brains, bawss-captain-sah. That unpeopled moon's dangerous, then? With . . . ray-ray?"

"Firm. The ray-ray's so high the whole thing's as eroded as procheese. People call it The Sponge. More caves and holes in the 'ground' than stratistone. TGW couldn't even run a proper finder fix on it. I've snuck *Slicer* in there before, when I've come around on . . . business."

Excitement brightened Jesti's eyes. Sure, this was a brand of piracy he could accept, with ease. All he had to do was think the TGO way: The End Justifies The Means (employed to achieve it). "So we just grab *Fluve* and ride her down!"

The sparkle in Hieri Jee's eyes was wicked. "You're jumping to conclusions, purple playmate."

Jesti forced a grin and pointedly held his bare arm near Hieri's purple-shirted one. "Nice shirt. How'm I wrong?"

"We grab *Fluve*, all right. Only you don't ride 'er down. *I* do."

"And leave me here? Nega-*to-ry*, Hieri."

"*I* am going, I said," the man from Outreach said coolly. "One thing you tend to forget, my purple pal, is that *Slicer* is my ship."

"Which you wouldn't even have," Yahna reminded him, "if Jesti hadn't saved your skins back on Croz."

Hieri, looking relaxed and smug and comfy in first chair, the master's chair, only glanced her way. He nodded.

"True. He busted us out to help hisself, and we've helped him, too, Goldie. Plenty. For another thing, none of us's laid a hand on you, me proud beauty. Ner any-thing else—a hard slicer, f'rinstance. Here we are, real *desperate out*–laws, alone in space with a real doll, and ain't a one of us so much as pawed yer tits, much less fucked ya. That uz for Jesti's sake, cake, not yours." And without waiting for her to reply or prove that she would not, Hieri returned his attention to Jesti.

"Musla 'n' Twil 'n' me stick to a pattern of self-interest, Eilonger. We're outlaws. We've taken certain goods from good ole CongCorp. Now we want to convert that stuff inta stells and cred. Since I'm the one who knows Jasbir and the Jazzes best, I'm the obvious one to go down to market. And finally . . . well—I remind you that Musla and Twil are my boys. That means that there are three of us to"—a less than cordial glance at Yahna—"two of you *at most*. So. If you want to live to see your beloved Eilong again, stand aside while I make arrangements for transport. With *Fluve*'s captain."

He was smiling when he finished. That didn't stop Jesti from noting that Twil'im had moved forward just a jinkle, while Musla had his hand on his kris-hilt and was glowering even more ferociously than usual. It was a situation, Jesti decided quickly, in which discretion constituted the usual cliché. Besides, he was glad Hieri had said so much. It was plain and in the open, now, just how matters stood. They weren't allies, not really. Hieri was a sneering bigot—and an enemy.

With a smile every bit as broad as the Outie's, Jesti threw out his arms and bowed surrender.

"Of course, Captain Jee-sir. All that wasn't necessary—I just didn't understand. I ask only that you bear in mind that I too have a goal on Jasbir."

"Your search for the fobber you call the Handsome Man?" Hieri's voice was brown with scorn. "You live in a galaxy of dreams if you think you can find any one individual who's hiding on a planet the size of Jasbir, no matter how handsome he is. He ain't Lance Sessakimey—or Akima Mars!"

Jesti shrugged and compressed his lips. "You may be right."

" 'May' meaning I also may not? Well, we'll leave that for time to decide. But I can't wait on it, Eilan. CongCorp and the superspooks are on our trail by now. I'd just as soon not meet their ruffos." And Hieri swung back to busy himself at his console.

Jesti was both intrigued and disappointed. He had anticipated that capture of even such a vessel as *Effluvium* would hold at least a few dramatic elements. Instead, it proved only a matter of a few words spoken over the short-range comm, after which *Slicer* snugged up to *Fluve* and linked airlocks by means of Slicer's S-tunnel.

Hieri blew Yahna a kiss and flipped Jesti the finger. "Enjoy yourselfs. I'm off. My boys will find a hole in The Sponge to bed *Slicer* down."

And he was gone, Twil and Musla with him.

Yahna said, "The word is betrayal, Jesti."

"Uh. As I told Hieri, you may be right." Jesti drummed his fingers. "And maybe not. Either way, there's still a road open."

Her dark eyes widened. "A way out? No dream?"

"Betrayal works two ways. I *am* going down onto Jasbir."

"On Jas–" Yahna stared at him incredulously, ripe-sullen lips half parted. "Jesti, you're talking lunacy! You have no way to get there. Even if you manage it, Hieri would be onplanet ahead of you. He'd have policers waiting. And you actually hope to find one man, a man whose name you don't even know—let alone his identitag or puterlabel."

Jesti gave her his most cheerful grin. "Golden, when you've got a problem and no answer, there are two ways to attack it. One's to beat your own brains out. The other's to get help."

She shot him a sidewise glance that clearly questioned his sanity. "And who do you propose to have helping you? TGW? CongCorp, maybe?"

Jesti made it his business to keep his face sober. "Actually I had it in mind to ask help from the local policers. Jasbiri."

"The policers!" Yahna's expression said she couldn't believe her bedangled ears. "The only help you'll get from them is your neck in a noose. They'd sell out their own mothers if CongCorp made an offer."

"Could be." Jesti finger-flipped. "Even on Eilong we've

heard how things work on Jasbir. So—I thought I might go about it all from a little different angle.''

"But you said–''

"And you jumped to conclusions.'' He let that easy grin break out again. "Just don't try to second-guess me, Yahna. Either what I've got in mind will work, in which case you'll have to listen to my bragging. Or it won't, and you can water my grave with your tears—that is, if there's enough of me left to bury. And if you have tears.''

"Either is doubtful,'' she said angrily. Swiftly, stiff-backed, she crossed to the equipment cabinet. She selected three fingernail-sized units and held them out. "Here. At least take these with you.''

He eyed them suspiciously. "What are they?''

"What they call a silent siren, Jes,'' she said, not realizing that she had just used an intimate name for him, a name all hers. "You wear it against your skin. Anyone wants to alert you, it gives you a *mild* shock.''

"Ah. Cute. These others?''

"This is a minicomm. Fits behind your ear so I can talk to you. This other—this is a throat-speaker, see, so you can answer.'' And then, when his face showed incredulity: "They work. Hieri wears a set.''

Jesti had his doubts. Rather than argue the point, though, he took the units, muttered a quick "Thanks, Yahna,'' almost touched her, aborted that, and redshifted the concabin. He shoved off down the ship's tunnel that led to the airlock. He was surprised to see that an *Effluvium III* crewman had come along the big metal worm connecting the two ships.

The loutish-looking jacko lounged there, radiating a stench that told where he worked more clearly than words. The garbage scow odor well-nigh choked Jesti. Fighting off queasiness, he squatted beside the ridiculously spotless pale green coveralls. Equipped with a field that kept them so, of course.

"Your boss's gonna make an account fulla cred from this little stopover,'' he said conversationally, and as if enviously.

"Gah! You're *purple*!''

Jesti looked. "You're right. Happens, on my planet—Eilong. Makes me an Eilan miner. Doesn't rub off on anybody."

The other man chuckled. "Eye-lawng, huh? Live 'n' learn! I'm from Luhra, m'self. Anyhow—much good my *boss*'s fortune'll do me. That sunuvagrat won't cut any of the rest of us in fer so much's a ministell."

"Really? Huh!" Jesti raised a sympathetic eyebrow, then let his eyes narrow to a pretense of thoughtful speculation. "Huh! Y'know . . . it wouldn't *have* to work that way."

"Shit."

"No, really. Suppose somebody else wanted to get onto Ruby—and Jasbir."

"I still hear ya. Why?"

"There's a great daktari down on Jasbir. We know all about 'im on Eilong because he can make us look *normal*—you know, like your skin. You gotny idea how tough it is being purple? So—that someone might be willing to pay enough to take your mind off your captain."

Jesti looked straight ahead. The man beside him stared at the deck. His scowl deepened. His mouth worked. "Huh. You, ahh, got cred, Eye-lan?"

"Got cred," Jesti said. "If somebody was to be able to figure a way to get a man onboard *Fluve* on the sneak. And off again at the Ruby wheel without the guards there throwin' him a party."

"*Fluve*!" the Luhran chuckled. "Pretty good." He sagged back against the airlock wall, lowering his squat so his rump bumped the deck. His struggle to use his brain grew clearly and painfully obvious. Luhra was a planet high on poets and boasted several of renown. Jestikhan Churt was sure that he was not in the presence of one. (He also crossed his fingers.)

Abruptly the strained lines vanished from the face of the spacegoing garbageman. Big teeth bared in a leering grin.

"Got it! There's a crap-hatch aft. You know—regs say we can't dump shit in space, and nobody spends cred on nice stuff like recyclers for conwaste carriers. So we got this big tank unner our sitter, you know? We drop it into our slot when we dock. Maintenance picks it up, sells it to farmers, and sticks in another'n. They're the only ones touches it. Oh—Ruby's got no wheel, by the way. Ruby's got essin' little of anything, includin' gravity.''

Jesti met the Luhran's grin with a piteous look. He sighed.

"You're telling me I'm gonna get to Ruby on a garbage scow, disguised as so many kilos of human waste.''

"Nicely put. You got it. Best I can do.''

Jesti said, "Shit.''

"You got it.''

Jesti did not choose to smile. He shuddered. It had to be true: the universe held no justice. The word, like the concept, was a human invention. And . . . *virtue and good intentions get paid off in fecal matter. Yukh!*

Beside him, shoulder touching shoulder in manner comradely, the Luhran was growing more enthusiastic by the moment:

"It'll be great, honest! There's air an' all. You won't get burned because ole *Effy—Fluve, Fluve,* haha—don't use no chems. There's a trap in the sitter, too. I can even drop you down some dinner . . .''

Jesti sighed. "Used or otherwise?''

13

Detached reflection cannot be demanded in the presence of an upraised knife.

—*Oliver Wendell Holmes*

It worked. The mask contrived by Jesti and his benefactor even kept the cess out of his face and orifices during the unfortunate freefall interlude and in Ruby's low-G, and the suit the garbageman sneaked him (in return for the bonus of Jesti's clothing, such as it was/had been) emerged spotless. Jesti did feel that his sense of smell had overloaded and departed to hide somewhere under a rock.

Ruby lived up to its name. Some weird twist of cosmic chemistry, some winking trick of primordial physics, had produced a medium-sized planetoid whose surface glistened with great glassy patches that were fused gemstone-red. They were not ray-ray and they had nothing to do with iron ore.

Jesti thought the moon was pretty handsome. The hard part was coping with the .4G. With each step he had the feeling that he was going to float up and away, to become one more lifeless piece of debris between the stars that, from Ruby, were very, very bright indeed. Being able to *see* the curve of the horizon was weird, too.

He did like the fact that security at the station and shuttleport were so lax as to be the Saipese twin of nonexistent. Red-tunicked guards were sloppy and casual. Not even Jesti's purple skin affected their complacency. His effluvium did. He was ordered into Medical for a quick sonishower and desepsis. He emerged antiseptic and odorless, and was on his way.

Once out of the shuttleport and into Jasbir's planetary capital, Marmot, he faced a world more complex than he had seen or envisioned. Just a countryboy miner within a great tinted safetyplas dome that controlled atmosphere pressure and temp. Tinted off-amber to reduce the glare and heat of Jasbir's sun, Huygens, it also filtered out the bulk of the cosmic radiation that had been such a plague during the planet's early period of development. Huge cone-shaped catalytic converters, each topped with a gigantic crystal globe, reared in two neat rows through the center of the metroplex. A network of multi-leveled transitways—tubeways in three colors—zigged and zagged about and among them in all directions. The tube-transport system radiated out from the city's heart past commerical and industrial districts through estates and parklands, clear to the mammoth bionarium on the farthest edge.

Water, Jesti had heard, could be a problem on Jasbir. Marmot's answer was a central reclamation/recycling/pumping/purification plant. That seemed a promising place to begin is program—his quest. The man he queried told him he liked Jesti's dye-job, and directed him to a kiosk called a spacefarers' friend. The cybernetic directions-giver there pointed him to the rec-rec plant.

On the way someone else told Jesti she liked his dye-job and asked the name of the hue he'd chosen, and whether he'd done it himself or gone to a cytological chromatician. Jesti had no idea what that was. Without stopping he muttered that his color was a special skindye blend and was very big on Sekhar right now. He made his way to the vast water plant.

Apparently the reclamation/recycling facility was something of a showplace. Fountains and cascades—Marmot's watery bragging—and fantastic dioramas were drawing a multitude of visitors. Jesti wandered among them, relaxed and casual in his spotless pale green coverall, until he reached a corridor marked AUTHORIZED PERSONNEL ONLY. It ended in a bright-red door an outsize KEEP OUT! sign. Authorities had emphasized that by locking the door.

Jesti pounded on it with his fist. Hard. Persistently.

At last the door was opened. An irritated-looking tech in a blue dress and yellow sandals—and a Rahmani fez, red—looked out. "*What?*"

"Sorry to bother you. The brass ought to install a buzzer or something, huh."

"Slice off," the man in the dress said, and started closing the door.

Jesti grabbed his arm and helped him close the door. On the man's wrist. He yelled and jumped back, pulling free and grabbing his wrist with his other hand. Jesti followed, kicking the door shut behind him as he moved in, and hit the bug a hard hand-blow just below the jaw. The man's eyes rolled up and he fell down. Since he didn't move, Jesti checked the lock on the door and inspected the chamber.

Valves were its predominant feature. Valves on panels, on pipes; valves linked to dials and pressure gauges in several colors. Off to one side, set into a wall socket, he spotted a control wheel as big around as his body. A metal bar locked it in place. A sign beside it identified it as SYSTEM EMERGENCY FLUSH.

Jesti looked about some more, smiling, purposeful now.

On the opposite side of the room from the big wheel, he smiled even more at a plass-fronted tool case, mounted on the wall. Its contents included a sledge hammer, handle neatly arced and angled so that even a child could handle it—presumably. Jesti borrowed the sledge hammer and attacked the locking bar of the wheel.

It took three blows before the bar broke. Jesti dropped the sledge and spun the wheel to full ON position. He crossed to the door and opened it. Far off, he heard the roar: gushing water. He also heard wild screams of panic.

Grinning, Jesti returned to the wheel and used the sledge on it.

The wheel made a sick and sickening noise and twisted-bent. Another blow snapped most of it off at the hub. It was going to be a long repair job.

From down the corridor, clamorous voices rose. Jesti tossed aside the sledge and sprinted from the control room. He was thoughtful enough to slam the door after him. The man in the blue dress snoozed on.

Three service personnel were racing toward Jesti. At a dead run, he raced toward them. He also gestured wildly. "Did you see him? Which way'd the sisterslicer go?"

"Who? What? Who?"

"Handsome man—*Very* handsome man! He's sabotaged the pumping system!"

"Holy shit!"

Well, Jesti mused, running on, *it's useful, pos, but I wouldn't go so far as to call it holy . . .*

Out in the plant's main court, he was pleased to see that water was rising fast. Already it swirled ankle deep, cascading out the main door into the street. A small lake was forming down toward the shuttleport, covering at least one spur of the tubeway. Good, he thought, traffic will be fobbed, too! And he made more noises about the culprit— the Handsome Man. The words spread. Even robed Xan-clanners were hitching up their skirts and running. Jesti joined that flow.

They were a tiny sect, but enough of them were about to provide cover. (A corner loudspeaker boomed out the message: *Handsome Man . . . lunatic . . . escaped from Croz.* "There he goes," Jesti yelled, pointing.) More importantly, the flowing multicolored robes and full-face masks the Xans wore under their hoods would provide anonymity: the order decried the importance of the individual. Jesti definitely did not. He had just spent a few minutes demonstrating the enormous power of an individual who didn't give a damn what he did.

Xan regalia would, however, certainly provide a disguise for purple skin!

"Quick," he said, shoving a tall Xan-clanner, "in here where it's dry."

The two swerved into the open doorway. The crowd-noises drowned the sound of a blow or two. Less than two minutes later a very tall Xan emerged, alone.

Jesti felt guilty about this gambit, but didn't extreme cases call for extreme remedies? Was it not a Xan maxim that humankind was born to suffer? (Suffer embarrassment, in this case. The former wearer of Jesti's new robe, gloves, and mask was not likely to enjoy coming out in public with nothing but his shorts.)

Meanwhile Jestikhan Churt was free to continue his project of bringing chaos to the city of Marmot. And, in the process, sharpening the eyes of policers, outraged citizenry, and visitors to the presence of any really handsome man newly in from planet Croz.

Just as he started forth, robe rustling, the silent alarm at his hip shot a small, stinging jolt of current into him. He grunted and repaired hurriedly into the nearest alley. And punched in the comm-button behind his ear.

Beat, beat, waiting . . . How high in Jasbir's sky was the moon called The Sponge—and spaceship *Slicer*? How many secs for sub-light communication?

Yahna's voice came into his head, taut and urgent. *Jesti! The reader/coder's "talking." All about "Hajji." They're making a deal, setting up some sort of meeting. We need to cover it if we can, somehow. If you can just get up here—Jesti?*

"Don't worry. I'll get there." As an afterthought: "I'll be wearing a Xan-robe." Already he was moving back into the street.

He was aware that getting back to *Slicer* wouldn't be quite as easy as he made it sound. It was one thing to play Xan here on the streets of Marmot. Making it past the shuttleport security would be quite another. *What I need's another Eilan!* Another purple man to distract attention from him. Might that be arranged? He looked about for a spacefarer's friend, to ask directions, and saw a hardware shop. Robed, smiling behind his mask, he walked in.

Yes, they had spray-squirts, uh—sir. Yes, they had green and purple. Ignoring curious glances, Jesti counted out the few stells, tucked his purchases within his rainbow robe, and headed for the spaceport. He had no purpose in mind for the green dye. Purchasing two colors, though, might prevent the clerks' remembering that someone had bought purple—and a streetcorner loudspeaker was putting out the word right now on a Handsome Man *and* a purple one.

A line of travelers was queued up at the shuttle. That was good.

Guards were checking IDs. That was not good.

A distraction, then, Jesti mused. He drew back into the cover provided by a parked cargo hauler. He surveyed the situation, and he thought. And saw the spacefarer leaning, alone, against a shuttleport pillar. He had the look of a dummy who had drunk too much of something very alcoholic, and without popping a red antintoxicant pill or two. Behind his mask, Jesti smiled. Ever so casually, he started toward that lone spacefarer.

The voice came from the wall-niche: "Welcome, purple playmate."

Jesti knew that voice. He froze. Slowly and carefully, he turned.

In the niche stood Captain Hieronymus Jee, pirate. He wore his mocking Outie smile. The snout of a stopper protruded ever so slightly from a cape slung over his arm.

"Naturally you have a stopper, Eilan. Kindly drop it." A twist of lip. "Bearing in mind that if you try to use it my hand will squeeze reflexively—and Poof you. Redshift one bothersome Eilan, Fried."

Wordless, Jesti dropped his weapon. Started to raise his hands.

"None of that, now! Keep your hands *down*, Eilan. We're not looking to attract attention, now are we?" And after a moment: "Your cute Xan outfit is a bright idea, of course. How better could you conceal that ghastly purple hide? Yet it also held a certain *weakness*, you see. It told me what to look for, once Yahna put out the message I ordered."

The words were a body blow. Grimly, Jesti gritted his teeth behind the mask. Yahna! *Ordered*!

"You didn't guess?" The triumph in Hieri's voice told

Jesti how badly he had failed. "Clever girl, that Yahna. Prideful. Rape doesn't set well with her. When I pointed out how she could get back at you, she jumped at the chance." A tight gesture with the stopper. "Shall we go now? We have an engagement with a certain corrupt Jasbiri sub-prefect of policers. He gets you—quite a prize, in view of all the damage you've done today. You do have a resourceful talent for serving the great god Havoc, don't you! I remember that from the prison . . . ah, the things the Jazzes will do to you, Eilan! Try not to think about it. Maybe, though, it'll make Petri rest easier. As for me—I get the opportunity to market my CongCorp souvenirs without policer interference. *Move*."

Numbly, still unspeaking, Jesti turned. He moved toward the gate.

To be betrayed by Yahna! To end his life in a trap sprung by the golden bitch! His hands shook. His belly knotted. He wanted to kill . . . no, what he wanted to do was throw up. *And yet . . . and yet can I be sure? Couldn't this be another trick of Hieri's?* A sadistic lie, told in vengeance for his brother?

Those were questions without answers. For now, at least. Only one thing was dead certain: when Jasbir's policers got their hands on Jestikhan Churt, death would be the least of his worries.

Which means I'd better not let Hieri turn me over to them. Think, *Jes!*

He pushed bitterness and bitter thoughts of Yahna to a rearward chamber of his mind. Tight-lipped, he touched the spray-squirt beneath his robe. Coinage jingled as he brushed his garbager's coverall, and the sound brought inspiration. Fumbling out a clutch of coins under cover of the robe, he let them fall.

They jingled and rolled and instinctively Hieri's eyes flicked down. Jesti ducked and spun and lunged in close to wrench at the cape that hid the stopper. The weapon flew high and wide. Jesti squeezed the squirter's bulb, straight at Hieri. Purple skindye drenched the Outie like the burst of a violet bomb. As his hands started for his eyes, Jesti shoved him away.

"*Eilan*!" he screamed, pointing at Hieronymus Jee. "Purple man! Eilan!"

Then he hurried, rustling, over for a certain dropped object. Everyone else was as if struck by paralysis, every eye focused on the stumbling, empurpled Hieri. The violet hands to his dye-splashed eyes made it seem that he was trying to hide his face.

Jesti tucked away Hieri's stopper. "*Purple man*!" he yelled again.

Two guards, a security woman, and two policers were heading for Hieri from three different directions. Jesti yelled it again, but this time his voice was drowned out by theirs. "PURPLE MAN! EILAN!"

Jerking his head, staggering, Hieri got his first (dye-bleared) glimpse of his hands, covered with instadry dye. With a curse, he lunged away. He rushed into the crowd and somehow no one was grabbing him, he was getting away—until suddenly a tall, almost unbelievably handsome man twisted away from the half-blinded pirate's rush. One hand snapped out at Hieri in what appeared more thrust than blow . . .

Except that Hieronymus Jee's entire body seemed to convulse. All direction and drive went out of him and he spilled to the pavement.

The handsome man let himself be engulfed by the milling crowd, and somehow was no longer there. Policers bulled their way to the fallen "Eilan." So did guards—those who were supposed to be checking IDs at the final gate.

Sweating within his rainbow robe, a Xan-clanner passed through the gate and headed for the shuttle. He was shaky, certain that he had just seen the man he had so long sought: *the* Handsome Man. The man who had murdered that hust. The man who had stolen Eilan blood and semen—*Jesti's* blood and semen—for whatever devious purpose. The double-dyed villain who proposed to *sell* planet Eilong to mighty and ruthless CongCorp.

The Handsome Man! *And so close, damn him!* And Jesti could do nothing. Surely Black Durga Himself protected the monster! Hiding him in the angry crowd around Hieri (Hieri's body?) so the bastard faded away, out of reach.

A cliché existed for the situation: So near and yet so far!

Raw of nerve and still shaking, Jesti sank into the first empty seat on the shuttle. At last he had seen his quarry— though at a distance, and while unable to do a thing about it. Who knew what another day might bring? Next time . . .

For now, though, he had other business. It began with that damned treacherous Yahna Golden.

14

Racketeering is one of the most ancient of human institutions. It is at least as old as any organized society of which we have historical records.

—*John McConaughy*

Thoughtfully, the Handsome Man considered the future.

The groundwork was laid. He'd made his offer to CongCorp. All that remained was agreement on details, and his Great Plan. *All*, Gelor thought, chewing his lip. The short word was blood-chilling. One miscalculation, one misstep would trip him into disaster.

He did have his background as compudator to serve him. At an opening move he had acquired one of the deservedly famous Badakeacorp calculators. Deviously and painstakingly, he had modified it to handle non-tech output. Tapping it in on CongCorp's beams with the skill of experience, he laid down his proposition . . . carefully. Obliquely. Glossed with equivocal terms and evasive phrasing. Deceptive verbiage enfolded sheer *temptation*.

The company reply came even faster than he had expected. The men at the level he'd reached were realists. Daily they coped with potentialities, with far-out extrapolation. Conspiracy was the dagger beneath their collective cloak, their tool of choice. So their contact was anonymous and less than open as to details of his outrageous proposition. What counted was the potential for outrageous profit for CongCorp. So—they would listen, and confer, and perhaps deal. They knew when a gamble was worth the taking.

Meanwhile, their anonymous contact's work proceeded.

DeyMeox finished the spore chamber. Already the cultures were maturing. Shemsi completed the Dravan dupladroid, even unto the Rahman-green birthmark and opaqued red optic. And she finished the nondescript 'droid, designed to pass unnoticed in any crowd of four. Now the Gelor-droid was taking form.

Slowly. "Face it," Shemsi told him equably. "A really good-looking face is harder. Ugly's easy!"

Gelor set up the meeting to take place in a bar in Marmot. For that "meeting" he sent the nondescript simulacrum, programmed to don a mask before entering the place. Immediately a pair of CongCorp ruffos seized the droid, tore off the mask, and began taking pictures. Enter a Gelor-bribed squad of Jasbiri policers. They seized the ruffos and allowed the dupladroid to "escape." Eyecorders/cameras "got broken." So did an arm, and it was not one of the uniformed nippers'. And all the while Shemsi was receiving her tribute: neither policers nor ruffos recognized that the dupladroid was not a person.

On releasing the prisoners next morning, the nippers handed the chief ruffo an edutape. It offered CongCorp the details of Gelor's offer. Now the company would know that "Hajji" had anticipated them and had the tape ready all the time. He had expected double-cross, and dealt with it—well.

The proposal was one to excite the greed of any multiplanetary or even smaller corporation. It included an automatic monopoly on kiraoun catalysts and tintinabulate alloys. The potential for profit was beyond imagining. And they had sicced the ruffos on this man! At a high CongCorp level, a head rolled.

(Never mind. Within seventeen days that ruthless, knowledgeable former executive who had bungled only once—was on a yacht. It belonged to the Joser slaver-pirate Manjanungo. Four days later a C-Corp spacer vanished.)

Negotiations proceeded. Maneuverings and manipulation. Gelor's skill at maintaining anonymity reached the fantastic level. There were times when he could scarcely believe that he was still alive and free. At last the time came when he could no longer hold back revelation of his secret weapon. DeyMeox's deadly mycotoxin, Teratogenesis Six.

As she had predicted, company experts balked. They demanded proof that Eilong could be made habitable again. (Meanwhile, Gelor was sure, other C-C experts were making feasibility studies of all-cyber mining and operations on a killer planet. Just in case.) By then, however, DeyMeox had come up with what she believed to be an antitoxin-fungicide of sufficient potency to deal with her brilliant creation. Fungal toxin T6.

A tiny XN satellite, long obsolete and out of the distant past, still circled Jasbir merely because no one had bothered to remove or destroy it. Gelor saw to the shipping of samples of T6 and its antitoxin to the tiny sat. With the samples went testing equipment . . . and enough high explosion to blast the entire satellite to atoms. (Should have been done long ago, anyhow.)

After that, Gelor got back to the corporation he'd been keeping on the hook. His message was brief and direct: C-C experts could proceed to the old XN and test both toxin and antitoxin. They were to comm results to their headquarters. If the results were satisfactory, CongCorp would pay the still-anonymous Hajji Kalajji, Gelor's chosen *nom de pillage*. (As a nonviable alternative, at the slightest hint of a double-cross the satellite, testers, and toxin-antitoxin would vanish in one eye-searing flash.)

Gelor specified the form of the payoff: 'Vocker ice emeralds; uncut Joser gemstones; and TGO credslips. All loot as anonymous as he was. All convertible in any corner of the Galaxy without fear of being traced. The only problem was the bulk of that massive ransom.

Gelor directed the solution: the payoff was to be loaded,

appropriately bagged, on a small spacer with subspace capability. It would cruise close by the old satellite. If the company decided to accept his plan and toxin-antitoxin, he would transfer from a charter carrier to the payoff spacer. The corporate reps would in turn take over the carrier, pick up their testers and toxin from XN, and go their way to megacred profits.

That was reasonable enough, and CongCorp agreed readily. Too readily. A grimly smiling Gelor could visualize the negotiators gloating and rubbing their hands at the stupidity he was at last showing. Now it would be clear to them that they were dealing with a flawed genius, a hyperclever fool. Once they had the toxin-antitoxin safely off the testing sat, they would snatch back the payoff ship, and him with it, before he knew what hit him. After that he would vanish, of course. CongCorp would have everything. The would-be planet murderer and seller would have nothing, including life.

So they were to believe. Gelor was not so insane, and he had his own notions. Furthermore, he had a superb and daring plan.

The nerve-knotting panic remained at bay within him now, washed away in the blood of Pearl *and* the Saipese thief *and* the Reshi ruffian. Boldness sang in him. Self-confidence soared, born of long and careful planning plus a touch of what had to be classed as inspiration. Genius, even.

Now it was time for him to put his true plan into effect. Time for the modified calculator and the ghastly Bleaker android. For so long, so long he had been waiting and sweating and preparing for this time!

He paced his palatial quarters in a long wine-dark robe, thinking, ever thinking. Now he reflected on what to do with the women who had indeed proven so competent and so useful; so indispensable to all his meticulous planning.

Once their work was done—the simulacrums and canisters of Teratogenesis Six prepared, the pair became a totally unacceptable threat; a continuing danger to Gel Gelor. DeyMeox could be counted on to pass on word of his masterminding the whole affair to all who would listen. That would include TGW and CongCorp.

Simple, then. I can't afford to allow them to continue to exist.

Although he felt secure in his plan for covering his tracks, he'd rather have no hint of his presence on Jasbir or even his existence leak out. *Firm, then. All that remains is the means. How to terminate them.*

He discovered that this time he had no taste for spilling blood. He had been too close to both women for that. Not a knife or club or stopper set on Three for Fry, then.

Pacing and thinking, he nodded. Inspected his hand. It did not tremble. Gelor smiled.

They had after all performed well for him, no matter how much irritation they had caused over assignments they naturally despised. He could afford to be merciful now, in their . . . execution. Good slaves. If they could merely go to sleep and not awaken. . . .

The perfect answer! Both their cells included ventilation ducts. He needed only to lock a little tank of monocyan gas to each, having blocked them off otherwise, then open the valves after the slaves had fallen asleep. And they would simply not awake. Ever.

Working out the details was even simpler than coming up with the concept.

"I have business over in the port tonight," he told them, each wearing a reward-garment purchased in a large store in Tenkilom, across the planet. "The cargo haulers come for the canisters tomorrow morning. That means early to bed for both of you. I'm locking you in until the action's over." The Handsome Man smiled handsomely. "I really am sorry, but there it is."

The glance exchanged by the two velour-jumpsuited women filled him with satisfaction. It said they still didn't realize that he knew they could enter and leave their cells at will. Good! Such a belief allayed any suspicions they might otherwise have had. He could move ahead at speed.

DeyMeox went to her lockbox first. She said not a

word. Equally silent, Gelor threw the bolt and went down the line to Shemsi's cage.

She . . . lingered at the threshold, in her nicely-fitted mauve velour. Eyeing him from beneath lowered lashes. Her lips curved in a small, cryptic smile. She seemed . . . flushed. Excited? He gave her a brows-up look and the corners of her mouth quivered as if in secret mirth.

"This is the end, isn't it?"

Gelor maintained that querying look. "The end?"

"Of our work here," she said, smiling openly. "I thought you might like to . . . celebrate."

At any other time he might have been tempted, and to hell with the frustration she'd given him. Not tonight. Not with his coup so close and his whole future in the balance. He shook his head with a sigh.

"Sorry, Shemsi," he said, as if wistfully. "It's not that I don't appreciate the suggestion. I–"

Her laughter interrupted. "I don't mean with *me*! I'm talking about Her Majesty, Gelor! Your own true love, right? DeyMeox."

"*What*?" Gelor stared.

"That bitch!" Shemsi's laughter died amid soaring rage. "You can't know how much I hate her! Working with her, day after day, while she puts on her crober's airs and looks down at her nose at me as if I were a–a hust!"

A stunned Gelor could only stare at her in astonishment.

"Tonight, though, tonight I pay her back! You're the only one she sneers at more than she does me. So tonight you're going to *have* her!"

Gelor had felt the beginnings of excitement. Now it was ebbing. "If I wanted to rape her, I'd have done it before now," he said stiffly.

"I'm not talking abour *rape*." Shemsi's eyes gleamed. "What do you know about aphrodizzies?"

"Sexciters? Like—Eros? Breeder's Friend?"

"Right! I slipped one into her drink tonight while we ate. It'll hit her now, any min. When it does she'll go crazy for sex. She'll have to have a man, and you're the one who's there. She'll give you a ride to make your bones ache! You'll be lucky if you can walk after *that* tryst!"

The excitement was back in Gelor's belly, and stirring him lower. It was all he could do to keep from quivering. DeyMeox!

He admitted it now. The crober genius was the woman he had ached for, day after day in this decaying old palace. Ached for her because he couldn't have her. And now he could. With her wild with passion, more than willing because Shemsi had slipped her an aphrodizzy. What did that matter? It would still be DeyMeox's body, her gasps and sobs, her writhing and spasms. Her *need*, for *him*. For that, his plan could be held in abeyance for a while . . .

Except . . . Except that suspicion was all at once a heaviness in him. He locked his gaze on Shemsi. "Why so eager to do me favors, Shemsi?"

"Do *you* f–I'm not! I don't care a jinkle about your pleasure! You might as well be a stray grat off the street, for all I care. You—you're a double-dyed villain, Gelor, a certified card-carrying member of Sadist Bastards Unanimous, surely! No, no—it's that DeyMeox bitch I'm after!" She stepped closer and clutched Gelor's quivering arm. (It wanted to hit her.) "Her High Majesty will remember this in the morning, all of it!"

No, she won't, Gelor managed to think, through his rising excitement. *Neither of you will remember anything, because neither of you will awake in the morning, you abusive little sourcake!*

"She'll wake up knowing that she soared with you like a mare in heat, even though you turn her stomach," Shemsi went on with some relish. "Any time she forgets, I'll be there to remind her. Every hour of every day I'll stick her with it, till she's ready to slash her wrists!" She paused, breathing fast, her color high. "Well? Do you want her or don't you?"

Gelor's voice was hoarse: " *I want her*."

"This way then!" Shemsi bustled him back to the other cell. She clutched his arm while he shakily unlocked the door. "I'm coming in too, Gelor. I want to *listen*; see her get it—and love it!" Her voice was as raw as his.

Together, they entered and paused in the small, very

dark room. In the stillness, Gelor could hear the sound of the crober's breathing. It came fast and shallow, as if DeyMeox were on the verge of panting.

Shemsi's whisper gloated: "She's ready. The sexciter's hit her!" She suddenly shoved him forward, almost violently. "Take her, take her, you thrice-cursed son of a bastard *jinni*! Take the high-and-mighty bitch and slice 'er till her eyeballs fall out!"

Gelor stumbled into blackness, groping. He found a bare, supine leg that twitched. Found a body open and hunching to receive him. The jumpsuit was gone. She was naked and ignited. He strove to get his robe out of the way while strong legs tried to lock around him. The body beneath his writhed, humped at him until he grunted with pain. He got the robe out of the way. Her excitement heightened his. High and hard, he sought and found in the darkness, and their gasping grunt of penetration rose loudly in unison. He did not have to slam himself home in her; she was lunging up with her body and dragging at him with both arms and legs.

The moments that followed were an explosive turbulence of flesh and lust. The odor of sexuality and joined groins arose in the dark cell, mingling with the scent of sweat. Gelor's mind blurred as he surged against her surging body and into it. *DeyMeox's body, DeyMeox, DeyMeox's* . . . God, the delicious obscenity of the wet slapping sounds they made! His body convulsed as in a seizure. Dimly he heard voices crying out throatily:

Hers: "I'm dying! I'm *dy*–inng! I can't wait. Quick, quick—ahhh—"

And Shemsi's: "That's it, you sickofobber! Ram it to her! Ream the whorebitchmare!"

He did. He rode and pounded, having to fight her clamping legs so he could move, realizing that she seemed anxious to have her breasts crushed out of shape beneath him. He felt the clawing of passion at his back and was glad the robe protected him from bloody scratches. He pounded, sluiced in and out of her. He bellowed out his climax and kept on pumping until she shrieked. Both of them were shuddering violently. He hurt, and right now he couldn't give a damn. What better hurt could there be? *DeyMeox!*

The clutching hands relaxed their grasp of passion. The straining arms softened and the legs slithered down on either side of his. Numb and shaking, he moved. His withdrawal from her inundated stash was accompanied by another obscene slosh-sucking sound. He rolled over, almost falling off her bunk onto the floor. Lurching to his feet, he groped his way doorward. Just to his right, Shemsi's voice spoke again, sounding hollow now to his staggery perceptions:

"Wonderful! Wonderful! You can walk! And you haven't the voice for any thanks to me, you handsome bastard stud of a double-dyed monster?"

"I—have—thanks for you," he gritted, squinting in darkness. "For all the things you've been calling me— here's my—thanks!"

His right arm swung out and around to smash her face— and he nearly fell. She was not there; must have ducked. Stumbling, he cursed and went on. Then he was out the door and into the passage. With both Shemsi and DeyMeox in the one cell. Good!

A panting Gelor was just strong enough to slam the cell-door and bolt it. He reached up to the niche that held the ventilation duct, already prepared. Tremulous fingers twisted open the valves of the minitanks that held monocyan gas. He could just hear the gentle, almost delicate *ssss* of gas forced into the duct, into the cell. At last he had possessed the so-brainy DeyMeox. Now he'd at last pay off Shemsi, too. Now . . . the Final Solution to the problem of his two *slaves*.

Hissing faint as a lost whisper, the deadly gas streamed into the cell.

Gelor shivered. It was a shiver of release, of relief. Just what he needed to clear his brain in preparation for the climax of his duel with a corporation equally as treacherous as he. Now for the final step of his brilliant climb toward wealth and the power bought by wealth.

He managed a chuckle. "Double-dyed and card-carrying

villain, am I? *Yes*! And I'll beat the corporate villains, too!''

He left the old dungeon that was now the execution chamber of the two who had made his plan reality. The charter carrier came first. He contracted for it by remote comm and ordered it to a locked slot up on Jasbirstation.

He sealed the Bleaker dupladroid, the converted calculator/comtrol box, and the two-step canisters of Teratogenesis Six in standard shipping cases. Those he sent up to the space station's freight ramp. They were marked to be picked up by a nonexistent Dhofar Ishutin.

Well attired in grays, he took the shuttle up to Jasbirstation.

There he paged the pilot assigned to the carrier: one Rafi. Gelor had Rafi pick up the cases in Ishutin's name and bring them to the carrier's private cocking berth. Of course that meant Rafi must die, since he could link Gelor to the cases. . . . Well, Gelor was working on a fine big omelet, and he awaited the pilot-turned stevedore. One more egg.

A single stroke of the spring-thing attended to that unthrilling and necessary killing. He even tucked Rafi's raffish jacket under his head to catch the blood from his crushed face and mouth. Then Gelor uncrated the droid, calculator, and canisters. Gingerly, he piloted the carrier himself. Rafi's helmet and standard mlss spacesuit barely fitted him.

He swept out to the off-satellite location where CongCorp was to deliver the System Speeder spaceship.

It arrived, brought piggyback and left hanging in space, as he had instructed. He nudged the carrier over, failed twice, bumping the other craft, and smiled when he had locked the two ships together with EM grapples. He double-checked his spacesuit, took a deep breath of canned air, and boarded the bigger speedcraft. When he found the loot and checked it, he went shaky again.

It was as specified. An absolute fortune. Gelor's knees gave way and he sat down suddenly, bouncing a little in freefall.

Knowing that he had to get up and go on, he did. "Swimming" through the silent ship with stopper in hand. No need; it was empty. Here was the special compartment, with its hatch designed to separate the T6 canisters from the rest of the System Speeder. No contact would be necessary between the ship's supposed pilot and whoever picked up the toxin.

Helmet off in the ship's good air, Gelor installed the simulacrum droid and his special calculator. The late Rafi replaced the dupladroid in the case. Gelor saw to it that all semblance of address and instructions were charred off the big crate. HOLD FOR CONGCORP PICKUP, he marked it clearly, and with a sigh he looked around. Oh. He reprogrammed ship's computer.

Done! He donned the helmet, clamped it, checked its seals and used the suit's air to check for leaks. All secure. He pushed the crate back to the carrier. Cutting the electromagnetic field, he let carrier and spaceship have plenty of time to drift apart, despite his anxiousness to be away from here. At last he powered up, executed a long curve, and returned to the wheel.

The suit he left in its slot on the carrier. The crate he eased down and abandoned for a stevedore to find and store. Gelor ducked into the scanning room. Everything had gone so smoothly!—so far.

It continued smooth. He watched a carrier (CongCorp's testers, of course) peel off from the old XN-sat. It eased out to the speeder and locked onto the T6 hold. Gelor grinned. Obviously the company analysis had accepted the T6 and CongCorp brass had decided to go through with the pickup; the trade.

The System Speeder's SIPACUM actuated the commscreen. Shock and horror!

A man leered out across all grids, onto all screens. A monster of a man. His was a terrifying face, hideously scarred, with a single rolling, glaring eye. The other was an electroptic, opaque and flaming red.

"*Done then, you bastards, and see me now!*" he snarl-shouted in a voice no prettier than he. "*See me and know*

*you've dealt with Dravan of Bleak—Dravan the Marked!
Back from the dead to carve a new life in your blood! Get
away from my ship you bastard grats! Cross me at your
peril!''*

A mean laugh erupted from the awful face, and an
armored Bleaker glove rose and thrust forth in wordless
threat. Gelor's grin died and he shuddered in spite of
himself. Oh, Shemsi—the late Shemsi—had done her work
well!

And CongCorp had something to think about. So did
those on the company carrier. It parted from the System
Speeder with alacrity—while Gelor sagged back in his
scanning seat. Even with elation soaring in him, he was
breathing hard. So many things might have gone wrong!
Dupladroid programming had its limits, and . . . but the
real test-moment was still to come.

Now the System Speeder powered. It moved. Sec by
sec, its velocity increased. As per plan and programming,
it swung off in a wide loop. That course would ultimately
carry it out between the star of Ghanj and those of the
Tri-System Accord—if continued. Gelor grinned tightly.
That course would not be continued.

It was then that he saw the other spacers. Two of
them, lancing into view. If they weren't RT-Quads,
Janissary class, they rated as next best thing, surely. As
surely, it spoke something about CongCorp's power and/or
relationship with The Gray Organization: those ships were
the ships TGW used! They were forbidden to private
operators.

A tightness came into Gelor's belly. He leaned forward,
staring at the scanner and trying not to blink. New sweat
formed.

Blurs on the screen, the Janissaries closed on the speeder.
A lance of evilly greenish light said that one had zapped a
beam close to the quarry: a warning and a command:
Power down. Stand by for *Red Rover* to accept boarders.

*The treacherous lying sisterslicers! They've got the T6
they wanted—I dealt honorably with them! Not they—all
the time they've planned this: to take back ship, loot, and
. . . me. That is, Dravan. Red Rover, my ass!*

The tightness in Gelor's belly knotted. The palms of his hands were wet. Unsteadily, he wiped them hard along his pants-leg. Go! Go! he urged silently, staring at the onscreen scene: approaching intercept of *his* fortune.

For a moment the speeder seemed to slow. Another, and it flashed so fast that Gelor was hard-pressed even to see it. The Janissaries leaped after it–

The speeder vanished.

His modified Badakeacorp box and SIPACUM had done their work. The sleek System Speeder had jam-crammed into subspace. Straight to Forty Percent City, the CongCorp crews would report. Except that with a speeder, the odds had to be on the order of 99.99-to-infinity that no Galactic could survive such stress. What anyone onboard would throw up would be his life, not just his dinner. So long, Dravan. Say hello to Corundum and Artisune Muzuni!

So that was that. The megabillion multiplanetary corporation would write off the payoff in this venture and know it was safe from the not-clever-enough creep it had dealt with. Not that the loss would particularly matter to the company's top command. CongCorp could simply shrug and slide the loss over into the slot reserved for the Expense of Doing Business: Developing New Enterprise.

Eilong's kiraoun catalysts and the men who mined the ore would cover the loss and move into the profit column in the long run. Sooner.

This of course left one Gel Gelor in an enviable position, involving incredible wealth and official non-existence.

That was the virtue of his scheme, his concept. It eliminated Forty Percent City from the list of hazards. A speeder could convert instantly to tachyons and jam-cram "into subspace" with virtually no danger. After all, Gelor's speeder had no human onboard to die or be bollixed. From start to finish the operation would be conducted by computer, cybernetics, and—an android. Shemsi's computerized, cyberneticized, cross-circuited simulation of life that performed its programmed functions with no distress whatever from pressure or gravities or lack of either or both.

So: it had been part of his plan all along. The speeder would disappear—*had* disappeared—into "subspace"—

along the Tachyon Trail the hard way. CongCorp would write it off and go on about its business.

Gelor was aware of an obscure theory. The bindingpost/boomerang hypothesis, it was called, by those few who'd heard of it. Rooted even further in the past, it sprang officially from the work of an ignored and nearly forgotten psyanalyst, Tzentis Querumen of Gelor's own world.

Querumen's belief was that the dangers and unpredictability of what was called subspace could be circumvented. Given proper correlates and sufficiently advanced computational unit, a jam-crammed ship should surface predictably at any desired place and time . . . provided that no living life form was onboard, according to Querumen—and another inexplicable: provided also that a sufficiency of a specific chemical composition was involved/onboard. Someone had observed that he had described *almost* the chemical composition of emeralds, and T. Querumen's "Emerald Road" theory was laughed into obscurity.

Gelor had studied Querumen's theory for months on end. He wondered if anyone else had discovered what he had: that the so-called "ice emeralds" of planet Havoc were not only technically not *emeralds* because their composition was not *quite* that which specifically officially identified that form of uniaxial beryl called emerald— $Be_3Al_2Si_6O_{18}$—but *was* precisely the formula described by Querumen . . . who had apparently never heard of the icy-green 'Vocker gemstones.

Gel Gelor came to accept his fellow-worlder's theory. He believed in it. Accepted it as fact—and stood ready to gamble his fortunes on it. So long as that fortune contained some of the Querumen composition: $Be_3Al_2Si_5O_{18}$. 'Vocker ice emeralds. And so long as he had his ability, and the modified calculator he had shipped out with the Bleaker dupladroid. It would instruct SIPACUM, no matter what CongCorp might have programmed it to do.

He had scheduled the loot-laden speeder to surface a week hence, off Shankar's second satellite. When it did appear there, to orbit that moon—worse-than-barren Phapanom—he would be there to pick it up and move on to the delights of wealth and power and prodigious pleasure.

If it did not show . . . Gelor shuddered.

He would not think about that. At least he had the handful of uncut Joser stones he had thoughtfully taken off the speeder. And the rest was days away. He had other uses for that time. For one thing, there was the matter of disposing of the gassed corpses of Shemsi and DeyMeox.

15

A shape of doom; a Vengeful Judge—A dreaded mystery.
—*Laura Simmons*

So what difference does it make if a man's skin is violet,
Yahna Golden asked herself. What was beneath the hide
was what counted, and always had. Courage, character.
Intelligence! Cleverness; a sense of humor.

She brought her reverie up short. Such thoughts were
dangerous. Especially for a woman of her strange disposi-
tion (and she admitted to that freely, now), no man was to
be trusted. Least of all a purple lunatic up out of a mine on
a skungeball planet and wanted by the Powers That Be for
everything from murder to subversion and piracy to advanced mopery.

Twil'im came knocking, just then. She heard the familiar birdlike whistles of its truly alien language, saw it
adjust its translahelm as she opened the cabin's door.

The translation helmet said, "Want to make it with a
horny Jarp?"

"Not today thanks—and that's redundant."

The system of straps and devicery did not translate Jarp
laughter worth a jinkle. It only tried. Twilly had come to
advise that a small charter carrier was hanging in limbo
somewhere off The Sponge. Presumably it bore one Jestikhan
Churt of Eilan and was seeking a coordinate signal to ride in

to the cavern where *Slicer* lay hidden. And—Hieri was taken, down on Jasbir.

Yahna approved transmission of the signal and told Twil that if it did *that* again she would kick it where it would do the most serious damage; the Golden bottom was not available for six-fingered gropings. Twil'im accepted that philosophically. Mins later, carrier locked to *Slicer*. Jesti came onboard. (Yahna was not exactly delighted to realize that her heart was beating more than a trifle faster.)

An hour ago, she had persuaded Twil'im to *loan* her a cream-yellow halter and a pair of trunks, pinstriped in green and cream-yellow. Her attributes bulged out of the halter, for no Jarp was truly big of breast. On the other hand she tugged the shorts up and contrived to take a tuck in the waistband, for though Twil's penis and testicle were necessarily also not huge—there had to be room down there, after all, for a vaginal opening and ovary, too—the crotch was cut for male parts, not hers. Still, she was aware that she looked pretty damned good.

Then the rainbow-robed Jesti came stalking in, and *stalked* was the word. He had removed the mask and she saw eyes that were afire. The skin around his lips was as pale as purplescent skin could become. His voice was hoarse as he slammed the door behind him:

"Well, brotherslicer?"

It was hardly a greeting to evoke cordiality. Startled, Yahna made the effort and refrained from answering. Instead, she made a show of peering here and there behind her. Furiously, Jesti caught her by the wrist, and clamped.

"Hoy! I spoke to you!"

"You did?" She met his eyes and despite pain to her wrist she held herself very erect. She made no effort to pull free. "I thought you were addressing someone who makes it with her brother. I don't even have one."

His face worked with rage. "How'd you like to have that smirk knocked off your treacherous face?"

She stared at him, face composed. Waiting.

Jesti's other hand moved—and he remembered. "Oh no, Golden. No *rewards*, bitch. I am *not* going to hit you—so why did you tell Hieri I'd be wearing this Xan robe?''

Ah, she thought—and considered it a stupid question. Perversely—perhaps predictably so—she reacted to his belligerence rather than to his query.

"And what makes you think I betrayed you?" Her tone was as imperious and disdainful as only she could make it.

"That should be clear enough, damn you. Hieri told me."

"Oh *well*, then. And sure, Hieri is an honorable man who'd never lie to his beloved Jesti—whom he's never even called by name! And so you chose to believe him rather than me."

"You haven't said anything to believe or not. So—Do!"

"That insulting order in that peremptory tone I do not deign to answer, *Churt*."

"Oh you do beg for violence, don't you!" He clamped both arms now, and renewed her knowledge of his strength. "*Tell* me!"

She twisted fiercely. "Jesti—you're hurting me!"

"I know! I said answer me!"

Yahna's control gave way. With a sidewise twist she brought up a foot and raked it down his shin, with force.

Jesti let out a yell, let go her arm, and struck. At the last moment he remembered to pull his blow so that he only cuffed her—and she seized that hand in her teeth. When he tried to jerk free, she hung on while letting her legs go limp. Already offbalance, he was dragged to the floor with her.

Cursing, he let go her other arm and seized her by the hair. He wrenched her head backward. Pain popped her mouth open to scream and his released hand leaped to her throat. The scream died in an ugly gagging sound.

"Answer me, damn you! For once don't challenge and sneer—*answer*!"

Her eyes bulged and she sobbed for breath. He eased up on her throat. She swallowed twice before she snap-gasped her reply.

"Damn you, I *told* you Hieri had a caller and silent siren too! All he had to do was tune in to your grid-line and listen to my transmission. *You* said you'd be wearing that stupid robe—he *heard you*! He didn't need me to betray you! But since he thinks you're stupid, he saw he could cause more trouble by making you think he and I had struck a bargain. *I'm* the one stupid enough to think you weren't that stupid, damn it, oh damn damn you!''

What came next was a foregone conclusion. It went with passions up and blood running hot and bodies writhing, on the floor.

He ruined the halter to paw and chew at her warheads, got the robe out of the way and his coverall open, and discovered that he didn't have to ruin her shorts or get them off. A tug lowered their crotch enough to allow his invasion of them and her. Impaled, she lurched violently and forced him to grab her flailing arms.

He forwent telling her that she was wet as a lake; excited, as usual, by violence and force. He thrust forward with all his might, powering into her from the tips of his straining toes. Violent spasms of shuddering leaped all through her and she writhed in little undulations that grew into bigger ones as she bucked under him. Filling herself. Her freed breasts became loose balls dancing on her chest, rippling and swaying. Spreading inner warmth turned her cleft into a humid morass of seething lust that oiled itself and tried to snatch at his impaling shaft.

Their sweat-shining bodies ground together. She was jerking her hips in spasms now. Twitching and moaning beneath him while need sluiced throughout the length of her squirming long body. His presence inside her was an internal fuse that sputtered heat into her very womb. It flared, exploded.

They lay still for a long while, still panting. Eventually he moved, to lie beside her. He chuckled.

"So that's what you wanted, you sly sexpot. I should have known a psychist would sneak up on my off-side!"

"Why you—damn you, damn you, you damned . . . *Eilan*!" She beat at his chest.

"Lord, the positively awful name you call me!" He smiled, watching the way her breasts danced and jumped with her exertions. Then she blinked, stared.

Realizing belatedly what he'd meant, she said, "Oh."

"As in 'Oh how right you are, Jesti you rapacious stud?' " He grinned and cupped her breast . . . with, almost incredibly, real tenderness.

"Uh. Those toothmarks'll be sore for days."

"Hope so. But I'll lick 'em to make the hurt go away."

"Oh, Jes, damn it. . . ." She looked away, then back. "Listen. The last word we got on the reader/coder is that your man Hajji Kalajji was slated to meet CongCorp. Might be worthwhile to see what happens, don't you think?"

"Ah!" But he grinned. "Sure you don't want to rile me up again, brat?" (She hit him.) When he started to rise, his "uh" was in recognition of pain. He examined his shin. "Glad you don't wear spike heels. Couldn't we just, uh, screw every now and then, Golden?—take it easy on each other? Just for a change."

She hit him. Not hard. "Oh damn. You've ruined Twil's halter."

"You should be delighted, Yahna-psychist ma'am. It's a sin to cover that beautiful set of inhalation halators of yours. Why not make a deal with Twil . . . both of you just go bare-topped. Tell you what—I will too!"

He grunted as he got to his feet, then turned to offer a hand to her.

She batted it away and bounced up—to catch him watching the further exuberanterant bounce of her "inhalation halators." Putting on a grim face over the smile that started, she crossed her arms over her outstanding attributes.

"I could make a nice top from that robe," she said reflectively.

He had taken it off and was opening the comm-waste coverall. "Uh, well, I'd like to keep it intact. It served me well, and might again. Here." He found and handed her his old tunic. She saw the stopper in his coverall—Hieri's.

That wasn't why she stared, blinking, with both of them thinking she was about to start leaking tears. At last she swallowed and got words out:

"First thing you ever offered me . . . can we . . . can

we stand such an encroachment of creeping tenderness into our pardon-the-expression relationship?''

Jesti chuckled. He also took back the tunic and started to put it on.

"Here, gimme that!" She snatched it and headed for the reader/coder. "Got a good chest and shoulders on you, you know that . . . pirate?"

The minutes after that were baffling. The machine pulsed with top-priority CongCorp communications. C-C had made a tentative deal with the mysterious Hajji Kalajji. If it went through, a small spacer with the payoff would pick him up in the vicinity of an abandoned satellite. Enter fortuitous circumstances: from *Slicer*, hidden in its cavern on The Sponge, Yahna and Jesti were in a superb position to watch the whole affair as if they watched an episode of a holomeller. They watched, an amazing clear picture.

A charter carrier came onscreen. Close by the dead satellite, it rendezvoused with a little speeder already there. Some sort of business went on between the two craft. Eventually the carrier unlocked and swept away. Just as Yahna began her "Is that all?" another carrier moved, onscreen.

This one departed from the XN-sat, cruised to the System Speeder as the first had, and locked on. Almost immediately came terror! It burst luridly out of the speeder's transmission screen: the face of a man with a single eye. Teeth bared, he glared and roared out a challenge. The sight of that awful green scar running from eye to mouth to ear was itself enough to chill blood. The man must have *chosen* to leave it there; why else, when scars were so easy for daktaris to get rid of? And that rubicund optic replacing his other eye!

Jesti reacted with a shocked identification: "Dravan! Dravan the Marked! We've heard of that devil even on Eilong!''

Yahna could only shiver and wish she were being held by the powerful man beside her. How could she, from her background and with her intelligence and talent, have come to this? Trapped in a nether world of pirates. Murderers. Madmen. Outlaws. Engulfed in terror and even draped in a nowhere male tunic. Swept from one whirlpool of panic/excitement/passion to another.

(And loving it. Loving every pulsing, petrifying moment of it.

(*When I'm not too paralyzed with fear to know how I feel about it, that is.* All those Akima Mars dramas she'd worked on—people thought *they* were exciting and fraught with peril and violence and derring-do!—not to mention rape. . . .)

They saw the rest of it. The attack on Dravan of two spacers zooming in out of the purple abyss. So much for Dravan the Hideous, Yahna thought . . . and then the System Speeder vanished from screen and from space.

That incredibility came as a shock that left Yahna gasping, staring. Nothing wrong with the scanner disguised up above their cave; the two attack craft were still there.

Jesti stood frowning at the screen too, with narrowed eyes. Abruptly he gave his head a jerk and headed for his clothes. "I'm going back down."

"Down? To *Jasbir*?"

"Firm."

She had to scramble up and follow him out the door. "*Why*? You saw what happened. That speeder simply . . . vanished. Disappeared."

"Uh. Had to be Forty Percent City. Hieri told me about it," he said, striding to collect the discarded robe. "What you call it when someone uses the tachyon converter—*bam*, just like that—without waiting to make sure it's safe. Odds are forty-something per cent that you won't live through it."

"Yes, sure, I know about jam-cram," she snapped, walking (rapidly, to keep up!) a tightrope between confusion and irritation. "But what's that got to do with your going back onplanet? You're not going to find Dravan *there*!"

"Dravan's the least of my concerns, Golden One!"

"Then what—Jesti-i–!"

"Someone was with him, Yahna. The same someone who brought him and piloted the carrier back. That's who I'm after. Someone who can tell me what's going on. How our Handsome Man and CongCorp's Hajji Kalajji contact fit into all this. Are they the same man, or two different people? I want to know. I *have* to know. So—back down to Jasbir for me.''

Yahna cringed at the determination she heard in that strong voice. It was a moment she had known instinctively would come. She had dreaded it. Now, for an instant, she hesitated. Wondering if it might not be wiser to let him go ahead, regardless.

But no; her brain wouldn't let her do that. That was the trouble with logic, with education. They got in the way of empathy and impulse and emotion. Tautly, she matched the firmness of Jesti's tone:

''Negatory. You're not going, Jes.''

His face froze. ''*What*? Why not?''

''Because you're you. She gestured to her friend, the mirror. ''Look at you. You're Eilan miner *purple*. Anyone sees that with one glimpse.''

''Not if I wear the Xan robe, mask, and the gloves. No color at all—no me showing!''

''Especially if you wear that rainbow robe! By now the word's out on it, Jesti.'' She was practically pleading for understanding, acceptance of good sense. ''Every Xan in Marmot is being searched and questioned, and probably released with some policer ID—a visible something. Show up down there in that outfit and policers and ruffos will fight each other for the chance to grab you.''

The difference between Jestikhan Churt and a fictional hero was that he could not and would not argue with logic. She saw that from the shadow that fell over his face. It made her feel better.

''Damn. You're right. But it's our only chance to get the scrute—to find out what the vug is going *on*!''

''No, it is not our only chance, Jes.'' She stared directly into his eyes. ''We can both go.''

''Both–!'' Pure incredulity crossed his face. ''You're out of your mind, woman. They'd have the two of us in irons before we hit the port gate.''

''Not if I had you sealed in a contagion sack,'' she said sweetly. ''A body bag out of, say, Shankar. Don't you see,'' she said, coming close to rest a hand on his arm. She indulged herself in a small, triumphant smile. ''It's the perfect answer. No one wants to take a chance with *Shanki Fever*!''

''Shanki Fever. Is it bad?''

''The worst,'' she told him. ''It terrifies everyone. Look, we're immunized against nearly everything ever thought of and a few that haven't been. But Shanki Fever's worse than the famous old Plague—and there's no vaccine. No one is going to want to *touch* me, or even be near. All they'll want to do is make sure the bag's sealed and puckpass me on to the next clerk, who'll do the same, and—''

''I see all that. Brilliant. But if there *is* trouble, any slip-up . . .''

''There won't be. I'm a registered psychist. No one—''

''No.'' He shook his head. ''Negatory, Yahna.''

Her heart sank. This time, she knew that no words could change his damned bullish head. She didn't even cover; seeing her reaction, Jesti patted her shoulder. A little clumsily; the ''encroachment of creeping tenderness into their relationship.'' She didn't flinch, either. Much.

''Don't feel too down, Golden One. It's a beautiful idea. It just isn't quite good enough. I left things in an uproar in Marmot. Everybody's going to be edgy. And no man in his right mind's going to let himself be sealed in a sack so that any nervous fobber can Fry him. Besides . . . there's a better way. You've sparked it from me. All we need's a breathing helmet, the kind spacefarers wear when they're on a planet way out of sync with what they're accustomed to in the way of air and grav. Put a faceplate with the right filter polarizer in it and I can have any color skin you want.''

''Your hands—''

He held them up, showing her the skintight, breathing gloves. ''Come to think, I can stain-squirt these green in about one min. Less.''

Even knowing she'd lose, Yahna tried to argue with him. Yet . . . strangely, she was glad he wouldn't let her dissuade him. It gave her something approaching a sense of security. As if she needn't fret any more about anything because, whatever happened, this man would protect her.

Shades of that infamous Kenowa! I'm thinking like a—a woman!

That was a species of insanity to Yahna Golden. It belonged to ancient eras of female subservience to "protecting" males—who accordingly dominated. That was anathema in any psychist's book, and never mind Mama Nature's (long outgrown) Plan!

Besides . . . he needs me. He can't protect anyone if they kill him on Jasbir or lock him away in durance vile for the next century!

She sighed. "Let's get it going, then. You have to promise to buy a bandeau or two for Twil. I'll try to explain to the horny creep and beg another something to wear."

"If it gives you any trouble, we use this." He slapped his stopper, and headed for the con.

A few minutes later, braced by an anxious-unto-surly pair of crewmembers, Jesti felt no compunctions whatever about lying.

"Hieri's been taken," he told Musla and Twil. "You two are the ship experts—the real spacefarers. It's up to Yahna and me to go down onplanet and try to find him—rescue him if we have to. I'm not too bad at that, you'll remember."

Surprisingly, Musla grinned. "I do, Jesti," he said, and while Jesti tried to remember whether the dour Sek had used his name before, Musla went on to his fellow crewmember: "Strip, Twil! Give 'er yer clo'es. Shit, it's for all of us, an' no matter how great she looked with 'er warheads hanging out on the bounce, she can't go down onto Jasbir like that! Shit, she'd be grabbed by thirteen slavers in the first seven minutes!"

Jesti laughed; the Golden One looked shocked. The Jarp went along, looking un-overjoyed. When Musla looked his way, Jesti gave the Sek a friendly look with a carefully measured dollop of gratitude in it.

Soon Yahna wore a good-looking lace-front jerkin in a rust hue, and tights the color of old wine seen in dim lighting. And she and Jesti went down. Down to Jasbirstation in their tiny charter carrier, while Musla and Twil'im stayed on *Slicer*. Whether the Jarp clothed its nakedness neither Golden nor Churt cared. They went down, with Jesti in a breather helmet whose faceplate he didn't dare open lest it reveal his purple Eilan skin. And green gloves. Down, with Yahna absolutely skin-sheathed in Twil's seductive clothing, sure to distract attention to from her companion.

"Musla's full of shit," Jesti observed. "You're sexier in that laced vest than you were bouncy-bare."

"Oh, disconnect your helmet's speaker."

That friendly sarcasm turned out to be an excellent idea. If she did all the talking, it would enhance the image they were trying to create of Jesti as an offplanet visitor with a breathing problem. Too, it would enable her to field questions that might call for knowledge he lacked.

They had little difficulty locating the carrier that had carried Dravan out to the System Speeder. The question of who had brought it back to the big docking wheel in space was another matter. It should have been the portside pilot called Rafi, they were told. But Rafi appeared to be missing.

Jesti chose not to mention the crate he had seen near that carrier's umbilical "door" into the station; a huge one marked to be held for pickup by CongCorp. He wanted a sneak look at and in that one himself, if he could sidestep station security and stevedores who belonged to a greedy and touchy union. That proved not difficult; a big flap developed on the station, and security people scrambled to that berth. Some maniac had blasted a lander or pinnace or something *right through a docked spacecraft*—one *Coronet*—and was away.

Jesti didn't know good guys from bad, didn't know who *Coronet*'s captain was, or whether the monster who had holed the ship had been escaping durance vile, slavery, or justice. Therefore Jesti didn't know who to feel for. He did know what to do. He hurried in the opposite direction of the big flap, and opened the box. *Dam' thing looks like a coffin*, he mused . . . and of course discovered that it was.

This, he assumed, was carrier "pilot" Rafi—the late

Rafi. His neck had been broken by a blow so savage that the shattered vertebrae stuck out through the skin.

It was hardly a time for reporting anything to the authorities, even a murder. Instead, Yahna struck up a few minutes' conversation with some of the dispatchers in the off-duty lounge. One of the women recalled that the last time she'd seen Rafi he was deep in conversation with one of the handsomest men she had ever seen. It was the sort of thing she remembered, she chuckled, and Yahna smiled and nodded.

Inside his disguising helmet, Jestikhan was not smiling. A man too handsome to be believed? Uh-huh. They checked, and a shuttle ID-checker/"guard" remembered the fellow. He had passed him. No, he didn't remember the fellow's name. All he paid attention to was ticket and ID picture. He did remember that it barely did the big good-lookin' man justice.

So. The Handsome Man was back on Jasbir, presumably back in Marmot. And still with no clues as to his identity or his whereabouts beyond the shuttleport.

Sharing Jesti's frustration, Yahna dragged him into the lounge for a beer or saufee. That did nothing for his frustration, since he couldn't drink through the breather helmet. They ordered one of each anyhow. While she sipped hot saufee she heard his plaintively helpless "Why—*why*?"

"Why what, Jesti?"

"Why'd he come up? Why take the risk of bringing up that monster Dravan?"

Suddenly the breath seemed to go out of her. She felt as if she was going to red out. The moment passed. "Neg," she whispered. "Neg, Jes, that isn't the question. Listen . . . the real question is *where did Dravan come from?* How did he get up here? How do you disguise . . . *that*?" She actually felt a little *frisson* at memory of that face, the absolute barbaric aspect of that animalistic man.

They sat frozen for a long minute, staring at each other.

"You've got it, Golden! An animal like Dravan . . . he *couldn't* come up here. Not openly. Yahna—I've got it. He was in that box!"

"Shh."

He lowered his voice but the excitement remained. "He was in that box. The Handsome Man *brought* Dravan up here. Come to think, *he* must have taken Dravan out to the carrier and returned on the first carrier we saw. The pilot was already dead—boxed! He had to be—he couldn't be allowed to see Dravan! Not for long, anyhow . . . Dravan looked big enough and savage enough to break the poor bug's neck that way."

She had known that she was caught up in his excitement, but now she clouded over and sighed. "Damn. There's a hole in that, Jesti. He couldn't have brought Dravan up on the shuttle. Not in a box that big—it's against the rules."

"Rules? Against bringing up belongings?"

She nodded. "Stevedore's union! They have the contract to bring up everything except carry-on things. So . . . he had Dravan *sent* up and held for pickup, while the Handsome Man came up on the shuttle. And let him out. Then . . ." She trailed off.

He banged his fist on the table hard enough to attract a couple of curious glances and one stare, from a Terasak spacefarer who sat alone at a table toying with a Habibula Sphere and a beer.

"Dravan would've had to be dead," Jesti said. "That box has no holes in it. None. He couldn't breathe."

"An . . . air tank, maybe?" Her tone was plaintive. They were so clever and so close—*couldn't we just get it? Can't we work it out and Do Something?* "The weird thing is that last I heard, Dravan the Damned was dead."

"Dravan the Marked. Well, he didn't look dead to me."

Once again she was staring, almost glassy of eye. He saw a new revelation behind those eyes, and he stood it as long as he could in silence: about three secs. He demanded words.

"Jesti . . . he *was* dead," she said in a dull voice, narrow-eyed in thought. "He—I'm sure of it. And he still is. That wasn't Dravan! That was one hell of a good dupladroid! We've used 'em in the Akima Mars holos . . .

and that was one of the very best. That must be what we saw! He—the—I mean . . ."

He touched her hand with his green-gloved one. "Easy now, you're doin' great. Go on—how what?"

"The ship. We saw that speeder go City! It didn't seem all that *necessary*, Jes, not right then. Believe me, going Forty Percent City is an absolutely last resort. Unless . . . there was no *person* on that spacer!"

"Ah! Sure, a dupladroid wouldn't be affec–you've got it!"

Triumph . . . while the Why, Where, and How of it were separate questions whose answers remained beyond deduction. Even the near-euphoria of this much progress had drawn Yahna's muscles so tight they ached. Unfortunately their deductive breakthrough gave no hint as to the whereabouts of their quarry. The Handsome Man. Looking down at the tabletop, Jesti pointed that out. Bitterly.

Yahna shook her head. More than ever, she felt calm and in control. "Negatory, Jes. It isn't that bad. We're closer than you think."

"We are?"

"Pos!" She smiled. "You see, a simulacrum has a heart, Jes." She paused while he frowned and groped mentally. "Not the mechanism that powers it. The mnemosyne." Again she paused; in her mind, she was back at the Psychesorium at Koba, listening to the lecturers explain the subtleties of such matters. "The sort of dupladroid we make today was made possible by the biochemist Hee Sun Hsu's development of the gel we call Hsu's Colloid. What makes it special is that it has a sort of memory (someone coined the word *mnemory*). A human mentor can transfer his own reaction patterns to—well, it's installed in the droid in a synaptic globe, and the droid will respond to stimuli according to the instructions conditioned into it by the mentor."

"Half-understanding that doesn't help me find my man."

"Yes it does, Jes! Hsuloid's hardly a mass production synchem! Not many places stock it. All we have to do is–"

"Let's go!"

•   •   •

They went. As it turned out, the only outlet in Marmot for either Hsu's Colloid or mnemosyne was a rather shabby dispensolab in one of the older precincts snuggling around the shuttleport. The creep in charge was small, spindly, rouged, and with a tendency to stroke everything he touched, whether animate or in-, as if it were a pet. His complexion was an unfortunate gray-rust.

Yahna found him worse than distasteful. He eyed her speculatively, ignoring her faceplated companion (which was fine with Jestikhan).

Hsuloid? Pos, he carried it. Not too much call for it, of course. Androids and droidal servomechanisms weren't too popular; people preferred created helpers that didn't look like people. Yes, he *had* sold three, not too long ago. To whom? Oh my—it had been a call-in and pickup. Cash. Sorry.

A stell-note, not of the lowest denomination, transferred itself from Yahna's bosom to his hand. The little downer tucked it away, pursing his lips, eyeing her even more interestedly than before. Uh, well, maybe the runner who'd processed the order would remember more about it . . .

The runner was as big and chocolate as his superior was spindly and grayish. He remembered the call. Rush order out to the zoo—the bionarium. Left the package with the gate-guard. That was all. . . . Knowing he'd never smell what she'd given his boss for nothing, Yahna slipped him a one-stell note and was almost knocked down by his bow.

"Oh good," she said to Jesti. "We'll have to go out there some day."

"Uh," he said disinterestedly, and they thanked and ambled out and along to the corner, rounded it, and ran like hell to the tubeway station.

The bionarium was Marmot's pride and a nice source of revenue, the most respected interplanetary zoo in the Galaxy. Huge and echoic, equipped with life-support systems to fit a Galaxy-wide range of specimens, including a few off uninhabited and uninhabitable worlds. The gate-guard, spiffy in red with black piping and skin-hugging tights, knew nothing about the Hsuloid. She was, after all, new here.

New?

Firm. The old boy who held this job had suffered a fall down the marble steps not long ago. Cracked his skull. Tragic. Just one of those things, though. Must've tripped over his own feet. A visitor had seen it happen and called for help. Too late. The fracture had been too bad, almost as if the old man's head had been smashed in with a plasteel club.

Like Rafi, Jesti thought, while Yahna said casually, "The visitor?"

"Whew! Never forget *him*! Named Dhofar something-or-other. Name's on the report of course. What a handsome devil!" She rolled her eyes at Yahna, who smiled. "Too good-looking to believe, you know? He was here at the bionarium quite a bit for awhile, studying alien life-forms. Dull work for such a doll. Lives somewhere close—he's from offplanet—probably the palace." She gestured. Used to be some Ghanji prince's palace, you know? About the only place available around here. Boy, I know one that handsome dog could share!"

"Well, thanks. That's not of any interest to us, of course."

Leaving the guard looking embarrassed at having rattled on because the man was *so* handsome, Jesti and Yahna left. Outside the park-like bionarium, Jasbir's dome-controlled darkness was descending. Yahna squeezed Jesti's hand.

"Same man!" he said. "Killed the old guard, killed Rafi. Same man!"

"In a palace, no less! We're close, Jesti! Tomorrow, we can—"

"No. Not tomorrow. Now!"

Yahna sighed. His tone told her not to bother trying to dissuade him. She wondered what she was doing here. It would be different if she were in command of her own feelings. It was so hard, hating Jestikhan Churt and wondering if she didn't really love him. Her destiny had got itself tied to a driven madman's! Worse, now that she knew she could walk away without his stopping her—she didn't want to. Couldn't. So—here she stood beside the fixated madman in his bizarre disguise, in the bionarium's lenghtening shadows.

Stood? No, already he was moving, on his way, eyes gleaming fever-bright behind the faceplate that made his face midnight black.

As she had known she would, Yahna Golden moved with him. Out into the ruddy dusk toward the distant, white-walled compound indicated by the guard as housing Prince Somebody's palace. And . . . the Handsome Man at last?

16

When Fortune flatters, she does it to betray.

—*Publilius Syrus*

Gelor returned to find light gleaming at the windows of the Inner Palace.

He stopped with a jerk. Every nerve was instantly on edge. To Gelor the power of life and death brought with it a sense of surging strength and elation. Murder, that ultimate power, calmed him. The unanticipated stole away that calm. It infuriated him that he was so constituted, but apparently there was no cure for it. He swallowed hard, and closed the compound's outer gate behind him. He saw to its lock. Keeping to the shrub-shadows that fringed the curving walkways, he moved toward the light.

He was very sure of one thing: he had left no lights on.

A woman's voice rose merrily. Someone said something and a burst of laughter followed. The words were too indistinct for him to understand. That did not blunt the impact of the situation. Women's voices could mean only one thing: somehow, incredibly, Shemsi and DeyMeox were still alive.

Damn them! This added up to menace. Alive, they would be working against him. Scheming. Plotting. And at a time when he had thought he at last had a chance to rest!

Would there never be an end to tension? Must he live

out his life this way? It was a bitter prospect, particularly since he had so successfully brought off his coup—*Surely I have a right to enjoy it!* To bask, at least for a little while, in ease and luxury. *Damn them!* His nerves deserved rest; the freedom to range the universe for his pleasure and intellectual stimulation. His every letch catered to by willing women. Instead, he was trapped here in this moldering palace with two too-intelligent and all too dangerous women.

Damn them! He crept closer, reached the Inner Palace. There could be no peering in at these light-radiant outer windows. They were set far too high. If, on the other hand, he entered by the postern door . . .

Ghosting around the building with as much speed as silence would permit, he pushed through the bushes that shrouded the cramped rear entrance, unlocked it, and eased it open. He stepped into darkness.

The passageway to his left followed the exterior wall to the main hall, the big room he used as a central workshop/lab. The corridor ended in a heavy door. To its right, a stairway rose. Halfway up it, a window looked into the sprawling workroom. Gelor crept up that stair, and peered through its inward-giving window.

Shemsi and DeyMeox sat at a cluttered table. DeyMeox was drinking the volcanic mineral water called Alive. Shemsi waggled a pottle of bose, the Franjese wine. Both wore their fine velour jumpsuits and both still laughed in hilarity. Unfortunately their words remained indistinct.

Not that it mattered. Gelor went back down the stair, trembling with anger, and flung open the door into the workroom.

The door hit the wall with a crash to shatter crystal. Both women whirled. Shemsi fell half off her chair. Their laughter cut off as if sliced by a knife. They stared. So did Gelor. He said nothing.

Shemsi's voice was a whisper: "We–" She tried again, "We–" She seemed unable to find or form further words.

DeyMeox: ":You . . . did return."

"Unexpectedly to you, that's plain." Fists knotted, Gelor

moved in closer to tower over them. "No doubt you have reason for all the laughter."

DeyMeox wetted her lips. "We–were telling jokes."

"Of course. *Hilarious* jokes." He bared his teeth. "I need to laugh, too. Tell me one."

That elicited only silence and large, staring eyes.

The tension in him burst into fury. His lashing out at DeyMeox was a savage blow that caught her across the jaw. She was knocked to the floor with a crash. Her plass of Alive cascaded down to drench her. Gelor had already whirled. Seizing Shemsi by the hair, he jerked her to her feet.

"Talk, you hust-bitch! What have you done? *Why were you laughing?*" He snatched up the wine pottle. "Or would you rather have this up your ugly stash—all the way up to where it *pours out your mouth*?" He added emphasis by slapping her, back and forth. That felt good, and he did it again, watching the blows jerk her head this way and that.

"No, no!" she was screaming, choking, sobbing. "We–oh, oww–"

"Stop it, you animal!" DeyMeox yelled. "Leave her alone! I'll tell you, damn you!"

Gelor pivoted. He kept his fingers knotted in Shemsi's hair, dragging the squirming, sobbing andrist along with him.

Clutching at the table, DeyMeox clawed herself to her feet. Blood dribbled from the corner of her mouth and her eye on that side was closed. She kept blinking, as if she were having a difficult time hanging onto consciousness. Yet somehow, grotesquely, she was smiling. Sneering, he realized. Her good eye gleamed with a light that could only be labeled triumph.

"What we've done," she whispered hoarsely, reeling, "is cost you Eilong! Eilong and your *life*, you melanomous monster! You gave CongCorp dead spores, not living ones! They will not reproduce and they will not infect. And the word on you is out, Gelor, out, over your own relays! CongCorp knows who you are and where to find you."

Oh, Shiva, how he wanted to kill her in that moment!

Fear prevented him. Fear for his own neck; fear of CongCorp. And above all, fear for what she might not yet have told him. His gaze jerked around the room, eyes raging, glaring, less than sane.

One of Shemsi's dupladroid frames stood across the room. With a snarl, Gelor dragged both women to it. He locked a droid-claw about the wrist of each, double-checked, and hurried into the loading room adjacent to the spore chamber. He found the spare two-step canisters still in their neat row, precisely as he had left them.

Breathing hard, he checked the homeostats. It was true! Temperature, humidity, pressure—all had been changed. Temp upward, humidity down—and G-pressure right off the dial.

His brain rocked and he raged. Dead spores! The plague that was Teratogenesis Six had been reduced to mockery. Dead spores. He wanted to rave, and he could not. His mouth had gone dry as a waterless moon. His tongue clove to the roof of his mouth. Whirling, he ran for the relay room; the communications center.

There, a loop was endlessly transmitting:

"The man who cheated you is named Gel Gelor. Identitag is in your banks. Former employee CongCorp, compudator at Lanatia Station. Presently onboard speeder you gave him, bound for Shankar. (beat, beat) *The man wh—"*

Over and over it pulsed out the message. Over and over and over. Through three replays, Gelor stood frozen. A roiling haze hung before his eyes. Rage such as he had never felt churned through him so that he felt vomitous.

(Rage? Perhaps it was panic, he almost-thought almost-coherently; a panic so deeply rooted and pervasive that his brain dared not acknowledge it lest he fall apart completely? The concept of such fright was in itself a frightening thought.)

Gel Gelor began to shake. His teeth chattered. The room swam lazily about him. It came to him that he was on the verge of fainting. Staggering, he slammed his elbow down onto the metal tabletop. Pain blasted through him so sharply as to blow away the haze. His panic ebbed. Somehow the throb of pain sent a new thought: *There is still hope. Damn them, damn them* . . .

The women had made their play based on a false assumption. They had taken it for granted that he was on the speeder and gone forever. Even they had not guessed at his true plot, the final genius-level twist. He was here and Shemsi's simulacrum was onboard the speeder, racing along the Tachyon Trail to surface again at a predetermined time and place.

That twist held his salvation. The speeder would still surface out off the Shanki satellite. Since only he knew where, he could still claim the booty his brilliance had earned. He could still live out his dream of wealth and power . . . *the wealth and power I deserve!*

Yet life would involve far less tension and apprehension if CongCorp's ruffos weren't searching for him in a killing rage.

Besides . . . it was not in him to let these two women bring him down. They had to die knowing that all their efforts had been in vain. That Eilong's doom was sealed just as he had planned it.

"Uh," he grunted, remembering. First came the matter of how they had tricked him! He hurried to DeyMeox's cell. His finger found the light and darkness vanished. And he stared. DeyMeox still lay on the disarranged vibrabed where he'd lain with her and left her.

It was the clever work of that sluttish Shemsi: a dupladroid in the crober's image, hitched to a sexulator. No wonder she had called for so much material and equipment! Grinding his teeth, Gelor actuated the . . . thing. The thing he had so passionately sliced.

"I'm dying, I'm *dy*-inng! I can't wait! Quick, quick–ahh–" he heard DeyMeox's voice say, and then, from behind him, Shemsi's: "That's it, you sickofobber! Ram it to her! Ream the whorebitchmare!"

Gelor pivoted—to stare at the powerful minicorder across the little room. From it emerged Shemsi's words. He had no doubt that when he walked toward the cell's door, it would split out her "Wonderful! Wonderful!" and so on. While he had made a fool of himself, wallowing with the false DeyMeox attached to a mechanical sexulator, Shemsi had slipped away to help the waiting crober reset the homeostats on the spore-cans.

After that he had made it simple. He had lurched up from the clutches of the *thing* half-blind with his own lust and satiation. He remembered lashing out without hitting Shemsi. Of course! Anticipation, too, had warped his thinking. He had gloated too much over the final twist he had planned for them: murder of his two helpful *slaves*, and to Sheol with his pledge to them.

Once he (thought he) had locked them in and started the flow of killing gas, he had assumed their deaths. Except that they had been carrying out *their* twist, upstairs. While he rushed to deliver harmless spores to CongCorp, they had been here, safe. Laughing. Laughing at him . . .

They won't laugh any more. I'll tend to those swinish sows as soon as I'm through with CongCorp.

In the relay room he hooked up a fresh loop and spoke into it: "This is Gel Gelor, who was Hajji Kalajji. I have been betrayed. Through no fault of mine the . . . merchandise I provided you is faulty. I accept all blame and within one week of days-standard I shall undo the damage. Count on it! Your project will proceed as scheduled. I ask only that you hold off retaliatory action until I have proven this. A fair offer, surely: simply give me one week. I shall prove my good faith and skill before the time is up."

He swallowed hard, set it to turning. In the loading room, he locked a new can to the spore-chamber. He opened the valve and adjusted the homeostat; watched the canister fill in mins. Smiling now, he returned to comm to call Jasbirstation for a charter craft. He had to *move*!

It still wasn't his day. The only spacer available was an ancient ramscoop. Its captain was some hard-drinker off Jahpur. His rep was so bad that no crew worth having would ship with him. Gelor pondered sweatily.

"I'll bring my own crew!" he said. "We shall be on the wheel within a couple of hours."

"*Acknowledged*," Station Charter said. "*We'll hold the ship for you.*"

Gelor cut the comm. His smile was thin, but it was a smile.

He'd bring a crew, all right. An unwilling crew—and stoned to the eyeballs. How they'd hate him when they learned the duty he planned for them now! It was better by far than killing them here and now. Instead, they'd all ship out together: he and Shemsi and DeyMeox. And Captain Hard-drinker. Gelor would see to it that the captain screwed the hell out of both women, going and returning.

Together, the three of them would rain Teratogenesis Six down on Eilong!

Jesti and Yahna arrived at the old palace just as their quarry was leaving in a commercial loader. They did see that he had two women with him, and several big crates.

"Shuttleport!" Jesti snapped, and wheeled.

He wheeled and ran . . . and of course he and Yahna afoot could not match the loader's speed. By the time they reached the port, the enemy and his little hhareem had gone on to Jasbirstation. Yahna and Jesti had to wait, panting, for the next departure. And up they went—too late again.

The Handsome Man and company had boarded a chartered ramscoop and redshifted. A little more checking nailed it down: the Handsome Man had also bought a commercial flight cassette. Oh yes, sure, the clerk remembered—because it was a mighty, mighty unusual destination. Eilong.

"That's a nothin' planet way beyond Saiping. He sure was—"

"He was in a hurry," Jesti grunted, "or he'd never have settled for that old ship. A big hurry to get to my planet! There's only one thing we can do—get *Slicer* out of that cave on The Sponge and try to follow."

He arranged transport while Yahna entered an overpriced station shop. Since it was a clothing store and she emerged wearing a beautiful new outfit and carrying a large box as well, he was ready to sneer.

Next they had to convince Musla and Twil that they had *tried*. A 'fax from the station newscenter was proof enough that Hieronymus Jee was dead, but the Bleaker and the Jarp were hardly happy about leaving—especially for Eilong. That's when Yahna made Jesti ashamed of having sneered. Yahna Golden, MarsCorp, had plenty of cred. Easy for her to turn that and her ID into a lot of ready cash, in that shop onstation.

A couple of thousand stells in cash convinced Twil and Musla. *Slicer* moved out of its hiding place and into space. Sensors and scanners found no ramscoop trace. The quarry was long gone. The pursuit set course for Eilong.

"Yahna, I—about the money . . ."

"I seem to be with you," she said, and Jesti swallowed hard.

His throat went even tighter when he gazed at the screen, much later. That glaring furnace was his sun, no matter how little he'd seen of it from the mines. That growing ball was *his* planet. Had the Handsome Man been here and gone?—or could he be here now? Jesti chewed his lip. His homeland. The Handsome Man's goal—so he could *sell* it. How? Semen and blood . . . murder and murder, again and again. *My world. Blood and semen? Sell?* Whatever the plan was, it was enormous and concerned the welfare of the whole world . . . Jestikhan Churt's world. Personal vengeance faded to triviality.

"I have to go down there," Jesti said, because it wasn't in him to evade or deny what he perceived as duty. "Onto *my* planet."

"You're a fugitive," Yahna reminded him. "You can't just call in for a docking berth." She waited till he turned to stare at her, stricken. "So. *I* dock us, in my name. *I* go onplanet, because we *might* want to make a holomeller there—big money for the Eilan economy! *But* I want it to be secret right now. No 'dignitaries,' no guides. Just me . . . and my bodyguard, of course. His problem is that he has to wear a breather mask/helmet."

He blinked. "You know—I'd hug you if I thought I dared. Musla! This ship just became a chartered carrier for Yahna Golden-psychist, of MarsCorp!"

"Uh. One condition. Me an' Twil get off, too. Stationside bar, maybe."

Yahna covered her new formfitting suit of violet with her new cloak—long and mauve and hardly so eye-catching as her miniskirt and SprayOn kneeboots. She and her "unfortunate bodyguard" with his breathing problem went through Customs in a breeze, went down onplanet with no trouble whatever, and attracted only minimal attention, none negative.

(No, no ramscoop had docked here. Not for months.)

Jesti guided her through the blue-gray night of the world that had been—no, that always would be his. Some called it a troglodyte world, since most Eilans dwelled in the abandoned workings of Eilong's mines. It was not such a bad existence ("particularly before you know what there is elsewhere," the Golden One's companion muttered). Constant temp was a rule in the old workings. A stripped ore-chamber could be turned into an attractive enough apartment, provided one didn't mind recycled air. And never seeing the light of the sun.

None of that mattered. Eilong was Jesti's home, a miner's world of cliffs and drifts, pits and circuitous caverns. A people-ravaged world with surface streets that wound among mountainous slag piles where recycling machinery worked day and night at turning deadly methane into lifegiving power for the dwellers below. Jesti's world. His and Oo-long Eef's.

Once they reached the maze of streets beyond the shuttleport, his feet turned automatically toward the old man's home + laboratories.

Strange, how they had come together: the boy from the pits and the Council of Elders' top scientist and sage. Somehow a spark had flashed between them. They had progressed to sharing not just thoughts but feelings. Jesti might even have built himself a place of power in the Elder's structure, had he not become so involved with the plight of miners.

Yahna walked tall and confidently. Jesti felt an unpleasant prickling every time he glimpsed someone who even *might* be a policer. He had not been away all that long—*it only seems a century!*

They came to the familiar shaft and entered the lift. Jesti touched the indicator. Then smacked it. The unit responded to that by grinding into noisy life. Yahna said nothing and held back a smile as they descended into Eilong. Down to the the third level, and then along to the proper apt-unit.

Jesti had expected to be apologetic for rousing the old man from sleep. Not so: Eef was up, a man whose girth just missed matching his height. Yahna watched him clutch the (unhelmeted, now) Jesti to him, and was introduced to one of the few whose body reacted adversely to the enzyme that prevented weight gain, and who (unscientifically!) refused to curb his eating. *He was amazed, then entranced at his white beard.* Nearly everyone in the Galaxy was hairless below the eyebrows—or nostrils, at least—by choice, and here was a man both fat and bearded—and the beard was naturally white!

Also, he was not purple. No, only miners were, she remembered.

Their explanations left out a number of activities, but included the Handsome Man and their pursuit of him. Had he been here?

Eef went very grim and led them to his labs. Carrying his helmet and with Yahna pacing silently beside him, Jesti was in the chill grasp of foreboding. The culture case with rank upon rank of shallow nutrient tanks did not diminish his apprehension. (Besides, Yahna had opened her enveloping cloak and Oolong Eef showed no reaction to her leggy, singular figure.)

"What do you see, Jesti?"

Jesti peered and frowned. "Black specks."

"Precisely," Eef said. "Dead spores. Attempts by *someone* to culture spores of . . . an undetermined type. The spores turned out to be dead, and so the project failed. Whatever it was."

"Dead spores. Project. You've left us in the dark, mentor."

"Hmp! I don't understand it either." Oolong's heavy white brows drew into a scowl. He paced off a few waddly steps. "A few cycles ago, an unidentified spacer flew over the world. It merely cruised, and refused contact. You know our people—complacent. No one fired on the ship, or tried to back up demands for communication. It departed. Naturally the Elders wondered, and I set to work on the mystery. What I learned was that the ship dropped those spores onto Eilong. Why, I do not know. I do not know, Jesti . . . Yahna. But there is more. Come over here."

He led them to another culture case. Again they gazed upon nutrient tanks. This time the contents were very different. These spores were far from black. Bright orange, they massed in colonies that seemed to seethe and spread before their eyes. They seemed . . . malignant, Yahna thought. Sinister. *Obscene*, Jesti thought, with a twisting inner sensation.

"This is from another batch of spores," Oolong said, "similarly seeded by another ship, only a few hours ago. We have been on the alert since that other time, and we were ready when this lot rained down . . . in two-step canisters that actuated at ten kloms altitude. We managed to snag one before it opened—though the ship escaped our pursuit craft and fled into space. This time, well you see. The spores are alive. Very alive."

The old man shuttered as he flipped on a puter simulation screen. The image was frozen there; Eef must have been studying it when his visitors arrived. The image was that of an unborn child, presumably Eilan.

"This is a computer extrapolation of the effect these spores will have—are having." Oolong's voice quivered. "They are unique to our experience. So far as I am yet able to discern, they attack only the unborn child. You can see the . . . the effect, on the human fetus."

"I—I—" Yahna put her hand over her mouth and crowded close to Jesti. He saw, and he too was shuddering. Horror rose in him—and rage.

"The head is reduced to half normal size," Eef said, almost in a whisper. "The arms and legs lose hands and feet. They become . . . flippers. Grotesque, piteous monsters!" He turned away. "The ultimate in teratogenesis. The top of the ladder whose first rung was something now only an edutape memory—thalidomide, it was called. A plague to terrorize a whole world. The spores spread like gas through a mine. Already there is no corner of Eilong they have not reached. They will invade the womb of every pregnant woman—may already have done! *Someone* has attacked all Eilong. Some evil crober has deformed and crippled and blighted the life of every unborn child! And its desolated parents, of course. *Every* child. The whole world is thus blighted, Jesti!''

Yahna heard Oolong's voice break. Her stomach was lurching. Every horror she had ever dreamed was nothing, compared to this moment. *''Why?''*

Oolong Eef spoke to the wall, where lights flashed to indicate his superb putersystem's recording of incoming communications. Probably from Council members, Jesti assumed. Oolong had work to do and he and Yahna were only in the way. Here, there was nothing they could do. The horror of it was almost too much to grasp, but one thing was left to him.

I can still seek the Handsome M—onster. He did not merely seek personal vengeance now, but planetary revenge. It was a necessity.

''The answer came shortly before you two approached my door. It came from CongCorp Central—and I must soon stop talking and hear all these calls I'm receiving. CongCorp's comm said it was *rumored* that Eilong had been struck by a rare teratogenic mycotoxin. In other words, a monster-producing mushroom spore. A rumor, mind you—this less than six hours after the *dropping* of the horror! *If* such were the case, CongCorp is happy to advise that it is familiar with the horror and that its scientists have developed an antitoxin. CongCorp will be *so* happy to help us cope with the problem.''

''And to take over the whole world in the process,'' Yahna whispered.

''Cong . . . Corp!'' Jesti stared at the floor, then jerked up his head. ''Oolong! Your *must* deal with them, to get the antitoxin. *Please*! I know this: an unusually handsome man is somehow responsible. He *sold* that horror to CongCorp. He is totally ruthless, a man who murders casually. Again and again. Meanwhile, you and the Elders must tell everyone—tell all the Galaxy! Tell TGO! Spread the word! *Use* CongCorp to get the antitoxin . . . but *do not let the monsters win!*''

''Monsters,'' Oolong repeated dully, and turned back to stare at the extrapolative simulation on the screen. At an unborn Eilan . . . monster.

Yahna went up behind him and placed both hands on those bowed shoulders because she had to. ''I will try my hardest, my best, my bitchiest, to get MarsCorp to help, Oolong Eef. I will try. Certainly some help from the Akima Foundation. Beyond that . . . I will fight, I swear it, for the next holomelodrama we make to feature the murder of a planet—with an interplanetary corporation shown as the true villain. I will *fight* for that, Oolong Eef—and to make the corporation recognizable. CongCorp's funds are enormous . . . and so are MarsCorp's! And the influence the Akima Mars series has, the following . . .'' Standing behind her, Jesti saw the great shudder that ran through her, so that her long, long cerise cloak quivered. ''I will try, Oolong Eef—I will *fight* for it!''

My God, Jesti thought, insofar as he was capable of thinking. *I knew I had allied myself with a madwoman, tied our destinies together, but . . . my God! I think I must love the brave madwoman!*

''Yahna . . . Valkyrie . . . he has things to do,'' he murmured. ''And we have a monster to track.''

''Monster,'' Oolong Eef mumbled, staring at the horror on his screen.

Knowing that the only way he—fugitive and subversive, condemned to death here and fled—could help his world was to leave it again, Jesti swung an arm around Yahna and left in silence, leaving Oolong staring at the simulation of horror.

17

Death was now armed with a new terror.
                              —*Henry Peter, Lord Broughaam*

Always before, Gelor had thought of the palace on Jasbir as echoically spacious. Now he had the feeling that its walls were about to close in on him. Though shaking with fatigue, he couldn't sleep, since the raid on Eilong. Strain rode heavy on him. He jumped at shadows. Sudden noises startled him. Again and again he checked the compound's outer gates. The alarm system preoccupied him.

The women saw to it that he stayed on edge. His first act had been to lock them to the droid-frame in the great hall. He knew he was safe from them, totally safe. Yet still he hung on the ragged edge of panic every time he glimpsed them. Their eyes seemed to follow him wherever he went—and that included even those times when he was out of that vast chamber. Long sidewise glances probed/mocked/accused him.

Their words were designed not to help, as well:

"Why's he so nervous, DeyMeox?"

"Why indeed! Wouldn't you be, if you had that crazy Eilan on your trail?"

"The purple man–?"

"The purple man, Shemsi. By now he's seen what T6 is doing to his world."

"You mean he'll want revenge!"

"Revenge is a word. What that purple man will come thirsting for is blood. Gelor's blood. It makes me chill to think about it."

"Dey—you really think he can find Gelor *here*?"

"Pos. He'll find him. Us. One way or another, the purple man will find his planet's murderer."

Then, rather than act nervous, they laughed. All the devils of a hundred moons and planets rode their mirth. Gelor wanted to hide his head, plug his ears. He couldn't, and he could not shut out the sound and the truth, the tension. Bleakly, he wondered if he were going mad. He thrust the thought aside. Fear of the man called Jesti wasn't madness. It was facing reality. What bothered Gel Gelor most was not the doom potential of that coming, but the fact that DeyMeox had seen it as soon as he had—or sooner. Her brain, her mind—why had he let his ego lure him into using her? From the start she'd had him on the hip. A victim, not a victor.

He didn't dare let himself think too much about that. Jesti would come. That was what was important. Gelor was chilled, far colder than the room's temp warranted. He sank heavily into a chair.

He sat there motionless for forty minutes.

And he knew why. Fear. Fear, too long extended, had frayed him down into the near-paralysis of panic, of depression.

He could not afford that. That way lay death, and he didn't need to die. He would have the wealth he'd won from CongCorp. He had this place, and weapons. He had the two women as hostages and to help him, however reluctantly. He had life itself—*and above all I have my brain*. If only he could muster the energy and will to use it.

He did. With an effort, he heaved himself up and went back into the great hall/workroom.

Silently DeyMeox and Shemsi watched him from where they stood locked in the grasp of the droid-frame. He had the feeling they were smiling, both of them, ever so slyly. He smiled too—openly. Striding across the chamber, he drove a fist into the crober's belly. She doubled over, gagging and gasping.

Gelor turned to Shemsi. "Your turn."

She cringed. Her free arm came up to shield her breasts.

"You mean you'd rather have it another time?" Gelor grinned. "My dear, it's your lucky day. What I need at the moment is an andrist. If you would care to put your skills to use . . ." He let the sentence trail off. Already Shemsi's lips were parting and her eyes widening.

"Oh yes, master. Yes, yes. I'm yours to command. You know that.

"*Master*." Gelor liked that. A little of his depression lifted. A fraction of his panic ebbed. "What I want is for you to rework my dupladroid. If that is within your skill?"

The affront was deliberate: questioning her ability. She could brook no question as to her wizardry at her craft, and he knew it.

"Of course, master." She paused. "What change is it that you wish?"

"A simple one. It's to have a special circuit built in."

Her eyes widened and her voice faltered. "A . . . special circuit?"

"A kill-circuit!—triggered to the color purple!" That was DeyMeox, breath back, defiant again despite the blow. "That's ingenious," she mocked Gelor. "You're brighter than I thought, double-dyed villain."

"But–" Shemsi's hand moved in a baffled gesture. "Why? If it's the Eilan Jesti you want dead, why not just kill him? Why rework the droid?"

Just as Gelor started to slap her, DeyMeox's voice intervened, still mocking: "It's very subtle, Shemsi. Our . . . *master* can't be content just to kill the Eilan. He must prove his cleverness, too. More clever than a mere purple man. He needs to feel superior to his victim. A sick twist of *mind*, you might say. One in keeping with everything he's done here." Sarcasm dripped.

Gelor struck her in the breast this time. It was a typical male choice, and of course hurt less than the belly-blow. She pretended otherwise. She mocked him further, reminding him that he'd better keep her alive. Dead, she couldn't help. . . .

When the right time does come, he thought in rage, *you'll be a long time dying, you so-intelligent rotten mocking bitch!*

He had installed an electronic control to the droid-frame's lock. He took it out of his pocket now, and freed her. For a moment, shakily, she stood chafing her wrist. Then, stumble-footed, she moved to the workbench that held her supplies and equipment. She began.

There were delays, each an irritation adding to a massive irritation. Though she worked fast, there were more points to be checked than Gelor knew existed. He filled the hours by working out the new programming for the Gelor simulacrum. He had some ideas along these lines. If they worked, the Eilan would be a lot more fun than problem.

Jasbir's sky was deep gold-shot slate with artificial twilight when she had finished. Gelor stood beside the simulacrum before the mirror. With a strange feeling of unreality, he saw himself twice. Perfectly. It was as if he were just discovering that he had a twin brother. A brother programmed to act; not to kill but to seize and hold. A fit match for his anima.

With the re-secured Shemsi as hostage, he told DeyMeox what he wanted her to do, now. She closed her eyes as if the concept were something visible she couldn't bear to look at.

"Ah God," she said low-voiced, "but you are an evil, *evil* monster!"

He did not touch her. Instead, he slapped Shemsi's bare breasts, back and forth, four times—while DeyMeox clamored that Yes, she could do it; Yes, she *would* do it; Leave her alone! Shemsi was squealing girlishly, wailing.

"Sorry, Shemsi," he said, stroking her cheek briefly. "Her fault, you understand. If only she could control her senseless attempts at mockery."

With that message gotten across, he released DeyMeox. She went to work swiftly. The retained samples of Teratogenesis Six would make it a simple project, she said, and added no comment on him or the monstrous hideousness of his plan for the Eilan's ultimate disposal. Captured, Jesti would be a monster, an adult version of what the pregnant women of Eilong would soon be producing. A T6 monster; a thalidomide monster.

She had only just announced that she thought she had it, when the compound alarm honked. That shocked Gelor back to life from the new numbness that had taken him, and he raced to the relay room.

The flashing red light was the one keyed to the main gate. Hastily Gelor flipped on the scanscreen. He looked at the tight little quartet of people poised outside the entrance. One, taller, was clearly a Jarp. Another, cloaked, was likely a woman. The other two—

One left the group. A man. Broad-shouldered. Heavy-muscled. While Gelor watched, he moved off along the compound's outer wall. It threw him momentarily into light. Gelor saw the helmet, and he glimpsed purple skin. So. The Eilan had come. As Gelor had expected, and as DeyM–

Gelor raced back into the main hall/workroom/prison and found her at work on Shemsi's steel bonds. She had accomplished nothing, and was soon again in bondage beside the other woman. Gelor raced back to his screens.

The Eilan was at the second gate. He tried it, and a new alarm honked while the second gate's warning light flashed. The clamor locked Gelor's emotions in conflict. Part of him stood frozen in terror. Feelings of panic and impending doom clutched at his heart.

And yet there was another side to it. The aspect put forward by the crober. Here was Gelor's chance to defeat the Eilan, prove his supremacy. That brought a different kind of excitement. Panicked or not, he could hardly wait to take the next step. (The Eilan was at the third gate. He tried it. The alarms reported that. The gate was locked. The purple man moved on.) Only one entrance remained, to the compound. The rear gate. Hurriedly, Gelor activated circuits and threw switches. Punching final corrections into his dupladroid's programmer, he set the robopath in motion.

In perfect simulation of his own stance and stride, the

thing strode from the workroom. Off down the hall to the palace postern. Out, and across the compound to the rear gate in the outer wall. (Gelor checked the screen. The purple man was rounding the corner of the wall. Just ahead of him was the rear gate. Gelor triggered the dupladroid's action track.) Opening the gate, the droid left the compound. It turned right and headed along the winding road that led to the bionarium's grounds.

Back in the shadow of the wall, the Eilan stopped short, staring, then moved swiftly forward again.

Not swiftly enough, of course. The simulacrum was programmed to keep ahead of him. As it broke into a trot, Gelor laughed aloud. The bait was taken! Snatching up his pocket programmer and abandoning the scanner room, he sprinted down the corridor to the postern entrance. In seconds he was out of the compound and racing for the bionarium—ignoring the road. He would reach it long before droid and Eilan could hope to: the interplanetary zoo that was the pride of Jasbir.

He ran up the ramp to the third level, and the monitor cell. The control chamber. He couldn't wait for the lift to take him up; his nerves were that tight and his exhilaration that great.

From his past wanderings here in his guise of researcher, he knew the woman on duty. She was so old that she drooled. A pensioner, allowed to dodder here in a post long without any real function. She looked up as Gelor entered. Recognized him and smiled. Raised a hand in greeting. She might have spoken had Gelor's spring-thing not smashed her skull. Time was too precious to be wasted on words and besides now she could never tell anyone about him.

Heaving the old corpse out of the way, Gelor studied the monitor bank.

All was quiet in the bionarium. Deserted at this hour, save for the non-human specimens it was designed to display. With few exceptions, they slept. Swiftly he focused on the monitor that scanned the barracoons: the cage-stalls housing newly-arrived, behemoth-level exoskeletals awaiting classification.

They were no sight for a queasy stomach or a nervous man. A fair proportion of the creatures penned here were carnivores. Some were persnickety as to diet. Others were not. One must prefer liver and had broken into another stall. It was systematically ripping open a succession of smaller, hoofed creatures, rooting out the livers, and discarding the steaming bodies to die in shrieking torment. Gelor smiled. A lovely predator!

Barracoon number six was empty. With a grunt of satisfaction, Gelor switched back to the monitor that scanned the bionarium's entrance.

Just in time. The dupladroid was already coming through the door. Working with the pocket programmer, Gelor kept it moving. First to the lift. Then down to the bionarium's subsurface depths. The barracoons. Number six.

Back on the surface, the purple man called Jesti had just entered. He wore a baffled look. A moment's study showed him the dial above the lift. It was moving; it stopped at SubSub 3. The purple man's eyes narrowed. He veered left and, ignoring the lift, took the slide.

Gelor felt a sting of grudging admiration. *Decision comes so quickly for the Eilan!* He glimpsed the dial and in a moment he'd seen not only the peril that must lie in riding the lift-pod, but an alternative. And he had at once taken advantage of it. *If he had a lesser man to cope with,* Gelor mused, *the purple freak might even win!* Back to the monitor/scanner screen.

Down on SubSub 3, the Eilan dropped from the slide. His hands were already up and combat-poised as he emerged. Feet wide apart, body hunched into a partial crouch. In every way he looked deadly dangerous. . . . So dangerous that even situated as Gelor was, high up in the control room with monitors for every cranny down there, his breathing quickened and his nape prickled.

The purple man moved along the narrow corridor that ran the length of SubSub 3. Warily, he peered in at the viewplate of the first barracoon door.

Gelor smiled. Checking Barracoon 6, he triggered the dupladroid to turn its back to the entrance. He even made it more realistic: it bent forward, as if busy with something near the door opposite.

Jesti moved along, easing only enough of his face to the viewplate to be able to see inside, then moving on. To number five, then six . . . and Gelor held his breath as he watched the purple man peer into Barracoon 6. He stiffened, ducked. Gelor watched one purple hand move, very carefully, out to press the cage-door's lockpatch. The door slid back. Silent as a Panishi ocelette stalking a plithit, the purple man crept forward.

High in the bionarium monitor cell, Gelor gripped the waldo that controlled the locking lever of Barracoon 6. His other hand touched his pocket programmer, just enough to make the dupladroid twitch and shift. (The Eilan froze.) Gelor made the droid straighten, twist, stretch, as if totally oblivious to any intrusion, even the possibility of an intruder.

The Eilan eased forward. He was clear of the door now, his whole attention focused on "Gelor." With a shove, the real Gelor slammed home the cell-cage's locking lever. The door crashed shut and the bolt slid into its ward.

The Eilan's reaction was so fast it was hard to believe. He didn't turn to look; instead he pounced sidewise to the wall, half-turning as he did. At once he was in a position of defense in relation to both droid and door.

Not that it would do him any good. Gelor caressed his programmer. The dupladroid turned to face the Eilan. With a speed that praised Shemsi's work, it swung just as the real Gelor opened the door behind it, by remote. The droid dashed into the passage . . . which led into the bionarium. It ran.

Even then the purple man was clever enough to check the hall door: locked. With a swift nod, he whirled and charged after the droid. And the watching Gel Gelor smiled. He even chuckled aloud.

Now he had to keep his attention on the droid. He was able to make it put on a burst of speed sufficient to evade a red-haired arm over a meter long when it shot out of a barred cage to grasp at the fleeing "man" with a four-fingered hand. The dupladroid ran on while Gelor diverted his attention long enough to close the door behind the pursuing Eilan.

Gelor had to bring the droid back to him, and keep it sufficiently ahead of the purple man. Sound-monitors were turned up, and if an animal got the Eilan Gelor would know it and pause to watch that. Otherwise . . .

Thus he did not see the red-furred arm rush out to grasp Jesti and pull him toward its cell and the hungry jaws beyond the bars; heard nothing for Jesti only grunted—as he used his knife to slash the four grasping digits of some creature off a world never settled. The thing in the cell made a coughing sound and let go. Jesti staggered, caught his blance, and ran on after what he perceived as the Handsome Man. He kept to the center of the dim corridor, now, and he could not always keep the other in sight. Three turns and two menaces later the droid took the lift. That Jesti saw, from a distance; he waited to see where the pod went, then raced up the ramp.

He reached that level in time to see a door closing. He ran to it, winded, and slowed down to peer into the control/monitor chamber. He saw a hooded, narrow-shouldered figure hunched over the screen, back to the door.

Jesti cat-footed toward it. One step. Two. Three—and the lights went out.

In total and complete darkness a body crashed into him. Desperately Jesti clutched in a one-armed bear-hug and struck, again and again—and the lights blazed on again. Jesti stared into an old woman's dead eyes. Briefly; she was already sagging to the floor. Her face tilted forward as she fell. Blood-soaked gray hair matted across the back of her head told him he had not killed her; she had been dead before, and hurled at him.

Under the impact of her fall, the figure at the monitor collapsed into a heap of empty clothing. Jesti stared, gritting his teeth.

It was a trick, he realized. *All of it. A trap!*

With realization came the laugh from behind him. He spun, crouching.

After so many weeks and so many planets, so much

effort, he faced the Handsome Man. With a stopper, leveled at Jestikhan Churt.

"Do you know my name by now, Eilan? I am Gel Gelor."

"Do you know mine, monster?"

"I do, Eilan. Surely you're not surprised to see me?" Gel Gelor's smile was thin. "You shouldn't be. You have been following me—too close. I have a distinct prejudice against being taken prisoner. Pain distresses me. Under its influence I might even answer your questions. So—I prefer to handle the problem this way. A neat bit of distraction, the empty clothing, don't you think?"

Jesti shrugged. His brain was working, if not his mouth: *He isn't the least bit winded. Why?*

"You don't see it? You aren't thinking *yet*, purple man. No matter how much your pulsing purple heart desires it, you cannot afford to kill me. If you do, your planet's doom is sealed. I alone hold the secret of how to prepare the antitoxin that's the only answer to Teratogenesis Six."

No, Jesti thought. *A lie—CongCorp knows! They wouldn't have bought any of it if you hadn't sold them an antitoxin at the same time.* He tried hard to push a smile, and spoke; he had to keep the monster talking long enough to find a way to turn the tables on a casual murderer holding a stopper.

"You make a good point, Gelor, monster. In that case, the balance of power's in your hands. Therefore—why haven't you killed me?"

"Ah, there the issue is subtler, Eilan. You have caused me much trouble. Much nervousness, I admit. I consider that an affront for which death alone can hardly compensate. So . . ." And he squeezed the stopper.

A muscular spasm convulsed Jesti. Quivering, twitching, frozen in a strange paralysis that held him immobile yet constantly shivering, he hung on his feet, hardly aware of what was happening.

"Setting Two," Gelor said in a condescendingly conversational tone. "Jangles the nerves. Also robs the victim of voluntary movement and, to a considerable degree, of thought. It seemed appropriate for the course of action I have in mind."

Keeping the stopper's beam on Jesti, the Handsome Man moved to where a Gravco gurney hung in a wall-sling. Pulling down the mobile stretcher, he sent it coasting across the room on it hovercushions. Gelor followed, and toppled his enemy onto the gurney. That took swift timing; the beam had to be off the purple man before Gelor could touch him. Free of the effect only for an instant, Jesti was easily manipulated.

A casual touch sent the gurney skimming to the door. Another little nudge and it was gliding down the corridor and then the ramp that led to the big echoic building's lower levels.

"You've seen the barracoons and standard cages," Gelor said equably. "In addition, a really big bionarium also includes viewing pits, for the observation of the interaction of . . . specimens. On occasion, you can see anything from mating dances and sexual congress to rutting bouts and interspecies conflict."

They reached ground level, then SubSub 1. Ahead, a door loomed. Gelor threw it open and gave the gurney a final push. It sailed out into what appeared to be a small auditorium. Settled slowly, gently, onto a floor of loose sand. At the same time, Gelor inactivated his stopper. Jesti lay gasping. When he tried, he found that he could move again.

That was a welcome discovery. He sat up and looked about.

It was an auditorium—of sorts. More specifically, he was sitting in the circular pit of an arena. Shining plasteel walls rose at least three meters straight up above the sand, surrounding the sand. Above, a heavy wire grating formed a canopy. Beyond that, a half-dozen tiers of seats were banked to give spectators a clear view of any action in the pit. Lowering his gaze to floor level, Jesti saw—opposite the smaller door through which he'd been shoved—six massive portals. Jesti eyed them more than dubiously. He could have no idea as to exactly what lay behind each, but he could assume: a large animal that might consider him food, or a challenger, or even an object for mating.

Laughter drew his gaze to the seating area, and a lone

spectator: Gel Gelor. He took a place at the pit's edge, between the grating and the first row of seats.

"It's hardly fair for a man of your talents to keep his abilities as a combatant a secret, Eilan! Now you can share them with an audience, even if it is only an audience of one!" He raised a hand, chuckling. "You who are about to die—we salute you!" And he reached out to some sort of control board.

Over to Jesti's right, one of the huge heavy doors swung open.

A bellow blasted thunderously. Amost instantly a *Thing* charged into the arena. It was considerably bigger than one of those old *things* called *rhinoceros*. Jesti saw evil little eyes and a hooked horn the length of his arm and a chitinous collar thick as brickwork.

Jesti sat very still, busily hoping the one-horn had eyesight too poor to spot him unless he moved. (He had no other name for the . . . thing.)

(Gelor checked his chron. Yes; by now his simulacrum should be back in the compound. Programmed to kill anything not purple, which it was to grab. Just in case this purple freak escaped the inescapable fate of the pit!)

Jesti's was a forlorn hope and a bad guess. The one-horn took one quick look and headed for him like a tank with legs. Jesti moved—fast. He ran straight for the wall. He heard the thing pounding after him, gaining. Sinking his heels into the sand to break his own rush, Jesti slammed into the wall and made a right-angle turn so sharp the plasteel burned his arm.

He kept moving. Behind him, the one-horn hit the barrier with an impact that made the whole pit vibrate. Noisily.

Jesti kept on running. Adrenaline surged through him— and, incredibly, a weird sort of ebullient zeal. Pitting a man against a monster—this was a game for an Eilan miner! *With the Handsome Monster's neck for a prize if I win.* When, when—*when I win*! He had to. And the curse of the Seven Shikaris on silly talk about doomed Eilong!

Before him towered the first of five unopened doors. Surely it was the act of a maniac to compound his danger by snatching at the latch and heaving with all his might. That was Jesti's act.

Ponderously, the door began to open. Muscling himself up onto the locking bar, Jesti swung with it so that the door was between him and One-horn. The thing hit the door, though not so hard as Jesti feared. The set of the hinges saved him from being crushed. And now came the new development . . .

Already another creature was emerging from the passage Jesti had opened. A worm-thing, this time. Nearly a meter thick, lithe and sinuous and so long its tail-end lay hidden in the passage's shadows. It glided forward a score of sems and paused to glare this way and that with strange, multifaceted insectile eyes that seemed to radiate a mysterious inner light. Then it moved in another thirty or forty sems. About it was an aura of chilling menace that grew gooseflesh on Jesti's arms. When it was far enough out to look back and inspect him, he felt such an instinctive urge to flee that he dropped involuntarily from the locking bar.

Heedless of the brooding one-horn, he made a dash for the next door and opened it to take refuge behind it the same way he had the second.

Again, a shock. This time it took the form of a red-eyed, oil-slick black blob at least two meters across that *oozed* out into the arena/pit. It lay quiverily, bubbling on the sand.

One-horn had ignored Big-worm. The blob drew a different response: another of those bellows like thunder. It gallumphed into a lunging charge, horn lowered, straight into the blobby new freak of nature.

Even staring, Jesti was not sure whether the horn penetrated the blob or not. It surged suddenly upward like a living puddle of black oil that wrapped itself over One-horn's head, all the way to the chitinous collar. Yes, the horn came through. The blob tucked itself around it. Neatly. Air-tight. The one-horn braked. All four feet plowed deep to spew dusty furrows in the sand. Crashing into the unipolymer plasteel wall with a stone-shattering, deafening impact, it scraped frantically against it, trying to tear away

. . . what? A giant leech?—a smotherer-and-digester? Jesti had no idea.

As a matter of fact, he didn't give a damn. He was already moving, dropping off the door's lock-bar. Watching blood spurt from the blob and feeling confident that it was One-horn's. Glancing over at One-horn's doorway. Still empty. Squatting to squint at One-horn's underside (while the blob drew tighter, tighter and its spasming prey sank to its knees). Jesti watched the great horn snap off against the wall in a jagged fracture.

And from above, he heard the laughter of a fiend from hell. "See, Eilan? See what's in store for you? You're already dead—you just don't know it!"

The One-horn was male, Jesti had seen. Chances were excellent that it was not a monogamous animal, and no other had shown up, either. Jesti's life was at stake, and as usual he decided to try to beat the odds by intensifying them. He matched Gelor's laughter with his own while he snatched up the broken horn.

"You're right, monster!" he yelled. "I don't! And you'd better start running, Gelor, *running!*"

With that he slammed the huge bone at the indecisive worm-thing and took his own advice. Jesti ran. He raced to the gurney, piled onto it like a kid bellywhopping a sled, and went zooming out of the arena and down the corridor from which One-horn had come.

Staring huge-eyed, Gelor rose and started running.

18

In revenge and in love, woman is more barbarous than man.
—*Friedrich Nietzsche*

Looking down into the great hall of a dead prince's palace, Yahna Golden felt very, very good about herself. For one thing, she was taking strong action against the enemy. For another, she had parted from Musla and Twil and was doing it with no help or backing from Jestikhan Churt.

It was strange, the way she felt about Jesti. Did she love him? She wasn't sure. And that brought up another question, an ancient one. What was this thing called love? As a psychist, she had read and viewed tape after tape and listened to others. For her, the questions remained unresolved. Could it indeed be only another word for sexual hunger, need? Yet could it not be that shared feelings, sexual and non-, formed the element that bonded two disparate personalities? Indeed, to Yahna Golden it seemed possible that mutual antagonism might even form the core of a bond!

That brought her back to her own relationship with Jesti. *Do I love him?* Did he love her? Or did it matter, so long as they found something they both sought—*even if it's antagonism!*—when they were together?

And that returned her to dead center. Unsure of her own

feelings even while she wallowed in bristly, left-handed, unspoken bonding with him.

This is no time to be pondering that sort of thing, she told herself. Not here in Gel Gelor's makeshift headquarters in a drafty palatial banquet hall. Now was a time for action, not soul-searching. Briskly she advanced on the two women staring at her from where they hung shackled to a droid-frame.

"I don't know who you are and I don't need to," she said crisply. "The fact that you're locked here proves you're not included among Gel Gelor's favorite people. That's good enough for me. How do I get you out of this?"

"You ask me for the key," a man's beautiful baritone said, behind her.

Yahna whirled. "Who–"

"Need you ask?" The man smiled, a twisted, dangerous smile that turned his handsome—too handsome—face into a mask of sadistic menace. "You say 'Who' only to cover your panic, your confusion." He crossed to stand facing her. "Tall, aren't you. I am of course the man you and the purple freak have been seeking. I am Gel Gelor."

The woman locked to the right arm of the droid-frame spoke. A rather stocky woman, with wide-set, intelligent eyes and close-cropped black hair. Bruises marked the left side of her face, and elsewhere.

"He's also a monster. A handsome monster, cast in human form. No fiendishness is beyond him. For wealth and power, he'll lay waste to a whole planet—the planet Eilong."

The other captive was smaller; petite and delicate. Fine-featured with lavender lips and eyelids and nails. She cried out her words:

"DeyMeox! Stop it! He'll kill you!"

Gelor gave DeyMeox no time to answer. Wordless, he closed the gap between them. Drove a savage fist to her breast, then slapped her hard where the bruises marked her face. She'd have fallen had she not been locked to the droid-frame. Staggering, clutching her breast, she retched.

By pure reflex, Yahna started toward her. Choking, DeyMeox waved her back.

"No—don't tempt him." She gestured, and Yahna saw the shining rod in the man's hand. "He loves that awful spring-thing. He'd have used it on me long ago if he weren't afraid to kill me. He may not feel the same about you."

Again Gelor smashed her in the face. This time he used his fist. Again she lurched and gagged. Yet, reeling, she still pulled herself erect. Even though her mouth dripped blood now, the black eyes flashed.

"You see, girl? This is the sport he loves best. Beating women. Poisoning planets. Crippling unborn children!"

In an obvious fury, Gelor stepped a pace from her, whirled, and used the spring-thing. She did her best to hurl herself aside so that the awful head spent most of its force on her shackle, rather than the wrist it would have smashed. Still, she made a wretched sound of pain and sagged. That quickly, Gelor's hand clamped Yahna's arm. His fingers gouged so deep that she thought he must be breaking the skin. Dragging her with him, he stalked off through the great hall's gloom.

The rage seemed to flow out of him as he led her to a sagging divan.

"Ah, that evil woman—how she wants me to kill her! You saw me step away from her so that I would not? Sit down, do sit down. I assure you, you're safe with me. I have no designs on you and feel no animosity toward you. I do hope that as a favor you will grant me your technical assistance—you are Yahna Golden of MarsCorp, are you not?—registered psychist?"

She was regaining her poise, too. "Firm. Technical assistance?"

"Your acquaintance, Jesti, proposes to come in here and kill me, I have reason to believe. I have no wish to fight him—but a fear barrier would keep him away, would it not?"

She matched his charming smile, crookedness included. "Of course."

"And then I need not kill him—or be endangered. You will help me?"

"And if I refuse?"

"A woman of your intelligence?" He laughed—a cheerful laugh now, with nothing sinister in it. "No, you won't refuse, surely. You'd be saving us both."

She studied him. "But suppose I refuse, Mirza Gelor."

He sighed. "You too? You want me to threaten you?" He shook his head, actually looking amused. "I'm sorry. I cannot oblige you. I have no den of snakes available. No torture chamber. The spring-thing is not for such an intelligent beauty as you. Neg—the decision is entirely in your hands. I leave it to you to give it freely or not at all."

Yahna shrugged and smiled amicably. "In that case, I of course must refuse. You must find someone else, if it's a fear barrier you want."

"Uh. So be it then." Gelor's voice had lost none of its good humor and he still smiled. He gestured. "This way, if you please."

Yahna rose. She held her face immobile. "Where are we going?"

"I do like the way you avoid the cliché 'Where Are You Taking Me!' To a room more secure than this one. You do understand that I cannot have you running about loose, but am not so crude as to *bind* you." Again he signed her to precede him.

Yahna bit her lip, glancing pointedly at the awful device they called spring-thing. If only she could get him to get rid of it . . .

He lifted it. "This? You are afraid to precede me? My dear, my dear!" And he tossed it onto the divan.

Yahna let him see her sigh, then turned as if to walk in the direction he indicated—and whirled, that deadly fingernail rushing up. She pounced as she had at Petronius Jee—and ran onto the fist a suddenly squatting Gelor slammed into her midsection. Agony doubled her over, retching, and he had the exodermic syringe out and had injected her before she hit the floor.

A few minutes later she was helplessly unable to avoid answering his questions. To get her to erect the fear barrier against Jestikhan Churt, he learned her fears. That was not difficult: she could not lie, with that tetrazombase in her system. In less than a half-hour she was working, sweating to complete her job. She had to erect the electronic fear barrier against the dreaded Fahrood, who was purple and who was coming after her at any minute.

"It won't stop him," she had said once, but he seemed to pay no attention other than to tell her to hush and hurry. She had to obey. Her mauve cloak was thrown aside and the jacket of her purple suit was open.

In the grasp of the droid-frame, the other two women watched her. She heard muttered words about "TZ" and "subconscious memory projection" and "induced paranoia as different from mere hypnotism," and she knew that the words were familiar to her from the Psychesorium. It was just that they had nothing to do with *her*, or Fahrood, who had taken the pseudonym "Jesti." She heard Gelor strike them, too, both of them, but that was their problem. It had nothing to do with Yahna Golden. She had to prepare the room against the advent of Fahrood/Jesti. And she did.

Jesti had been right. The One-horn was alone in its tunnel, and in its cave. Furthermore the cage was easy to get out of—for any thinking being with a hand. That was for the safety of anyone who might become trapped inside. Jesti was, and he very quickly was not.

The trouble then was that he had to search the bionarium for the monster named Gelor. He did not find him. Over an hour had passed before the cursing Eilan allowed himself to leave the great zoo, and head back to the palace. He received another terrible shock—here were Musla and Twil. Or rather, here were their bodies. Both appeared to have been smashed down by incredible blows, and the Jarp's head was twisted half off. Jesti saw the fingerprints and marveled at the strength of Twil'im's killer—and then he remembered Dravan, and Jesti knew why Gelor had not been winded, up in the monitoring-control room.

"*Yahna*," he murmured, and started running.

In the relay room, an alarm bell rang. Hastily, Gelor switched on the monitors. He focused on the figure who was moving through the compound gardens, and without much regard for stealth. It was the purple man, and Gelor glanced at Yahna. He smiled, seeing her shudder as she looked at the Eilan onscreen.

That purple skin. Those bulging muscles. The shag of ugly, half-grown hair, ridiculously hued. Gill-slits, even! She must not let him touch her again! Fahrood, now called Jesti, disguised—her mortal enemy! The terror and nemesis of her childhood; the shadow on her life.

Gelor spoke into her ear: "Quick! He's headed for the back hall." Catching her hand, he led her back to the others. Thrust a stopper at her. "Here. Take this. Protect yourself!"

The skweez-tube felt good in her grasp. She must remember not to squeeze it until the right time. Against *him*. Fahrood/Jesti. Unresisting, she let Gelor position her just to one side of the entry.

"Stand here, Golden One. The stopper is set on three. Disintegration, and you'll never have to fear him again. Wait till he hits the fear barrier. If he can stand it as you say, he will emerge not two meters from you. That way he will see you, and know who it is who Fries him."

Dutifully, Yahna nodded and took her stand. She gripped the weapon gratefully, and waited.

A shadow came gliding along the hallway. A cat-lithe, heavy-bodied shadow. Numbly, Yahna bided her time. Her palms were wet and her mouth dry. Her breaths came shallow. Out in the corridor, the shadow resolved itself into a solid figure. The figure of the Eilan—no, no, of Fahrood, disguised as an Eilan. Her grip on the stopper tightened instinctively. A rill of sweat slid from her armpit. It felt cold. She shivered. The purple man reached the doorway, and paused. He peered this way and that.

Monster! Soon I'll fear you no more!

Yet her heart missed a beat. He looked so *alone*. So exposed, so . . . vulnerable. (*No! Absurd! His true image is what he is: lethally competent, a deadly menace! He wants me again, poor little Yahna!*)

Horrible ambivalence—why did she also have this feeling of fondness, of . . . of *love*? The conflict of it made her quiver in indecision. Then, somewhere deep within her brain, a pulse began to beat: *Fahrood . . . Fahrood . . .*

That beat wiped out all else. This was her nemesis. Fahrood-Jesti. How could she have forgotten, even for a moment! The thought put iron in her soul. Tight-lipped and tight-muscled, she sucked in air. And the purple man stepped through the doorway of the great hall. Through the doorway—and into the fear barrier.

The sense of anxiety hit him first, the subconscious anticipation of impending danger. Fear took the stage an instant later. Jesti wanted to whimper as paralyzing waves of it surged through him like a cresting wave. The impulse to cringe, to cower, to cry out was an almost palpable force. Then came the pain. Leaping like a phosphorus flame, it flashed a message of agony into every neuron, every cell of him.

Instinctively, within his staggering mind he knew what had happened: *I've walked into a fear barrier.*

A neuro-electronic wall, a powerful one designed to turn his reflexes and perceptions inside out and rob him of self-control and movement. A poison.

At the same time, he knew it was all inside him, and that so was the antitoxin. He had the counter to this induced horror because he was from Eilong, with an Eilan's unique nervous system. He simply had to fight the fear and ignore the pain. Force himself to keep on going . . . even while his lips hung slack and his muscles seemed made of syrup.

I have done it before. This is good. It must be Yahna's doing—he made her do it! She is alive! I can do it. I will do it! I will! I will!

He was. With efforts that shredded his equilibrium and rocked his belly with spasms, he forced one foot forward. The other. Another step. Another. (Or were they steps?) He could not be sure. Fear and pain could distort reality. *Maybe I'm only shuffling in place.*

He was not. All at once the fear was gone, and so was the pain. He was left with only a tendency to shake and a hammering in his ears. He was past the barrier and into the dim, echoing mustiness of the palace great hall, grimy with age and thick with clutter. And directly before him was . . .

"Yahna!" Her eyes—that strange, glazed look above the leveled stopper, as if she were seeing not him but someone or something far beyond him. "Yahna? You don't want to point that thing at me."

At that instant he saw hatred and loathing in her face such as he had never seen anywhere in his life.

The female voice, however, came from behind her: "Yes she does! She's in the grip of TZ! She'll *kill* you, Jestikhan Churt!" And with that screeched warning, DeyMeox surged desperately—and tore free of the restraint weakened by the crashing blow of Gelor's spring-thing. The spring-thing that lay on the divan just behind him, because behind his back he held a stopper, ready . . .

It was then, too, that Gelor's simulacrum came home. It came through the doorway and the invisible wall of fear as if it did not exist. Instantly it was aware of a heavy concentration of purple, and the dupladroid charged it. As it had been instructed to slay Musla and Jesti, and had, it had been instructed to seize and immobilize that which was purple, and it did. Jesti wore pale green coveralls and a helmet. The violet of his hands and face were as nothing in comparison to the concentration of Yahna's matched jacket and short skirt. Charging past Jesti and between him and Yahna, it seized her. The stopper spun away. Yahna screamed, but her captor was not programmed to hurt.

"You damned idiot droid," Gelor snarled, swinging his stopper around. "You were supposed to grab *him—damn* you, Shemsi!"

Then he leveled the stopper past Yahna at Jesti, the stopper that really was set on Fry, and from behind him his own spring-thing shattered his elbow.

His only sound was one of sharply indrawn breath. Then Gelor fainted with the pain, and behind the crumpled form stood DeyMeox. Smiling.

Jesti was trying to wrest the dupladroid's arms away from Yahna. It let her go with one long enough to sweep the Eilan two meters across the floor.

"Damn you, woman—what do we have to do now, wait for him to wake up and call off his droid?"

"Neg," DeyMeox said. "We merely release its maker." She squatted to thrust a hand into Gelor's pocket, and then another, and soon she was thumbing the impulse that cut the EM field to Shemsi's bonds. DeyMeox broke the shackles.

Shemsi was weeping, practically wringing her hands. "It won't hurt her," she cried. "It's programmed only to hold her until he–" She glanced at Gelor. "Oh shit. You'll have to hit it in its power-pak, dead center."

"Belly?" Jesti asked, wiping off his helmet to reveal freaky hair.

"Firm," Shemsi nodded, while DeyMeox bent over Gelor again.

"And what if I just break its damned head open," Jesti said, and used the visor of his hardhat in an attempt to do just that. It sliced into the back of the droid's head.

The thing continued clinging to Yahna, who writhed. Suddenly her eyes seemed to focus. "Jesti? What the— what's happening! Oh—Gelor!" And she bit at skin that was not skin.

"Just be *still*, damn it," Jesti said, and aimed, and struck again.

And then again. Unfortunately the dupladroid continued to grasp Yahna even after the back of its head was split open and its neck sufficiently severed so that it lay at an angle on its shoulder. With one hand it held her. With the other it defended itself. It swung a mightly blow at Jesti. Jesti went straight down with both legs while that mighty arm whished over his head with an audible sound, and that fast the Eilan was up and slamming his helmet's ridge into the droid's midsection.

Yahna, straining against the unnaturally strong hand that held her, staggered away several steps and fell when that hand dropped spasmodically away from her. Unfortunately the other had already begun its backswing, and even as Shemsi's creation fell, a couple of meters from the real Gelor, that arm rushed back and slammed into the side of Jesti's shoulder. Again he was flung across the room. This time, as the droid collapsed, Jesti's head banged into the wall and his eyes flared, crossed briefly, and closed.

"Check his pulse and the back of his head, Shemsi, Yahna," DeyMeox said, grunting as she dragged the unconscious Gelor toward a table. "We have this monster at our mercy at last, and I have no mercy for him at all. Just as we discussed, Shemsi!"

"Pos!" the andrist said excitedly. "Absolutely!"

"And if Yahna-psychist objects," DeyMeox said, "knock the snot out of her, Shemsi my dear!"

19

Sure, purple's all right—it's just that Orange is Beautiful.
—Tl' leoot' lee of Jarpi, in *The World According to Jarp*

Jestikhan Churt stood in the con-cabin behind Captain Fej,
gazing at a viewscreen he hardly saw. That yellow-white
ball a couple of sems in diameter was Kamo, Fej said. A
star—and Eilong's sun. That was exciting, with exiled
miner Jestikhan Churt returning as hero. The greatest hero
in the history of Eilong, most likely.

Yet Jesti hardly saw the eye-eez green screen, even
while he stared at it. Blankly. Remembering . . .

It really is over. (*Well . . . almost.*)

In destroying the Gelor simulacrum—and how good that
had felt!—he had also got himself knocked unconscious.
When he awoke, he was in a small squarish room behind a
barred door. A cell. A *dungeon* cell, in fact, and for a few
moments he thought the Jasbiri had caught up with him.
No; outside, her hair combed, cleaned up and poured into
a velvon jumpsuit, was one of Gelor's aides. The two Jesti
had seen secured to that odd metal frame-thing behind
Yahna and the Handsome Monster.

"Jesti, you are safe," she told him in a nice soft voice.
"You are not a prisoner. I am Shemsi-andrist. I've been
Gelor's captive, and I made the Dravan dupladroid you've

221

seen and the Gelor one, too. I had to. It was that or be tortured—or killed.''

"I'm not a prisoner? You could have fooled me, Shemsiann Drist. Open up, then.''

Her smile was tentative. "I'm sorry. Not just yet, Jestikhan. Not until DeyMeox is through with him. Gelor. She's the one he treated worst, Jesti. Hit her again and again, till she was all bruised.''

"Uh. What'd she do for him, create the plague?—the spores?''

She looked surprised, then nodded. "Pos. She is Dey-Meox-crober, Jesti, and she's the best. She is also one weird person—all honor and duty and guts. Yahna says that describes you, too. Well . . . Dey doesn't even hate Gelor the way I do, although he treated her the worst. Worse. She's all scientist. Still, we agreed on what we'd do to the monster if we ever got the chance, and we did, thanks to you. She's doing it now. After that—''

"So she's 'doing It.' What's that got to do with me in this . . . cell? I keep rescuing the most ungrateful dam' people—and what is she doing to him? Damn! All I wanted to do was break his neck. Slowly, maybe.''

Shemsi nodded, and her face showed understanding, sympathy/empathy. "I can understand that. You're here because we were afraid you would stop us. We all owe Gelor, you see. As to your other question, well, you called him a monster. He is. He is also just too perfectly, incredibly handsome. So . . . Dey is making his exterior match his interior, his personality. She's in the lab with Gelor, Jesti—making a monster.''

Jesti stared at her, blinking, while he tried to digest that. Just as he started to speak, the sensuous Shemsi did.

"Oh—as soon as Yahna Golden awakes, DeyMeox says, she'll be fine. Dey gave her an injection and a counter-hypnotic. As soon as she's finished with Gelor, out you come, dearest friend and ally. We have things to do, Jesti! None of us is qualified as ship's master, so we'll have to hire one, or charter a ship. Then we have to—no, no. You and Dey and Yahna have to go to Eilong. I'll stay here with him. Gelor.''

"Eilong?" he echoed, and that's when Jesti learned that he (with DeyMeox-crober) was to be the greatest hero in Eilong's history. She had all the surreptitiously-made tapes she had dictated while she worked. She had created not only Teratogenesis Six, but its antitoxin as well. She had not only created that antitoxin, she had devised a means to reverse the effect of T6. Eilong would be saved, and CongCorp thrwarted.

Worse than thwarted. CongCorp was about to be notorious and in one hell of a lot of trouble.

And so DeyMeox had finished, and Shemsi had remained in the old palace, with the *modified* Gelor. Jesti and DeyMeox and Yahna found a man to take them to Eilong—fast. That was Captain Fej. With him he brought two crew. The great DeyMeox-crober would save Eilong. She and Oolong Eef and a lot of others would be very, very busy for awhile. Jesti, meanwhile, would be being cleared, commended, and lauded by the Council of Elders and all Eilong.

After that they'd all space back to Jasbir, and the palace that had been Prince Palkivala's and then Gel Gelor's.

Gelor. A piteous, helpless creature, now. With the most careful of scientifically dispassionate vengeance, DeyMeox had removed his larynx and both his hands and feet. The latter she replaced . . . with flippers. A bit of *rearranging* of his head and face turned Gelor into an ugly, swell-headed monster . . . just the monster he'd have made of every Eilan baby. A thalidomide freak—and the toy of two vengeful women.

They would make him last for a long, long time. A lifetime.

Meanwhile . . . well, Yahna's plan was a little heady for Jesti, but he had decided to go along. He'd try anything once, and he'd try this.

Fully recovered, Yahna Golden intended to try filling a new role with her employer. Scriptwriting. She swore that her and Jesti's adventures and his derring-do transcended most of the fictional ones the writers had managed to come up with for Akima Mars. And Yahna intended to write it. To try to get her *friend* Setsuyo Puma—hyperstar, as Akima Mars—to tell the MarsCorp brass that she wanted to make *this* meller, *this* script. Yahna Golden's and Jestikhan Churt's script.

After that—well, surely Jesti could at least try out for the role of Akima's co-hero. He would already be famous, a celebrity.

"Better to combine your part and mine into one, for her," he had said, "and maybe there'll be a bit part for me. As Chief Elder, maybe!" He laughed. "Or as Hieri!"

"Big bucks as technical advisor!" Yahna had said, all bright-eyed with the excitement of her plan. And would CongCorp be sorry! (Which was the main reason Jesti had decided to go along. He thought about that now, in the con-cabin behind Captain Fej, en route to Eilong.)

Red-mopped Captain Fej interrupted his reverie.

"About one hour, Mirza Churt. One hour to docking. Are you serious about wanting to try to learn how to bring a ship in to dock at station?"

"I'm serious, Ship's Master. Call me when it's time, and call me Jesti."

He left Fej then, and made his way back to a certain cabin. He pushed in.

Here sat Yahna Golden, mostly naked and with her legs looking over a meter long. Seated before a mirror, doing primpy things to her golden halo. She looked up as he entered, and he was sure he saw the beginning of a smile. Then her eyes flashed and her face tightened. She yanked her skimpy negligee together over her breasts—mostly.

"You dam' tiptoeing Eilan—can't you even knock?"

"Ah," he said, resignedly fulfilling his role of dutifully launching his own attack, "fiddling with your hair again, hmmm?"

She sprang up, face working, eyes flashing and bosom heaving. (She was good at that.) "*Damn* you, you freak!"

Ah well, it's our relationship, he thought. *But I'll be glad when you and DeyMeox get you over this shit and we can just screw like other people, without all this mean-ass "foreplay!"*

But he dutifully snarled "Rotten bitch," and moved in, and of course one thing led to another, and after that the victim held her rapist for a long while, murmuring and crooning happily.

The Worlds of SPACEWAYS

PLANET	NATIVE	POSSESSIVE	CAPITAL	STAR (sun)
AGLAYA	Aglayan	Aglayan	none*	Thales
ANDOR (T.S.A.)	Andran	Andorite	Koba	Arkimedes
AREPIEN	Arep	Arepienese	none*	Alkoman
BLEAK	Bleaker	Bleaker	Zero	Ulubeg
CORSI	Cors/Corser	Corser	Newhope	New Altair
CROZ (Croz II)	Crozer/-ite	Crozite	Oddford	Thabit (Matana)
EAGLE (TSA)	Eagleman/Eagler	Eaglish	Starlight	Arkimedes
EILONG	Eilan	Eilan	Swayn	Kamo
FRANJI	Franjese	Franjese	Velynda	Chandrasekhar
FRONT	Fronter	Fronter;-ish	Graha**	Shapley
GEM (TSA)	Gemman/Jewel	Gemman	Diamond***	Eratosthenes
GHANJ	Ghanji	Ghanji	Starlit	Cospar
GINNEH	Ginneher	Ginneher	Deephole†	Alsufe
HAVOC	'Vocker	'Vocker	Sherazad	Brahmagupta
HELLHOLE	Heller	-ish; Heller	Golden	Menzel
HRALIX	HRal	HRal; HRalish	MRayl	Offa (Mlall)
ICEWORLD	Iceworlder/ Bluelip; Snowman	Iceworlder	Sunshine Lake	Kuyper
JAHPUR	Jahpurese	Jahpurese	Delirium	Aresebo & Algolyeh
JARPI	Jarp	Jarp	none*	Tomonaga (unpronounceable)
JASBIR	Jasbiri/"a Jaz"	Jasbiri	Marmot	Huygens
JORINNE	Joser	Joser	Komodi	Payne & Humason
KAUFMAN's PLANET/TSA	Cougher	Kauffmanish	Binary Junction	Fermat
KNOR	Knorman	Knorese	Survival†	Plato
LANATIA	Lanatian	Lanatish	Proc	Aminilari
LUHRA	Luhrese	Luhrese	Point Pleasure	Alkharkhi
LYON	Leo/Lyonese	Lyonese	Inapur	Khwarizimi
MECCAH	Meccan	Meccan	Muslallah	Abualisina
MIRJAM	Mirjer	Mirjer	Windbreak†	Zarkala
MOTT-CHINDI	Mottchin/Macho	Mottchin	SeeYou (Cu)	Kiddinu

T.S.A./TSA: Tri-System Accord
* no planetary capital
** *Graha:* "Disobedience"
*** all cities named for gemstones
† by default; only town or settlement
Star-names in parentheses are local names in language other than Galactic

PLANET	NATIVE	POSSESSIVE	CAPITAL	STAR (sun)
MURPH	Murpher	Murpher; -ite	Silver City	Jansky
NEVERMIND	'Minder/ Neverminder	Nevermindish	Newhope	Mizar II
NEVERMORE	Nev/Nevaman	-ish; Nevaman	Plughole	Skaparelli
OUTREACH	Outie/ Outreacher	-er; Outie	Forty Klom Hill	Razee
PANISH	Panishi	Panishi	Harmony	Kopernikos
QALARA	Qalaran	Qalaran	Norcross	Galileo
RAHMAN	Rahmanite	Rahmani; -ese	Ramadan	Lemaitre
RESH	Reshi	Reshi	Menre (Temple City)	Slipher
SAIPING	Saipese	Saipese	Payping	Ptolemy
SAMANNA	Samannite/ "a Sam"	Sammanish	Riverview	Fiel
SEKHAR	Sek	Sekhari	Refuge	Al-jebr
SHANKAR	Chank	Chank; Shanki	Medina	Hipparkos
SHIRASH	(jelly-blob)	Shirashi	? none* ?	Struve
SOPUR	Sopurese	Sopurese	Graymount	Herschel
SUZI	Suzite	Suzite	Suzi City	Albattany
TERASAKI	Terasak/Sak	Terasak; -ish	Yamato	Hubble & Durga
THEBANIS	Thebanian	Thebanian; -ish	Raunch	Janski A & B
TOKTAGA (TSA)	Tok	Tok; Toktagan	Point Pleasant	Arkimedes
TULA	Tulanese/Corper	Tulanese	Farrisberg	Tula's Star

T.S.A./TSA: Tri-System Accord
* no planetary capital
** *Graha:* "Disobedience"
*** all cities named for gemstones
† by default; only town or settlement
Star-names in parentheses are local names in language other than Galactic